I0616903

*The Mask of the Pontimax*

# AMAGON

## The Book of Man

*A History Past and Future*

A. Ûmaz

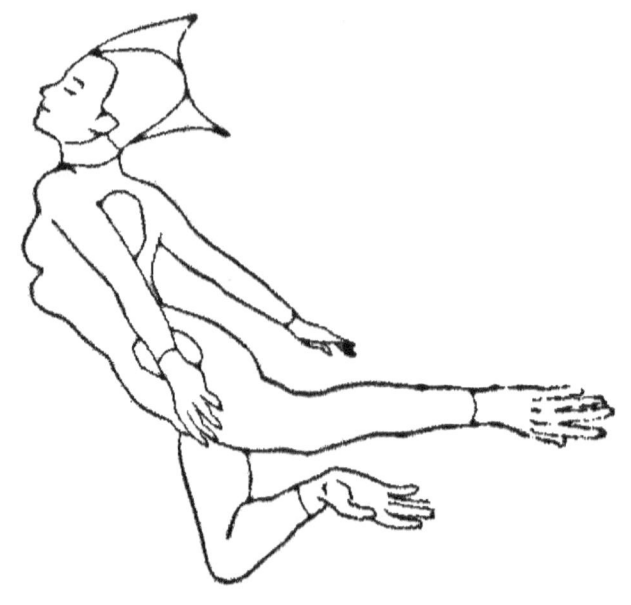

ISBN-13: 978-0692391266
ISBN-10: 0692391266
Library of Congress Control Number: 2015936115

Published in Cooperation with    **Helios  Press**

An imprint of IACP/Co-oPress

www.co-opress.org
Printed in the USA

CHAPTER 1

C ondo slipped into the Interface. As always, the sudden sensations of weight, wind, sunshine, and sand induced a momentary and terrifying vertigo. He gasp involuntarily, remnant of a primitive reflex common to the ancestral inhabitants of this ancient and turbulent world. The sudden inspiration gave rigidity to the torso and hyper-oxygenated the blood, preparing the organism for "fight or flight." But now there was need of neither. As the adrenalin metabolized and the panic subsided, Condo smiled at this sudden reminder of his less than spiritual origins. Excision spared this vestigial autonomic response because even in the modern age it saved many a life.

As the Interface's transducers came into proximity with Condo's peripheral nerves they automatically synchronized sensory transmissions with the neuronal responses from his central nervous system. These responses were in turn transduced and transmitted ethereally to the Golem on the planet's surface. Condo could in no way physically tolerate the true levels of force and radiation to which the Golem was subjected at the planet's surface, but the Interface created facsimiles of these conditions within Condo's nervous system - intense, unshielded solar radiation; unremitting gravitation; a tornadic, noxious atmosphere. As the sensations increased in intensity, particularly in his legs, it occurred to him how inconvenient it must have been for his ancient earthbound ancestors to have wasted the use of two good limbs for nothing more than the perpetual struggle against gravity. A brutish image painted itself momentarily on his consciousness, the frontal lobes of its cranium rising a scant 10 cm above a ridged brow overhanging small, squinting eyes, its limbs hirsute, stubbish, thick, and clumsy with muscle. He wondered how it must have smelled.

As the robotic Golem powered up a stark and inhospitable terrain came to focus in Condo's visual cortex, wiping away the atavistic phantasm. Windswept sand and yellow sky stretched in all directions – as far as his "eyes" could see. He marveled that this barren place had been the birthplace of his species. Devoid of its water and organic matter, which had long ago been take up by the Habitats, nothing remained but an endless expanse of sand and stone.

"This way, Holiness."

Condo heard the voice of his guide perfectly above the howl of wind and sand. He turned to look at Hersh'ma and saw the likeness of his archeological assistant's ocular presentations displayed on the eyescreen of a robot. For the sake of precision the physical reality of the robot was not disguised, though it well could have been. To see Hersh'ma's familiar gaze looking back at him from atop all that gleaming machinery and circuitry seemed so clownish it made him chuckle. Unlike the technicians who dealt with Interfaces and Golem on a daily basis, Condo relished these occasional adventures – the novelty had not worn out!

"Yes, Hersh'ma. Lead the way!"

Condo turned 180 degrees and found himself at the edge of a great pit surrounded by robotic devices of every description. His transmitted thoughts energized the robot's electro-static fields. It levitated and drifted to the center of the pit. Letting Hersh'ma lead the way, they began a rapid descent.

In archaeological jargon carried over from before the Ascent, the *excavation* measured approximately 100 meters in diameter, through *strata* levels 53.65 meters deep. Four tunnels extended in the principle terra-magnetic directions at the bottom of the excavation. Hersh'ma rounded off his descent and headed for the tunnel marked *East*. Condo followed closely, a sense of anxiety and excitement building within him. What lay at the end of this tunnel could, or would, have a most profound effect on the Species.

The ancient surface exposed by the excavation and traced by the tunnels lay covered with an overburden of sand. Consequently, the walls of the excavation and the vault of the tunnels had been fused into thick layers of glass to give strength and stability. As Condo and his guide moved down the main tunnel light sparkled and danced from these crystalline surfaces. At regular intervals side tunnels had been excavated in a systematic search for artifacts in the layer. Six hundred meters down the main tunnel its excavation suddenly terminated. A tunnel to the left was obviously the focus of attention and activity as a steady stream of Golem entered and exited. Condo maneuvered his Golem in these close quarters, not expertly, but adequately. He banked hard left and shot past Hersh'ma as their destination came into view, the robotic Golem wobbling a little uncertainly under his pilotage. What he lacked in skill he harvested in a boyish thrill reminiscent of his first soaring into the canopy of the Habitat.

A short distance down this side tunnel the excavation opened into a great, vaulted room. Condo brought the Golem to a stop just where the tunnel joined the larger space, and hovered while he examined every detail of what lay before him. Initial reports from the archeologists indicated that the artifacts uncovered at this site could establish once and for all the truth of the long lost Amygdalite city, and more importantly could reveal the location of Proffit's fabled New Jerus'lm Complex – the actual site of the Ascent!

Though the object of his greatest interest obviously stood at the center of the excavation, Condo deliberately turned his gaze to the side, slowly panning the view before him in the systemic fashion logic dictated. He wanted a most complete and accurate impression of the current find, though he could not deny feeling strongly that all too human urge to relish the found treasure. But he maintained his composure as befitting his office, and only when he had thoroughly examined the entire did he let his gaze and his attentions focus on the objects in the center.

Running at regular intervals in a straight line through the center of the excavation, skew to the line of the tunnel but obviously approximating a cardinal line east and west were a row of "post molds" – the cylindrical, charred, celluloid remnants of trees, whose woody structures Condo knew from his study of ancient history had been used by primitive men as "power poles" to support conducting wires against the force of gravity. Their original height would have held the wires high enough into the insulating atmosphere to prevent the conductors from coming into contact with Earth and discharging the electromagnetic potential they were designed to transmit. It was a primitive, inefficient method, but had served the ancient technology well, and had been employed everywhere on the ancient, inhabited surface of the planet.

A modeled planar surface with shallow parallel excavations to either side ran parallel to this line of post molds. These "ditches" had served to carry away the excess waters that once flowed on the surface of the planet. The modeled surface had been covered with a thin layer of "asphalt" to provide a uniform, stable medium upon which ancient men could propel themselves and their devices in the face of extreme gravitational force without becoming mired in the sometimes insubstantial materials of the planet's crust. This ancient road seemed so foreign to the modern concept, and yet even in those ancient days a road was a *pathway to somewhere*, though the methods of travel differed dramatically.

But all of these things had been seen before. In fact there were very few places on the old "continents" of the planet that did not contain such artifacts from man's primitive past. And in very many instances it was not difficult to align such archeological finds with the places referred to in the ancient writings, recordings and images. The last days of man on Earth had been filled with turmoil, however, and so much had been destroyed. But the legend and myth had survived, recorded in the letters of holy men for ten thousand years. Now it appeared that at last the myth would be revealed, or refuted. At last the holy city would be found in substance, or again relegated to the spiritual, the ethereal!

The geometric balance and symmetry of the road bed and drainages and row of poles testified to mankind's long pursuit of useful precision. All was nearly perfect in the uniformity of its measurement and dimension - save for one lone, seemingly incongruent artifact. This artifact's possibilities now quickened Condo's pulse in anticipation. His Golem approached near to the thing, its camera focusing narrowly on the details the multi-spectrum holographic illumination revealed, transmitting them through the Interface's neural transponders to Condo high above, deep within his Habitat; deep into his visual cortex; his consciousness; his understanding; his reason; his memory; his dreams – his hope!

The artifact was in poor condition. Though still firmly rooted in the ground, the two meter tall metal tube was badly corroded. A rectangular metal plate affixed to its top was little more than oxide held in place by static charge. Except for the preservative encasement of desert sands the object would have disintegrated long ago. Though badly degraded, yet much of its details remained. The various archaeological apparatus employed had microscopically sampled and analyzed the artifact. The resulting data was then sent to a set of holographic illuminators. His neuronal impulses now fed to the devices, Condo created holographic images of the artifact that transformed it from its present state to one that approximated its original condition. The transformation took places seamlessly before his eyes. The corroded pole took on the silver sheen of newly worked and treated metal, while the plate affixed at its top became once again crisp in its profile and embossments. It took on the smooth appearance of a freshly painted surface - white, raised letters and numbers upon a green background. The old letters spoke to Condo as they spoke to few men in this day. They were sparse, simple, geometric shapes, with little individual meaning. But taken together they shouted the voices of men long gone - of lives and dreams and hopes lived long ago.

The sign read: AMAGON 7 MI.

Condo let the emotion roll over him and through him! The myth, not myth, but grounded in reality! The ancient city - found! And not only found--but at precisely those coordinates suggested on the Mitsuzuki Disc. Now everything would have to be re-examined in this new light. Moreover, readings from the various spectrometers and particles detectors indicated residues that could have only been generated by the use of a Device – Proffit's Device – as an agent of destruction! And just when it seemed that man's knowledge was complete, the great mystery returned!

Condo withdrew from the Interface and floated to the corner of his Cell. He let the vista of Forest greenery beyond the Cell's portal bathe his senses. He felt thankfully humbled, awed! The Pontimax, and C.E.O. of Alhumana Corp., charged with the emotional and spiritual well-being of the species, found his faith in the truth of *The Third Testament* renewed, and the burden of *doubt*, from which it was his duty to protect his fellow man, suddenly lifted from his own troubled heart. Folding his hands and feet in reverent supplication, Condo curled himself in Prayer.

## CHAPTER 2

Condo emerged from Prayer spiritually refreshed and psychologically calmed. He straightened and stretched himself and yawned widely. He remembered vividly the dreams that had come to him during this short Prayer – dreams of conflagration, misery, and white veiled spirits rising in redemption. But now he must make his report. The Board of Directors had been expressing more than a bit of impatience recently with his "archaeological obsession." Now he had something concrete to give them. He dashed off a communique:

*10034.4.2.3 Ano Ascensu*
*Es'paul Condo*
*Pmx/CEO Alhumana Corp.*

*To: The Esteemed Board*

*Re: Amagon*

*Archaeological efforts have this day produced an artifact giving physical corroboration to the "myth" of Amagon. It is expected that further analysis of references in The Third Testament will result in validation.*

*Humbly,*
*Condo*

The drum sounded just as Condo confirmed transmission of the message. Another day's work done. He disengaged his backpatch and terminated his control of the Cell. The Comm ports and Interface de-energized and darkened. Condo snatched his Locator from its hook, slid into its harness, and gave it a quick preflight, checking to see that the propelletes at shoulders and hips were functioning. Once last systems check of the A-nav and A-cav indicated they were operational. Setting the A-nav to his home coordinates and the A-cav to one meter, he engaged the Auto and was immediately propelled out the Cell's portal.

All along the expanse of Cells other workers were also exiting. Engulfed by the growing crowd, all were gently sucked into the entry of a nearby Ventportation Tube. Atmospheric circulation and human transportation within the Habitats was accomplished by this vast network of transparent ducting, exchanging oxygen rich air from the forested areas with the carbon dioxide laden air of the urban centers, and transporting people from habitation to occupation in the AM, and occupation to habitation in the PM. He relaxed and let the current carry him along with the rest – anonymous, pensive, and reflecting on the day's find. But momentarily his Locator's A-nav sounded. Stirring from his reverie he navigated to the nearest exit, smoothly disgorging from the flowing swarm.

Above him spread a residential region in one of the Habitat's Forest sectors. The Forest Trees extended outwards from the Core Sphagnum nearly to the vault of the Habitat's Shell. Along the under side of their great branches a myriad of bioengineered Pods dangled at the ends of delicate, seemingly insubstantial stems, but all that was required to support such large fruit in the microgravity of the Habitat. Genetic modification during maturation of these woody fruits produced internal architectures suitable for human habitation. A few personal modifications and the addition of some windeyes quickly rendered a Pod a home! Spying his own, Condo disengaged his Locator's Auto function, and with it now set to respond to his neural outputs, he commanded his propelletes as effectively as a bee commands its wings.

As Condo approached home the smiling face of his wife Sar'ha emerged from the rising throng. Coming alongside him and joining hands and feet, they entered the blossom end of their Pod together. Transiting quickly through the lower chambers to the family room at the stem, they found their children already there availing themselves of manna, the sweetly nutritious, taffy like secretion which during certain months of the year flowed in excess, leeking through small fissures where the pedicel met the Pod's core. Competing good naturedly for the tenderest bits, they scarcely noticed their parent's arrival. Eight hours at the Corps exercised the growing mind and left a good appetite!

Smiling at the eagerness of his foraging children, Condo turned to Sar'ha, gazing deeply into her eyes.

These "windows of the soul" were the first avenue of understanding between them. He looked closely to see which of the five primary states she was presenting: (1) *I have something I must ask you,* (2) *I have something I must tell you*, (3) *I understand*, (4) *I do not understand*, or (5) *I am at peace.* He could see that she was presenting the first state: *I have something I must ask you.* Of course, he was himself presenting one of the primary states: *I have something I must tell you.*

She spoke first: "Do you have something you want to tell me?" He smiled, and said: "We have found Amagon." Sar'ha's eyes narrowed with more questions. "I visited the excavation today. The road to Amagon is no allegory. Its physical existence is confirmed with a simple signpost!

Sar'ha's delicate features blossomed into a smile. Condo could see immediately the state of peace glowing in her eyes. He reflected that of all the challenges required to maintain the Habitats and keep them flourishing, it remained inarguable that of greatest importance was seeing to it that the soul flourished. Life was no longer viewed as simple chemistry. Sentient, it required a soul and purpose to continue its evolutionary climb to ever higher forms. This was the duty of the Church and its Alhumana Corporation – and the soul and purpose of Es'paul Condo's life.

Condo reached out to Sar'ha, and their hands entwined. He turned an approving and affectionate gaze on the lithe and animated forms of his busily feeding children. "Stick some manna in your pockets, and let's go up to the canopy for sunset." His suggestion met with enthusiastic approval, reflected in the returned and adoring smiles of his offspring.

CHAPTER 3

From *The Third Testament*: "We can comprehend the physical reality. We can analyze it, dissect it, and understand its components and workings. We can know its properties and manipulate them. We cannot alter it. We cannot rewrite its laws. We can never fully explain it."

Like all men, Es'paul Condo had questioned Faith in his adolescent years. Those years of intense learning – each day a new problem solved; each day a new solution revealed – imbued a sense of confidence in the youthful mind that can only be attributed to ignorance. "For it is not until a man finally discovers his ignorance that he has truly learned something of value," says *The Third Testament*.

Unlike most men, Condo had come to this realization quite precociously. In fact, his first *philosophical* inclinations had revealed themselves while he was still enrolled in the Habitat's Maintenance Corps. This Corps, to which all children dedicated the second eight years of their lives, was a realm of hard science and harder physical realities. Here the requirements were absolute: for every problem that arose, a solution must be found! Survival depended upon it. It was the realm of chemistry and physics and biology and mathematics and dozens of other relevant disciplines by which men comprehended and manipulated the physical reality to insure the survival of the species. And yet, in the midst of all this precision and pragmatism, the young Condo and inquired of his Sensei: "Why does it matter if we survive?" On that day he was marked for the Church.

It would be years before his philosophical musings matured, however. At sixteen he signed on for a second eight years in the Corps and in that term he attained the rank of Sensei. In becoming a Master in the maintenance of the Habitat, Condo had to prove himself proficient in each and every relevant discipline, and further, to know and understand the Habitat's origin and history. It was in the study of the Habitat's history and origin that he would find the great calling of his life.

By their very nature the hard sciences must be complete and precise if they are to prove useful, reliable tools. But history is an amorphous thing, forever losing and finding itself, as useful in its bits and pieces as it is in its whole. It is a matter of individual interpretation and prejudice. Throughout the entire of its venue as a human occupation it has been woefully incomplete. It is a castle made of sand, falling down in one place as quickly as it is being built up in another. Given the nearly miraculous scientific and technological achievements of the species, it would seem that once and for all a reliable record of the course of human events could be achieved. But there are too many factors at play. *The Third Testament* tells us: "Man's recording of his deeds, his *history*, is forever incomplete and broken. Only Life, given by the Creator, is unbroken and eternal."

Condo first became aware of the uncertainty of history when he realized that *The Third Testament* attributed no actual physical point of origin to the Amygdalite city of Amagon, the site of William Proffit's New Jerusl'm Complex, where the first Habitats were conceived.

He confronted his Sensei with this fact and got a most unsatisfying answer.

"Sensei, in all of problem solving it is absolutely necessary that a "point of origin" be established. The forces of logic and reason cannot proceed in its absence. Without the forces of logic and reason we cannot achieve faith. And yet *The Third Testament* does not tell where we might find Amagon, the birthplace of Habitats. How can we accept as an article of faith what cannot be arrived at by logic and reason?" The gaze in young Condo's eyes presented to his teacher the primaries: *I must ask you a question* and *I do not understand.*

"Gaksei, in the Corps we have taught you that solving a problem is like putting together the pieces of a puzzle. Logic and reason permit us to see how the pieces fit together, and when we have joined two a point of origin is established from which we may proceed. What we cannot teach you is that the physical reality is but a small part of the puzzle. We cannot teach you that any two pieces made to fit are as good a point of origin as any other. We cannot teach you that the puzzle has no borders; that the pieces are infinite in number. You must learn that by faith." The Sensei smiled, and presented *I understand*, while his pupil's gaze only revealed more questions and less understanding.

In his frustration Condo worked doubly hard to master the workings of the Habitat. He studied its every facet down to the finest detail. He could recite every engineering detail required to repair, renew and maintain the great glass sphere that encased a Habitat. He understood and analyzed the biological processes within a Habitat and their precise and delicate balance. He could offhandedly run the mathematical equations which described the great osmotic forces at work between the Cylinder Sea at a Habitat's Core and the surrounding vegetation which produced the life-sustaining atmosphere.

In the evenings at home in his family's Pod he began his search for Amagon. He soon discovered that 10,000 years of recorded human history raised as many questions as it answered; that the longings of the human heart were as adamant in his day as they were in the days when men first cut notches in bone or wood, or fashioned impressions in clay tablets. Even where the record was complete, and the how and when and where and who were easily determined, he found little to truly understand the *why*. Yet, out of this swirl as out of a mist, the legend of Amagon arose, held in faith but uncertain in fact. Amagon, birthplace of the first Habitat - the site of man's last days on Earth. How could it have been lost?

The will to understand *why* remained unrequited. In a mind as well qualified and able in physics, mathematics and, chemistry as any, Condo's passions led him into history and thence into philosophy. His questions soon revealed to him that arena from which no physical certainty obtains; that realm where reason and logic are not masters; but wherein lies the destiny of man. For absent faith if in nothing more than himself, man's ability to reason - his very consciousness - brings no satisfaction to life. Yet, the simplest faith in things unseen or imagined spurs every talent he possesses.

Most young men become so enamored of the challenges and excitement presented by the frontiers of the hard sciences, so intellectually piqued by the *hows*, that their consciousness resides primarily in an action/reaction relationship with the physical world. Even in the more abstract realms of mathematics and theoretical physics, their thought processes originate in and revolve around real world phenomena. Rare are the young men who can eschew that dynamic and rewarding realm for the philosopher's lonely and introspective cloister. But the young Condo early noted that a spiritual crash within a Habitat could have as devastating an effect on its well-being as an imbalance in its environment, or the sudden appearance of some new virus. And so much more insidiously! For several generations might pass before the actual crisis was even noted, and by then the thought processes of those in the Church might have become so corrupted that disaster could not be avoided. Even more subtle than the theoretical physics of the Ether were the spiritual workings of the Ethos.

So Condo tackled the *why*. The first requisite in that quest, then, was to explore and understand the history of this solely human activity. His journey necessarily began with his enrollment in Seminary, and his study of *The Third Testament*, the myth of Amagon, and the enigmatic William Proffit.

CHAPTER 4

Condo and his family were citizens of Habitat 34 Beta, created in the year 8255 *A. A.* It was preparing for the birth of its 100th generation. It had experienced 8 major expirations.

34 Beta was one of the original *integrated* Habitats, with vegetation only minimally engineered into the structure. At nearly a two thousand years old it was in many ways an antique. Most of its younger citizens emigrated to one of the newer, more organic Habitats shortly after marriage or struck out as pioneers in a newly created one. But Condo's position and life's work was well-served by Habitation in this link between the old ways and the new. There were inconveniences, of course, and additional dangers, but they were far outweighed by the continuous visual reminder of transition this Habitat provided him.

One of the primary courses of study for all children in the Maintenance Corps was the evolution of human Habitations. That study began with the history of ancient man's *greenhouses,* those first attempts to master and manipulate environment. For prior to his Ascent man had been an organism totally subservient to the environmental vagaries of a planetary surface. He was compelled in his existence and evolution by the great geologic and atmospheric turbulences and gravitational stresses which obtain on the surface of planets, and by the occasional and always dramatic extraterrestrial visitation of rock and ice from the heavens. But the tide was turned, and with the increase in sentience and knowledge and the subsequent spawning of ever more advanced technology, what was once master, became the mastered.

It proved quite a balancing act, however. For the forces which man mastered were the very forces which had heretofore compelled his evolution. And in fact, some initial attempts at Habitat creation had ended disastrously. The dynamic of life permitted no stasis, such that a cessation in evolution resulted in an immediate devolution—of man as well as environment. The trick, then, was to create a dynamically stable environment which permitted permutation and mutation to a degree that evolutionary forces continued, and yet which did not wrest itself from the gently guiding forces of human intelligence. All the knowledge and inventiveness of the human mind proved requisite to approach that dynamic. It meant that the training and work of the Maintenance Corps was an endless, evolving task. Still, there were dramatic failures.

Every student in the Corps was required to study and to memorize the names and fates of the Habitats that had been lost down the long history after man's Ascent. There were exceptions, but generally the story told, the lesson learned, had very familiar elements. Too much pressure put upon a natural system by men too certain of their abilities ultimately led to wild oscillations in atmospheres or biospheres or temperatures or pressures or physiologies or psychologies. The arrogance of men who lost their respect for Creation never proved a good thing. It seemed nothing was ever truly gained when humility and respect for the Creator was lost.

One such spectacular loss was the demise of Habitat 17 Alpha. Created in the fourth century after the Ascent, it employed the principle of 24 hour rotation to mimic the radiation pattern to which life had been subjected for most of its 3.5 billion year history. Through procreation and immigration it had reached saturation in a mere four generations. As with all Habitats, its Elders enjoyed the autonomy of birthright and soon began to diverge from the principles established by the General Council.

One such principle agreed upon by the Council was the sanctity of human DNA. Through the ages too many experiments had resulted in disaster; in unacceptable outcomes; in extinction. For all his divinely inspired genius, man was not yet prepared (the philosophers and Holy Men argued that he never would be prepared) to tamper with the blueprint of his own creation. And yet, regularly, a generation of men came along who felt superior to this edict, this lesson learned. Certain of their accomplishments and abilities, they forswore this principle and trod dangerously in that realm reserved for God.

The Elders of 17 Alpha at the time of that Habitat's saturation were such a generation of men. The creation and fulfillment of the Habitat had been accomplished with nearly miraculous precision. So many of the environmental imbalances and biological and viral infections which generally assailed growing Habitats had been avoided that the Corps Sensei were certain they had mastered the art of life. The numbers of their enrollment in the body of Elders was sufficient that they were able to take control of the Habitat's destiny. Then, exercising the autonomy which every Habitat as an independent, self-perpetuating life preserve enjoyed, the Elders of Habitat 17 Alpha informed the Council of its intent to directly manipulate the DNA.

Of course, there was a great clamor. Those members of the Council who had themselves risen through the ranks of Corps Sensei pleaded with their brothers to take note and be forewarned by the record of disasters that the direct manipulation of the human DNA had brought about in the past. They recited the list of lost Habitats. The philosophers and Holy Men, the Board of Directors of the Church, the entire of the Ecumenical Board, warned of the moral consequences and the wrath of God. But the Elders of Habitat 17 Alpha were not dissuaded. Certain of the perfection of their own abilities, they were not content with the prospect of long, comfortable, and fruitful lives. They would reach for immortality. The genetic map of the aging process had been traced again and again. There was no one who argued that it was not complete. Yet, in the past every attempt to remove these coding corruptions from the sequence, though at first seemingly successful, resulted in unanticipated, unaccounted-for phenomena that led to the destruction of the organism by other means. Sometimes it resulted in sudden, unexplained biological cancers, or auto-generated virions. Inevitably it resulted in neural and psychological demise for those who lived *too* long. The will to live became the will to die. All of these arguments were put before the Elders of Habitat 17 Alpha. They refuted them all.

By general agreement of the Council, Habitat 17 Alpha was placed in isolation. The Holy Men called it *shunning*. No thing, living or otherwise, would pass between 17 Alpha and the other Habitats. There would be no sharing of seed, human or otherwise; no exchange of artifacts or material; certainly no contact of environmentals or organics. Nothing would pass between the isolated Habitat and all others, save communications via ethereal data impulses. The Council decreed that Habitat 17 Alpha was responsible for its own fate - and would God have mercy upon them. By their second year, the Corps Gaksei knew this story by heart.

Procreation within and immigration to 17 Alpha stopped immediately. The mature citizens of the

Habitat had the coding corruptions of the aging sequence stripped from their DNA. A stage of maturation was established for the children of the Habitat, and as each came of age, the sequences were stripped from their DNA as well. It had been reckoned that one generation, 24 years, would suffice to bring the Habitat to stasis; to see aging of the human organism halted – to see immortality gained!

At first it seemed quite a simple accomplishment. Communications from the Habitat were full of positive news and braggadocio. Totally isolated from the other Habitats, 17 Alpha seemed to have reached an environmental and biological equilibrium. A second generation passed, and those who had been in the fourth and final quarter of life at the outset of the experiment were now apparently successfully entering a sixth term.

But then mortalities began to rise beyond what could be explained by statistics or accident. There were cancers and virions that could not be easily contained. And with the loss of human life arose the need to fill the biological vacancies. Attempts were made to reinstitute procreation, but the genetic engineering that had been used to halt the aging process had adversely affected the procreative process and could not easily be reversed. Fertilization rates were low and too many of the offspring who did survive to birth were not viable. As the human population decreased, and the Maintenance Corps went undermanned, unwanted or at least un-preferred life forms began to proliferate and fill the biological vacancies. Habitat 17 Alpha appealed to the Council for assistance as a third generation passed, and its human population declined precipitously. But the Council stood upon its decree of isolation. Many who had sat upon the Council at the time of the edict had long since passed, but they had taken care to impress upon their descendants the gravity of 17 Alpha's transgression upon the sanctity of life (the Holy Men called it *sin*) and this prejudice now worked as a safeguard against those who tended toward compassion. In despair and desperation, 17 Alpha sank into a dark age.

Nothing violates the sanctity of life and of evolution as does the cloning of life. It is a certain dead end to the vitality of life. It is the period at the end of a sentence, the final chapter of a book. It can only copy what has gone before. It can only be less than the original. Yet, in desperation, the citizens of 17 Alpha resorted to this blasphemy – this insult to the Creator – to stabilize their population. As the first generation of clones came to breeding age, it was decided that the Sacrament of Excision would be abandoned in hopes that a return of the *procreative instinct* would provide the vitality needed to spur reproduction.

It is true that the abandonment of Excision permitted the return of the long-denied human instincts of territorial aggression in the male and sexual aggression in the female. However, these subconscious urges which had facilitated procreation in more ancient times now lead only to unproductive struggle between the males and un-reproductive sexual promiscuity by the females. For reasons that could not be medically overcome women spontaneously aborted their fetuses; for reasons that could not be psychologically overcome they committed in-utero infanticide.

For several years more generally psychotic and unintelligible pleadings were transmitted from the failing Habitat until presumably a want of expertise and maintenance to the systems finally silenced the pathetic cries. A decree of perpetual quarantine and abandonment of 17 Alpha was unanimously passed by the General Council.

Desperate genetic experiments had as well unleashed a myriad of horrors and monsters that could only be speculated upon. A mere four generations after its break with the General Council the last intelligible transmission was received from 17 Alpha. Moments before his suicide the reigning Elder of the Habitat transmitted this message to his brothers on the Council: "We are doomed. God forgive us."

Life did not cease within the Habitat, however. Though its sphere became murky and obscured, the occasional evidence of motion on its inner surface attested to the tenacity of the life force. But it was not known what form that life had taken.

In the present day, parents encouraged right behavior in their young by telling them that bad little boys and girls were sent to Habitat 17 Alpha!

CHAPTER 5

From *The Third Testament:* "No man who must breathe to live is ever *free*."

Condo awoke as the first rays of morning sun fell through the windeyes of the bed chamber. He reached out, grasped the handrail, and slid from the embrace of his bedclave. The morning air was pleasantly chill.

Pulling himself effortlessly along the handrail, he stopped momentarily before the bedclaves of his still sleeping wife and the four children of his second brood. All slept peacefully, and as he studied their familiar countenances, he felt deeply stirred by their gentle beauty. He relished this moment of sublime reassurance.

But today would be a day of challenges. He had no time to linger. He was meeting with the entire Board of Alhumana Corp., and though he had scheduled the meeting so his sector in 34 Beta would be in daylight while the Habitat sectors of his primary rivals would be in darkness, he wanted to be at his Cell long before the others came on-line. He would need every advantage he could garner in order to successfully defend his project.

He pulled himself along the handrail and into the Pod's central tube. The rich mahogany and honey hues of the woodworks seemed to glow in the early light.  Reaching the portal to the bathing chamber, he rounded-to and propelled himself to its interior. Sensing his presence, the chamber's embedded LEDs brightened.   Condo slipped from his sleeping silks and was immediately set upon by a Worm.

The undulating, translucent rope-like creature ballooned at one end and engulfed Condo's head and shoulders.  The sudden, bracing sensation of the millions of cilia on his scalp and face and neck brought Condo to peak consciousness and sensitivity.  As the Worm continued to swallow him, the cilia did their work – cleaning, exploring and examining every minute aspect of his exterior. Dead skin, unwanted or harmful bacteria and viruses, and a day's accumulation of residues were removed.  Genetically engineered to accommodate as nearly as possible the entire of human hygienic need, the creature expanded until Condo was totally encased. The Worm's millions of specialized cilia worked by degrees to clean, examine, and, if necessary, to apply healing antibiotics and medicinals to injured or infected areas. As its final function, the Worm stimulated Condo to excrete and then disgorged him in as clean and clear-headed a state as any man could hope to be.  Its work done, the Worm slithered out its exit portal, and with undulating motions began its descent to the Core Sphagnum, where it would spend the day digesting and converting its meal, and making its deposits among the roots of the Forest trees.

As Condo emerged from the Worm he momentarily regretted the rapid passing of this expedient affair. As with all things pleasurable it was a human weakness to long for more. But as the sensations subsided rational thought returned, and the day's challenges once again dominated his thoughts.

Again grasping the handrail, Condo pulled himself into the dressing chamber. He slipped into a set of clean khakis, then strapped on and adjusted the bandolier of his Locator. He energized its Device, and set its neural sensitivity. He conducted a short pre-flight check of the propelletes at his shoulders and hips, their gossamer flings responding precisely, setting him in the posture and position he desired. Then using them for thrust, he loosed his grip on the handrail and was propelled into the Pod's central tube and thence out the exit at the blossom end.

At this hour of the morning the traffic converging on the Tubes was primarily constituted of journeymen, technicians, and laborers. They were greeted by the *nocturnals*, whose day's work was just ending and who were heading home. Even on the dark side, a Habitat never really slept! Condo was the unusual element. Most professionals would not begin migrating to their Cells until after the mothers and children were off to school and the corps cadets had headed to their maintenance academies. But Condo needed this contact with the masses to insure that his human connections remained intact and that the direction of his reasoning did not become too abstract. He gave a pleasant "*O-hi-ogoz'm*" and nod of recognition to all whose gaze he met.

Condo headed for a Tube entrance that was not overly crowded, and once caught in the draft, engaged the A-nav, and set A-cav on his Locator and relaxed for the several minute trip to his destination. Freed from the need to navigate, he began to tune in on the murmur of the throng around him, picking out bits of distinct conversations. The heated topics of the day were Alecon's revaluation of the Life Credit, and Almanag's refusal to sit down to talks with the Brotherhood of Glass Workers. It was always so – the producing masses at odds with the parasitic managerial classes. But it was a symbiotic relationship that had proved itself too often and too well to be offhandedly disparaged or discarded. Even these working men were aware of that. So they complained, and continued toward their jobs.

As the CEO of a major corporation, Condo felt it incumbent to seek exposure to these reminders of the real business of humanity. It was all too easy for a man in his position to personify the corporation and devalue the humanity it was invented to serve. Sadly, this condition was prevalent among his colleagues: partly out of a loss of perspective; partly out of the remnants of aggression, territoriality, and hierarchy that survived in the human neural networking after

Excision. But here among the roiling masses so vibrantly engaged in the business of living, right-mindedness returned.

Condo's Locator beeped as he neared his destination. He disengaged the A-nav and A-cav, and at once the unit began to respond to his motor neuron outputs. He maneuvered himself to the outside of the flowing throng and deftly exited upon the draft of discharging air.

Just below him lay one of the vast honeycombs of Cells from which corporate management that eschewed the urban environment conducted its business. The Cells were fixed between long rows of titanium girders which were anchored at their ends to great bands encircling the boles of the Forest trees. This particular bank of Cells was principally occupied by lower level management, the Cells of upper management being secured higher on the trees (and were considerably more elaborate and often personalized). But in a true sense of humility, Condo preferred the greater anonymity afforded him by taking his work space lower on the trees.

As a Virtue, anonymity came naturally to Condo. The psychoanalytic reduction of his personality did not indicate any deep-seated inferiority, caused by physiological or experiential trauma. Rather, analysis indicated a very profound, objective understanding of the philosophical dilemma of existence. This understanding allowed him to intellectually subdue even the most tenacious of remnant instinctive behavior. The Id and the Superego bowed before the power of Ego's reason and compassion. It was the quality that had destined him for the Church.

Condo approached the transparent, hexagonal facade of his Cell, and stopped before the airlock that served his work space and the two adjoining it. Sensors in the airlock door scanned Condo, and making positive identification, the door to the lock opened. Condo passed through its small orifice and as quickly as the door behind him closed, the door to his Cell opened. The necessary quarantine measures were accomplished quickly and unobtrusively during this rapid passage. The sophistication of the apparatus contained within the Cells required this nearly surgical environment. This sudden transition from the highly organic environment of the larger Habitat to the sterile, metallic interior of the Cell conduced a *business* frame of mind.

At his presence the Cell energized. There was a perceptible change in the air, a noticeable charge, as the enslaved electrical quanta leapt to their tasks. This domain of conductor and semi-conductor, of logic circuit and pico-processor, of quantum theory and ethereal mechanics – this place where the much imagined and little understood marvels of Creation performed modern miracles – was a fitting place for the probing intellect and abiding faith of a man like Es'paul Condo. And it was the head office of the Alhumana Corporation, Church to the Habitats, espousing the General Theory of Religion, and bringing the strength of faith and morality to the masses.

As CEO of the Corporation Condo had on this day the unenviable task of appealing to his Board of Directors for funds. As a *service* corporation, Alhumana's revenues were legislated and subsequently limited and subjected to the strictest of budgeting by its Board of Directors, whose responsibility was to insure the efficient maintenance and continuing creation of Habitats through the faith and proper moral guidance of the inhabitants. Unshakable in his belief that faith was a fundamental constituent of the phenomena of human consciousness, Condo still felt his metal severely tested by having to sell the notion over and over again to a group of men whose motives ranged from the noble to the ignoble. He always found himself a bit nervous before these meetings.

Positioning himself at his console, he busied himself with the perfunctory check-list for establishing the communications links and with reviewing the meeting's agenda. His usually agile manipulation of the console controls were today punctuated with an unusual clumsiness, as his neurotic anxiety altered neural chemistry and response. With a wry smile, Condo thought to himself: "Boy, I'm all toes today!" Once immersed in activity, however, the clumsiness subsided. As he began to focus on purpose, his concentration narrowed and intensified. A passage from *The Third Testament* came to mind: "The life of the animal is the pursuit of pleasure; the life of a man is the pursuit of purpose."

A flashing light on the Cell's transceiver indicated that one of the board members was also at his Cell and establishing an ethereal link. Condo reflected on the irony in his current appeal to the Board for the funds to continue the archaeological and historical investigation of one William Proffit, whose revelations in the field of Ethereal Mechanics made possible instantaneous communication over tens of millions of miles, which fact allowed for the upcoming debate to occur. He wondered if the Board members appreciated the full gravity of the circumstance.

Condo glanced at his chronometer and saw that he still had some minutes remaining before the scheduled time to go on-line. It was generally agreed that in meetings where moral principles were involved, the participants would refrain from wearing their Caps. But as time still permitted, Condo reached for his Cap and pulled it snuggly over the great orb of his cranium. He wanted to review his "Proffit-isms." He wanted his quotations to be appropriate (more than appropriate – logically and philosophically devastating!) and correct.

A quick review of the extant libraries and databases had the sought after information flowing through Condo's consciousness. Those particulars he wanted to retain he relegated to short term memory. Others were bookmarked for later reexamination. His communication with the computer was only limited by the reaction time of the neural chemicals at the synapses. Within a few minutes he had what he was after and removed his Cap.

It had long been argued by existentialists and the like that consciousness was merely an epiphenomenon of neurochemical reactions. Likewise, it was argued that imitating these processes, first in the electronic computer and then later in the quantum computer, would result in creating an artificial consciousness - an *artificial intelligence.* But no matter how great the computing  Capability of the "machine" became, no matter how cleverly it could mimic human "logic" – it never successfully passed the Turing test.  One had only to turn to questions of faith, introspection, and moral judgment, and it was soon evident that the *intelligence* was not a human one - was very fundamentally less than human!  As a result, the early tendencies to give the machines speech  capabilities; to turn them into *someone* or *something* with whom or which humanity could commune, were abandoned.  What these machines became instead were extensions of the human mind--incredibly fast computing attachments, entire libraries and databases as random access memory directly accessible by the human consciousness.  And the Interface between the human mind and machine became known simply as "*the Cap.*"  As with most of modern technology, the  Cap operated on a version of Proffit's Device.

A chime alerted Condo that communications would commence in 30 seconds. He removed the Mask of the Pontimax from its beautifully hand carved box and placed it on his face. He then slipped into the communicator and ran a quick check of the neural transponders and camera. Though communications could be accomplished in a much simpler synapse to synapse transmission, it was long ago learned that completely bypassing the corporeal body and its inputs led to increasingly detached, unrealistic and therefore meaningless jabber. Most importantly, it was discovered that *eye contact* provided the greatest and most efficient method of social bonding, absolutely essential to the survival of the Habitats.

The Mask of the Pontimax was a golden sculpted affair possessed of an ambiguity that defied description. At one moment it appeared serene, the next aloof, and then perhaps dispassionate. One legend held that the Mask was created by Proffit himself and was in fact a melding of the images of Jesus the Christ, Buddha, Mohammed, and Moses. Whichever the case, the Mask in this day served to diminish the individual that wore it, and to reflect the meaning of the passage from *The Third Testament*: "What I offer here comes through me, but not from me." It was the suppression of the individual Ego, and its submission to the wisdom of the ages. Only the eyes of the wearer were revealed by the Mask.

Only for this need to have eye contact was the camera necessary to the communicator. The image recorded by the camera was reduced to digital data and fed directly into the visual cortex of the receiving party, so that the retinas of the eyes were not actually involved in the process. But what was crucial was that the image itself be an accurate representation of reality. As the visual cortex had the ability to process several images simultaneously, it was possible to make eye contact with several individuals at the same time. This was quite beneficial when groups of humans were interacting. Further, for all the billions of humans who filled the Habitats, no two pair of eyes were exactly the same, so that even where the Virtue of Anonymity was intended, the lay of the carpal fold; the fullness of the long, fine lashes; the arch of the brow; the striations of the iris, delicate and subtle in their variations – all identified a man (or a woman) as certainly as if they had their names and all their personal data written upon their foreheads.

CHAPTER 6

Condo donned the Mask of the Pontimax and eased his cranium into the camera's head stand just as its indicator light blinked on. The meeting began.

"By the authority vested in me as CEO of the Alhumana Corporation and as Pontimax of the Church of the Habitats, I call this meeting of the Board of Directors to order. Gentlemen, sign the roster, please." All eyes were upon the Pontimax; the eyes of the Pontimax were upon all. The individual board members uploaded the required data through their communicators into Alhumana data records. "Gentlemen, I have called this meeting regarding matters of the faith. Without faith, there is no call to Morality. Without Morality we are not the Children of God. Amen."

With the perfunctory opening statement of purpose and its relevance accomplished, Condo relaxed the formal stare and immediately began to process the subtle nuances contained in the gazes of the board members. He sensed the interrogation in their eyes. He began his presentation.

"Gentlemen, as you know, matters concerning the archaeological and historical record of William Proffit are fast developing. We are about to penetrate the great darkness which for nearly ten thousand years has shrouded the last days of man on Earth; the raising of the first Habitats; the demise of William Proffit."

A board member representing the banking and commercial interests spoke up. His name was Am'riah Redshilt. Heavily invested in pharmaceuticals, he was also one of Condo's principal opponents in the argument over Excision, declaring the practice a barbaric and unjustifiable practice in the light of human advancement and knowledge. "With all due respect, Holiness, in the current tight economy, can such purely scholarly interests warrant so high a position on the list of priorities?" His ocular presentation and the subtle nuance of his inflection betrayed ulterior motives. Condo saw the challenge in his eyes, a challenged proffered by the entire class he represented.

They were a marvelous class, these bankers, businessmen, and entrepreneurs. The ingenuity with which they manipulated and coordinated human effort into meaningful, productive activity never ceased to amaze him. But they could also be a highly individualistic, selfish lot. If left unfettered, they tended to rush to the extremes of exorbitance, superfluity, and the outright ridiculous in pursuit of their profits. They represented a class upon whom the blessings of Excision were least manifested. Condo knew his battle with this man and the group he represented was just beginning.

He was at once understanding and reproving in his gaze. "Kind sir, there is no economy without man; there is no man without morality; there is no morality without faith; there is no faith without reason. And our reason demands that we know what has gone before so that we may with certainty understand what obtains today." The logic of Condo's reply prevented Redshilt from further challenge at the moment.

A board member representing the scientific interests spoke next. "But there are so many more practical enterprises that are in want of funding. Why, the program to extract organics from Jupiter alone represents such challenges to science and engineering that at best estimates it will take several generations of effort and funding to bring to fruition. Some are already calling *it* impractical, an impossibility. Yet, it is more important to our further existence than this rummaging in the past."

Condo replied: "Our Brother in Science in his very remarks reveals the doubt that is the great devourer of our purpose. Reason seeks knowledge not only to feed the body, but to feed the mind. *The Third Testament* tells us that "The mind *is* the soul." The mind must have understanding in order to defeat *doubt*. We must have knowledge if our soul is to have purpose." Again Condo successfully warded off the challenge.

A representative of the Schools spoke up next. Her remarks did not challenge Condo's plea, but were intended to convey to the board a feminine view point. "Life flows unbroken from the very beginning. It is likened to a tree. Many branches have sprouted from this tree. But only those that grow continually toward the light prosper and prevail. The others wither and die in shadows and darkness and are no more. I and my Sisters are the branches of that tree; you are the gardeners. Tend us well, and see that we and our offspring grow always toward the light."

"Amen." Condo's addendum was simple but appropriate and complete.

Finally remarks issued from the quarter from which Condo anticipated his greatest opposition. A board member representing the Subsidiaries of Alhumana Corporation, Church of the Habitat, spoke up.

"May God have mercy. Amen."

From his opening remarks, it was apparent this board member was an affiliate of one of the transactional congregations. The call for mercy evidenced his belief that life was a transaction between good and evil, and that a final judgment was based on the bottom line balance of one's life. One ended up either in the good or the evil column and enjoyed the unspecified consequences thereof. These congregations tended to be very fundamentalist and very demanding. But they were an absolutely quantifiable asset to society. Condo could anticipate the board member's remarks.

"We find this preoccupation with the persona of William Proffit a bit disconcerting. We fear that the head office may have some inclination towards the demystifying of this persona. We believe that *The Third Testament* clearly directs our right behavior in this regard. 'Up from the Ether are we raised. To the realm of quantum reality. A single event in God's Creation, and no more. Anonymous individuals; elements of the Sacred Whole.'

Condo listened carefully to the board members remarks. He saw in the man's gaze a deep, underlying sincerity. He also saw in the gazes of many of the other board members an allegiance with this man's fears. How ironic that the very passage quoted had probably been penned by Proffit himself. Condo answered carefully: "It is not our intent to create doubt where none existed, but only to dispel the cloud that surrounds William Proffit. When seen clearly, we believe he will be a better example of God's handiwork to us all. We believe we must have the facts so that understanding by reason will dispel doubt and strengthen faith, inspiring us in the purpose of God's Creation."

The final challenge also came from within the Church. This member was unquestionably a member of one of the metaphysical congregations.

"We can see no end to the mystery, save that God himself should reveal. Until that day the state of knowledge shall be incomplete. Does his Holiness recommend that we should not honor this precept? Perhaps the veil of mystery which surrounds William Proffit is God's intent."

Condo had anticipated this challenge, and from this quarter: "My Brother in the faith, to clear away the dust which men stirred in the wild abandon of their animal past does not presume on the greater mysteries of God's Creation. It was no divine act which conceals the fuller history of William Proffit. Though desert sands long ago buried the truth of Amagon, giving birth to the legend, we have cleared away those sands. We shall soon see what part of truth there is in the myth. We have already discovered that Amagon did not "die from war, degradation and disease" alone. We must now face the fact that no simple version of an Armageddon occurred. We have proof that a Device was used!

Condo's little revelation about the Device had the desired effect. The ocular presentations of the board members betrayed curiosity. All theology aside, human inquisitiveness, author of the "greatest of God's gifts," had been invoked: *Third Testament*, Book 2, line 133: "From inquisitiveness shall man pursue knowledge. And from that knowledge shall man ultimately arrive at faith, the greatest of God's gifts."

Before the vote was taken, Condo sensed the victory. He continued quickly: "Alhumana respectfully requests the sum of 64K Life Credits to continue its archaeological expedition and historical inquiry."

It was no small sum. The entire value of the productive lives of sixty-four thousand human beings, even spread across the multitude of Habitats, would be felt. As closed environments, the Habitats could not run deficits – such spelled disaster and death. But likewise, the ecologies could not run excessive surpluses either. Though not as immediately detrimental as a deficit, surpluses inevitably lead to wild fluctuations within the Habitats. Every expenditure had to be carefully calculated to maintain the delicate balance.

After a short debate among the board members, in which Condo observed all manner of subtle negotiations and power plays by the exchange of glances, a favorable vote was returned. Condo closed the meeting with a prayer.

"God has given us life. God has given us purpose. May it ever be so. Amen."

Once off-line, Condo breathed a sigh of relief. He removed the Mask of the Pontimax and carefully replaced it in its hand-carved box. He found these highly staged, extremely formalized confrontations with his Board of Directors exhilarating yet daunting, particularly in these days of economic cut-backs, which found Alhumana Corp. always struggling to find the funds for normal daily operations. True, the vast majority of the populations of the Habitats still participated in the corporation's spiritual functions, but Condo was not fooled, and realized full well that this participation was more force of habit than an expression of belief. There were a few of the more radical subsidiaries that still managed to incite a bit of fervor in their congregations, but even these lacked the real philosophical depth that was the sign of true religious health. The total contributions from the faithful did not come close to meeting the operating expenses of the corporation.

As had been the tradition since before man left Earth, the Boards of Directors of major corporations were to a great degree membered by persons who were themselves the CEOs of major corporations. It was a demonstration of the hierarchical tendencies in man. And so it was with the Board of Alhumana Corporation, whose members represented the major corporations involved in biologicals, mechanicals, planetary mining of both organics and inorganics, and nearly all the other major organizations engaged in the businesses which served the needs of the Habitats.

Condo was well aware that most of the board members did not truly view serving the spiritual needs of the Habitats as essential in the degree to which the more practical industries served - particularly Am'riah Redshilt and his congregation of investors and entrepreneurs. They found the morality, which was the primary product which the Church dispensed, as an irritating and unnecessarily limiting protocol in their quest for new products and markets. It was required, then, that Condo and the rest of top management at Alhumana continually find ways to entice these businesses to contribute – by appealing to their sense of justice, their sense of pride, their sense of guilt (via the Power of Audit),or, as in this case, by tweaking their curiosity. After all, Proffit had *tweaked* the Ether, and marvels had unfolded!

At any rate, Condo was glad the meeting was over and had gone well. He was about to turn his attentions to the more mundane matters of the corporation's daily business when his communicator bleeped again, and then by its amber light indicated that a one-way communication had just been received. Condo touched the acknowledged sensor and the message appeared holographically in the air above the communicator – in ancient kanjiscript! He noted immediately that the top lines did not include the name of its author, or its point of origin. The message read: *"There are perhaps truths about ourselves we should not know."*

CHAPTER 7

From *The Third Testament*: "God's Law *is* the Natural Law."

Generally the historical record is quite complete. And yet, long after the advent of the scientific and technological ages, long after the techniques of record keeping had reached nearly divine perfection, a horrendous gap appeared. And that gap occurred at precisely the moment when mankind had made a quantum leap, evolutionarily speaking. It occurred around those events that were mankind's migration from life on a planetary surface outward into Free Space.

Given that in Condo's day the historical record since the Ascent spanned something on the order of ten thousand years, an obscured century, a misplaced decade, or an occasional missing year or two seemed inconsequential to the masses. The good interpolative and extrapolative skills of an experienced historian could satisfactorily smooth out such inconsistencies. But for men who lived life at the intellectual level of Condo precision was everything. It was Reason's sword in the battle for knowledge. Yet, for millennium this missing piece of history had been avoided by scientist, historian and theologian alike. It was an unspoken corporate edict originating in the General Council of the Habitats, and pervading every subsidiary organizational structure, including Alhumana Corporation.

Condo's predecessor and mentor at Alhumana had made allusions to the missing history prior to his sudden death. It had proven a clear break with the tacit understanding extant during Condo's apprenticeship that the "accepted" history regarding Proffit should be left to stand. The current "history" clouded the fate of Proffit and Amagon in a mist of tragic destruction and insinuated divine intervention – in a word: Armageddon!

The previous CEO went to great pains to establish a secure link with his successor for these final communications, using a channel reserved for the Pontimax alone. Dispatching the necessary code by special courier on the appointed day, Condo received the code and entered its esoteric symbols into his Communicator. With his Cap affixed, his head firmly cradled in the Communicators head stand, and camera resolution set to maximum, Condo prepared to receive what would be the final admonishments and blessings from his patriarch.

"We are seen by many to be the pariah of the corporate world. We produce nothing. We survive on handouts and the market support of the faithful. And yet they fear us. For the faithful place in our hands the power of the Audit." The intensity of the old man's gaze revealed a well of wisdom, and yet at its very depth betrayed a hidden place where thoughts existed that could not be shared, save with the Eternal.

He continued: "I have examined the darker secrets which forever attach themselves to the histories of men. It is argued that such truths as these secrets hold do not benefit the upward progress of man and could adversely affect the markets. And yet it is often at man's darkest moments that the Creator reveals Himself. Perhaps you as well will be called upon to penetrate the fog and to bring into clear view the events which have for so long been obscured. And to find the courage to do what must be done…. Or perhaps not."

Condo did not miss the allusion to the mystery surrounding Proffit. That courage entered into the mix implied danger. The Pontimax's sudden death, however, and the Corporate Conclave's as rapid selection of Condo as the next CEO and Pontimax of Alhumana meant that any further inquiry would be his alone. Ever faithful, and yet ever inclined to reason, Condo could not tolerate the missing puzzle pieces, the historical gap. To allow such circumstance admitted of doubt - doubt that the pieces could be found; doubt that the pieces were of value; doubt that the pieces were even a part of the puzzle. And doubt, once permitted to germinate, spread like weeds among the Sphagnum, and choked the life-giving tree at its very root. Condo was certain of his moral obligation to eliminate this pernicious seed. Like the humble Gleaners far below, Condo's task was bound at times to be unpleasant, unappreciated and even hazardous. But by faith, through reason, he knew it was his job to do.

As a theologian, Condo subscribed to the philosophical inclination to seek out the universal unifying force - the godhead. In effect, he wanted to put the puzzle together; to get a glimpse of the big picture constructed by all those myriad pieces. And yet the analytic part of his mind wanted to examine each piece, reduce it to its fundamental properties apart from the whole. It was the tension between these two proclivities that provided the dynamic of his inquisitiveness. The paradox that complex systems (such as life) are invariably more than the sum of their parts provided the fundamental stepping stone between his ability to reason and his abiding faith. But a puzzle, or a complex system, cannot be fully understood until *all* of it pieces are known!

Condo felt certain the mystery surrounding man's last days on Earth, the fate of Amagon, and of Proffit was no accident. He also believed that in the labyrinthine corporate structure of the Habitats there no longer existed anyone who fully understood the nature of the mystery. He believed the lack of curiosity in most quarters concerning the subject had become an instinctive avoidance in the corporate organism. But crises of faith had begun to plague many of the Habitats in recent generations. A certain existentialism had begun to creep into the philosophies of several of the most essential corporate structures. In many areas management was beginning to question the basic precepts. Was human life and its continued expansion truly the essence of all economies? This skepticism was creeping into the litanies of the laboring masses as well. Why build another Habitat? Why work so hard to bring the organic elements together in the Habitats so that biological processes might mold them into a man, when man, though marvelous in his sentience, was but a creature that lived for a only a short time and then died? These crises were becoming epidemic, and the *doubt* they engendered threatened man's very purpose.

*The Third Testament* says: "If you would understand the foundation upon which a house is built, you must go to the basement." That is what Condo intended to do. Amagon *was* the basement. He knew therein he would find the strengths to shore-up the house. He believed he could find the truths that would dispel the growing doubts.

But there had been the anonymous message.

## CHAPTER 8

Condo set the A-cav on his Locator to automatic and lapsed deep into thought. Once caught up by the entrance draft to the Tube the propelletes at his shoulders and hips fluttered alternately, like the tiny wings of fairies, deftly maneuvering him through the mash of evening traffic. He had run a trace from his communicator and determined that the anonymous message had come from his own Habitat. In fact, it appeared to have originated from a mobile communicator located somewhere in the Core Sphagnum. He knew that Gleaners eschewed the use of most technical devices. Generally the only persons in that region who had communicators were the Salvors. He was still puzzling over the matter when his Locator beeped, indicating he had arrived at his exit.

Condo could have taken one of the vertical Tubes to a location nearer his home but instead preferred the free flight up to the level of the Pods. His wife Sar'ha also generally preferred this route on her way home, so he rotated slowly as he ascended, seeing if he could spy her among the others free flying in the great open spaces between the boles of the Forest trees. He didn't see her, so he began to prepare for the ritualized evening encounter with his offspring. He let his mind begin a review of the *facts* learned during his years in the Corps.

Though these facts were readily and easily retrievable under the Cap, Condo knew his children would quiz him on their studies for the day, hoping to find some bit of information that he didn't have stored within his own brain. . .

Condo reviewed his compendium:

*34 Beta was of that first class of Habitats in which the vegetation had actually been engineered into the structure. The trees had been genetically derived from Earth-bound conifer stock, but unencumbered by intense gravity, uncertain climate or marginal soil, they far surpassed the timid 100+ meter length of their ancestors. At nearly a thousand years old, they generally exceeded 500 meters just in their boles, with overall lengths reaching 700+ meters from the surface of the Core Sphagnum to their uppermost tips. As the trees had matured, titanium girders were removed, these structural members of the Habitat replaced by the living trees. Longitudinal wedges of these Forests alternated with the great terraced Hydrofarms and urban panels under the great glass Shell. The trees were anchored by their roots in the Core Sphagnum, which covered most of the length of the Cylinder Sea, and absorbed fresh water from the sea through great panels of permeable membrane.*

*The great Cylinder Seas were the heart of every Habitat. They provided the axis of rotation to the structures, and by their sheer volume, were the primary source of the minute gravitational forces experienced within the Habitats. This attraction, countered by minuscule centrifugal forces created by the rotation, did little to interfere with the nearly effortless transport within the Habitat, but did create a settling, such that anything lost or left unattached slowly drifted downward to the Core Sphagnum. There it became the property of the Gleaners, and as recovery or salvage, was traded to salvage brokers for a fair price. These salvage brokers reintroduced the materials to the general economy.*

*For reasons of nostalgia, culture, and psychological continuity, the Habitats were constructed commensurate to the old Earth dimensions an oblate spheroid: equatorial diameter - 12,756 kilometers; polar diameter – 12,713 kilometers; which translated to Habitat dimensions of: equatorial diameter - 12.756 kilometers; polar diameter - 12.713 kilometers. The Cylinder Seas, which provided the axis of rotation, contained 90% the mass of a Habitat, but represented only about $10^{-9}$ the mass of the old Earth. For all intents and purposes, gravitational attraction was imperceptible.*

*To mimic the eons-old radiation cycle of one revolution per 24 Earth hour day, the rotational velocity at the Shell's equator was 1.68 kilometers per hour, producing minimal centripetal forces at that location, which reduced as one approached the Cylinder Sea. The seas were open at their polar ends under great glass domes, whose interiors were fitted with great mirrored prisms from which extended living, light conducting fibers that continuously directed the solar radiation deep into the body of water. This accumulated energy, besides supporting an extremely fecund aquaculture, provided the baseline thermal gradient for the Habitats, served to stabilize the internal temperature as the structure rotated, with the internal environment alternately exposed to direct absorption from the sun, and re-radiation into dark space. These organoptic fibers also permeated the Sphagnum, which constituted the majority of a Habitat's biomass. At any given moment, 98% of the organic mass of the Habitats was directly involved in its living organisms.*

*The electrical potential between the Shell and the Core/Cylinder Sea, generated by the photosynthetic/osmotic processes of the biomass, naturally occurring and engineered photoelectric effects, and the air currents and weather patterns, both naturally occurring and those created by the ventilation/transportation system, proved sufficient to provide the electrical needs of the Habitat.*

Having gone from the Corps directly into Seminary, Condo had gained no practical knowledge of the industrial and mining sectors. As these activities were all conducted on or from platforms remote to the Habitats, and operated completely by automatic machines and Golem, his knowledge of them remained limited to that retrievable from the Cap. His only experience in operating a Golem was his occasional visit to the archaeological sites. For the sake of his children and to better understand the complete functioning of the human social machine he always intended to learn more. But in the hectic pace of the modern day intentions very often went unrealized. He hoped their questions tonight would fall comfortably within the realm of his expertise.

As his home Pod came into view Condo could see the eager countenances of his brood of four peering from the blossom end. As he approached nearer they all propelled toward him, their adoring faces coming so close to his that he could smell the sweetness of manna on their breaths.

"Hello, father!"

"Oh, what an adventure we had at Corps today!"

"Father, I want to ask! I want to ask!"

"Tell us father! Tell us! Is it true that someday they will be able to grow an entire Habitat from a single seed?"

The four children of Condo's second brood swarmed around their father like bees around honey. There were the two boys, Io'sak and Jo'suf, and the girls, Mar'oi and Beth'ha. Now in the eighth year since their births, they were Tyros in the Corps and did not yet wear the tonsure of Excised Cadets.

Condo laughed warmly and fully at their unabashed inquisition. "Such a question! Grow an entire Habitat from a single seed? I think that is still very much the stuff of science fiction!" He winked at them ostentatiously, and tilting his head jauntily nodded an affirmation to the possibility so as not to dampen the enthusiasm of their imaginations. It had the desired effect. He could see by the expressions in their eyes that they pursued the idea within the gedanken realms of the creative mind. He reached out to embrace them, feeling the warmth of their bodies next to his. Then, gathering them up in his arms and legs he propelled upward through the blossom end of the Pod.

"Is your mother home yet?" he asked as they ascended the Pod's central tube.

Mar'oi answered. "She has sent a message, Father. She will be at Hospital till late finishing a class, and won't be home till after Ensymphonium."

After graduating her second brood from School to Corps Sar'ha had returned to her profession as a physician. It had been a nine-year absence and Condo understood that she was working very hard to review and to learn the latest in procedures so she could resume practice. Just the innovations and new techniques employed in Excision were a

formidable challenge, let alone the advances made in neo-natal care, nutrition, disease prevention and treatment, and the ever-expanding programs for the maintenance and care of Unfortunates.

"Well, we shall have to fend for ourselves then. I am sure you are all starved. Or have you got your bellies full of manna already?" Condo pretended a stern look.

"No, Father!" they chorused. "We've only had a little nibble."

"To the Kitchen, then. And let's prepare a feast!"

They swirled up the central tube to the common rooms at the stem end of the Pod. The boys threw open the windeyes to the kitchen; the girls began to ransack the compartments for ingredients. Mealtime, and particularly its preparation, was a very important family activity. They would manage this evening without Sar'ha. Within an hour they had prepared a meal of 27 courses, consisting of fruits and vegetables; nuts and grains; pseudo-meat, pseudo-fish; sauces, gravies, beverages, and breads. The canister for each course was appropriately heated or chilled. The portions of each were no more than good nutrition required and the various courses would be served in an order such that the taste and texture of each course anticipated the course which followed, creating a crescendo of enjoyment with each ensuing morsel.

With the meal prepared and the canisters set, Condo and his children took their places at table within the kitchen ring, attaching to its inner cushions with the back patches of their Locators. They curled themselves in Prayers of Thanksgiving.

As it was Io'sak's turn to lead, he recited a simple and common verse known to all children: "As is His purpose, we take the bounty of God's creation into our bodies, and make it Human Life." Jo'suf, Mar'oi and Beth'ha chorused: "Amen!" The family took up their feeding tubes, and dipping into the first canister, the feast began!

Later, Condo and his brood gathered in the family's balcony ring atop the Pod in preparation for Ensymphonium. The children had put on their Caps and were beginning to exercise their fingers and toes on the pitch holes of their recorders. They were just beginning to participate in the ritual and would contribute only an occasional note. But they were enthusiastic and anxious. Condo on the other hand had become quite accomplished on the violins. With his Cap on and activated he was beginning to visualize the flow of melody and harmony which was being created moment to moment by those already in Ensymphonium. He was just beginning to hear the symphonic swell approaching from the east as the sun was rotated out of view to the west.

At its onset, Ensymphonium gave one the effect of a very distant and yet visceral chorus, warbling between the joyous and the melancholy, not quite melodic, but possessed of a growing and irresistible harmony. As the light faded and one entered into the longitudes of participation the feed from the Cap and the audible contributions from the nearby participants led one into the current theme of the music. As always, it ranged from the sweetest, most joyous of lilts to the darkest and most forbidding of dirges. This regular cycle exercised the emotions to a totally satisfying exhaustion within the space of no more than 20 minutes. Then, as one passed out of the longitudes of participation Ensymphonium once again reduced to a distant murmur and faded into darkness.

During this Ensymphonium, Condo's children each ventured a note or two in contribution, and after having done so would look to the others in childish delight and uncertainty, their eyes dancing between pride and fright. Condo himself had managed a four note phrase that for an instant was picked up in the Ensymphonium, and then sped away in a myriad of variations, happy and sad. He noted Sar'ha's empty place, missing her harps, and wishing with the bit of vanity and pride that survived in his psyche that she could have been there to hear his composition.

As the music faded, that warm fatigue that always follows exertion glowed on the faces of Condo and his brood. They removed their  Caps, and after storing their instruments, began to assail their father with appeals and requests. Mar'oi took the lead: "Can we go up to the canopy tonight Father? You promised that we might. We haven't any homework to speak of and the dishes are done."

Like so many fathers, Condo's promises to his children were too often a long time in the realization. He needed to be in his study preparing for Sab'hath and catching up on the reports from the archaeological digs. And there was the matter of the strange message from the Core. Besides, with Sar'ha absent he felt it wouldn't truly be a family affair. Still attached to the balcony ring he was about to reply when Sar'ha's voice whispered in his ear. "You really should keep your promises you know. What must the children think – what must *I* think when the number one Holy Man doesn't keep his word!" Condo turned in his place to find Sar'ha hovering behind him. Giggles from the children informed him that she had been there for a while. He blushed at being surreptitiously observed, even by his beloved Sar'ha.

"Ah! What a fine piece of work! The anger and lust cut right out of the man, and yet he blushes!" Sar'ha's observation was astute. The process of Excision had advanced greatly from the crude removal of tissue to the delicate dividing of distinct neural connections, not only in the amygdala but in the hypothalamus and hippocampus as well. Yet, it was rare for the blush response to have survived the procedure in someone from Condo's generation. As a skilled Excisionist, Sar'ha appreciated the exception her husband represented and the vast unknowns that still faced her profession. But that was a matter to address during regular working hours. Now was family time. So Sar'ha washed the pensive look from her face and turning to the children encouraged their appeals. Vastly outnumbered, Condo gave in.

"All right. But let's swim up. I haven't had enough exercise all week. Getting flabby." Condo distended his abdomen, blew out his cheeks, and began a wallowing undulation, acting as if were impossible for him to move because of his bulk.

Sar'ha and the children laughed at his antics. But the children's interest in his clowning was quickly lost to a flurry of activity as they shed their back patches while Sar'ha retrieved the family's set of fins. As quickly as each had slipped limbs into fins, the children began the rhythmic undulations by which they pushed against the air and propelled themselves forward. They circled their parents like a small shoal of fry while Condo and Sar'ha donned their attunements, which process, do to age and lack of exercises, was not so easily accomplished. Once all were outfitted the children led the way, beginning an immediate vertical ascent from the balcony, deftly swimming in, out, and around the overhanging foliage. Es'paul and Sar'ha struck out horizontally to avoid the excessive maneuvering (which would have been taxing to their mature physics – or at least his!) seeking the open space between the trees to make their ascent. As yet more agile, and better exercised, Sar'ha quickly gained a lead on her husband, glancing mockingly over her shoulder. Then, with a burst of speed she joined the children as they emerged from the vegetation.

Condo was so enamored of the scene that he stopped and for a moment floated, gazing up at the sheer beauty and grace of this mother and her offspring. It was as if pixies and their fairy queen had emerged from the pages of a fairy tale to take residence in his world.  So beautiful and supple were their movements as every muscle was employed in this act that on one hand it seemed the most natural form of locomotion for this delicate species and yet had something of the otherworldly – the angelic – about it. He momentarily lamented its surrendered to the mechanical Locators, for it had been the principle method of propulsion in the first Habitats to go weightless.  But differing abilities had created problems as populations grew. It was not practical to let everyone swim at their own speed and in their own direction. Efficiency and safety demanded equalization, however, which led to the development of the Locator. Condo abandoned his pining when he realized his wife and children had become mere specks in the distance.

The last light of day reflected off the interior of the Shell far to the west as Condo, well exercised and severely winded, reached his family.  The photo-sensitive plaques coating the interior of the Shell's glass regulating the penetration of radiations were returning to optical transparency, at the cost of some thermal opacity.  The family huddled together in the cooling air and growing dark as the vast panorama of the night sky opened before them, sparkling with a myriad of starry jewels, all framed in the grid-like girding of the Shell's global frame. The air was fragrant with the blossoms of the parasitic, arboreal orchards which grew upon the uppermost limbs of the Forest trees, and the barely audible strains of a now distant Ensymphonium mingled with the chirp of grazing aphids and the lazy whir of spiraling bee's wings as the last of the pollinators swarmed in vortexes of circus ballet back to their hives.

The Faith did not abjure all primitive emotion. In fact, the awe which Condo and his family now felt beneath the great vault of the firmament was hailed as good and true reverence. But the nearly disastrous loss of so many of the good emotions in the early centuries of Excision had almost lead to extinction. For it was discovered that even love, the most lauded of human emotions, had to have its origins in the primordial neural networking if it were to become an element of the rational mind. And the early butchery of the amygdala and surrounding tissue too often destroyed the very roots from which this mature and rational emotion could grow, particularly as it was deemed in those early days that Excision should take place in the child well before sexual pubescence. For several generations it had been necessary to implement a very severe form of brain-washing just to keep reproduction at levels sufficient to maintain the population of the extant Habitats.

The human race had come a long way since then. And yet, in this awe-filled moment Condo realized the journey had only begun. As keeper of the Faith and dispeller of *doubt*, he was humbled by the vastness of Creation. He looked down at his as yet un-excised children and marveled at their innocence. He looked heavenward and marveled at its mystery.

Condo recalled this passage from *The Third Testament:* "The thing we seek lies beyond the farthest star; beyond the furthest moment."

## CHAPTER 9

As an executive and a professional Condo was exempt from the social regime of "8 hours of work; 8 hours of play; 8 hours of sleep" for the six yobi of the week, not that anyone adhered perfectly to the regime or were any longer persecuted or shunned for failure to comply. His adherence to strict observance of the Sab'hath had to be exemplary, however.

Having seen his children into their night silks and tucked securely in their bedclaves, and having left Sar'ha at her desk studying for her re-entrance exam, Condo retired to his study off the central tube at the lower end of the Pod, just inside the blossom end, to work late into the night. The embedded LED's illuminated on his entrance. His desk and console energized as he approached. His back patch engaged its counterpart at his chair, and thus stabilized, he reached out and removed his Cap from its box. He slipped it over the great, bulbous orb of his cranium.

It was the sixth yobi, and tomorrow being Sab'hath, he was in need of a sermon. But his mind was on the archaeological digs and Proffit and the strange message from the Core. So he scanned the data files of past sermons, and finding one that had not been logged onto for several years retrieved it and entered it into the Sab'hath program, hoping no one of real importance would detect the repetition, and find cause to criticize him for underperformance of his duties.

The sermon accomplished, Condo retrieved the anonymous message from the Core written in ancient kanji script and with it floating before him quickly reviewed the latest reports from the digs. He began a systems search for all the data files concerning one William Proffit.

Condo was thoroughly familiar with the extant Proffit files. They represented one of the principle courses of study at Seminary. Yet he was also aware that the files had been sanitized over the years as a succession of Pontimaxes and Elders had found reason to sculpt the facts into a serviceable legend. But perhaps he might glean some new insight by reviewing the files. *Glean some new insight. . .* He looked again at the message from the Core. Could it have come from a Gleaner? What could a Gleaner have to say in this matter?

The lowest class of citizens within the Habitats, the Gleaners were seldom ever discussed or considered during regular business of any sort. They did not appear to participate in the general social structure. Their only know communications were with the Salvors, with whom they conducted business. Condo had seen pictures of them, but long ago. His curiosity piqued, he called up the image of a Gleaner. The Holograph on his desk created a lifelike image in the space before him.

He was involuntarily taken aback by the strangeness of the visage. The man was obviously human, if it was a man. The gauntness of the features and the billowy and pleated cut of the sack it was wearing made it impossible to determine the sex. A life-time spent at the Core Sphagnum, which the Gleaners referred to as their Bog, left its mark. The tannin rich, highly acidic environment darkened and wrinkled the skin. It left the hair a flaming orange color and the eyes eternally bloodshot. Eschewing the use of technology, the Gleaners did not transport via the Tubes, nor use Locators. Instead, in an almost comical imitation of their ancient, earthborn ancestors, they moved about by grasping the surface of the Sphagnum with the toes of their feet, tugging themselves along in a fashion they called" walking." This rendered their feet nearly black. They never used their feet for manual tasks; they did use them in Prayer. They were certainly nothing an ordinary man would want to shake or embrace!

The Gleaners lived in burrows in the Sphagnum. Receiving moisture from the sea by parasitizing the succulents, and supported in photosynthesis by the dim light delivered through a trellis of natural optical fibers produced by sponge-like organisms, the moss grew to a thickness of 150 to 200 meters in places. It was here these mendicants carved out their abodes. They were not the sole occupants of the Sphagnum, for it was here that the great bio-cycle of the Habitat began. It was here that the Worms resided, making the daily migration up the long boles of the Forest trees and into the great, open, terraced trays of the Hydrofarms, the clusters of the urban panels, the Forests of the management class, to find nourishment in cleansing humans and devouring much of the other organic detritus which daily accumulated, returning at night to deposit their excreta as nourishment for the Sphagnum and the Forest trees. There were hundreds of varieties of other annelids, insects, arachnids, and the larvae of various orthopterae that participated in the process, many feeding on the Sphagnum itself, converting the material into nutrient for the trees and moss, or to be collected for the Hydrofarms. It was said that because of the tannin, the Worms would not cleanse a Gleaner, nor recycle the corpse of a Gleaner. It was said that the Gleaners relished the flesh of Worms.

His thoughts had only incidentally turned upon the Gleaners, but with a Cap on, the memories stored in the vast array of databanks had begun to well up. Needing a moment to rationalize, Condo reached up and pulled the Cap off of his head to stop the process.

Though the transitions were quite smooth, still one could tell when a memory had its origin within one's own neuronal networking, or whether it was being accessed through a Cap. With the Device now removed, Condo was surprised to realize just how little he really knew about the Gleaners. But then, he was at the very apex of society, and they were at its very base. Still, as head of the Church, his paternal responsibilities certainly required that he should know more about this element of society; these lowly fellow humans. He recalled that on occasion the Church did send missionaries to the Core. He remembered seeing the memos. But he could not remember ever seeing or being sent a report by these missionaries or their supervisors or department heads regarding the outcome of these projects.

The implication of the Gleaners in his archaeological and historical query regarding Proffit, Amagon, and man's last days on Earth allowed only one reasonable course of action. Condo would have to visit the Core Sphagnum. He keyed his secretary, and when the program opened, instructed it to check his schedule and make the necessary appointments and arrangements for him to visit the Core. That done, Cond again donned the Cap and seeing that the search for data regarding William Proffit was complete, he set the filter parameters to allow his conscious editing of the data stream, opened a program to record his interpretations, and curling himself in his chair commenced the retrieval.

The record was constituted of narrations attributed to eyewitness accounts or contemporary news reports. Condo's review and interpretation of these files would be a lightning fast exchange between the micro-Proffit Devices that were the neural transponders imbedded in the Cap, and the synapses of his own organic, neuronal networking, as coordinated by the precision of the quantum computer – a perfect meld of the intellect of the man, and the speed, capacity, and accuracy of the machine. The following colloquially authored narrative emerged:

*William Alden Proffit was born to devout, working class parents in the city outlands in the tumultuous days of the second half of the third millennium of the modern era. Great chasms had opened between the social strata, and the upper classes argued that civilization existed only within the fortressed walls of their cities. But genius was still valued wherever it was found, and eagerly exploited if possible.*

*William Proffit attended public school until the age of 10, at which point the system could no long contain his academic abilities. He traded Grammar School for the Institute of Technology and received his B.S at age 12, his Masters at age 14, and the first of several Ph.D.s at age 15. Thence he commenced a career as particle physicist and theoretician.*

*At the age of 28, William Proffit suffered an apparent complete emotional and mental breakdown. He went on a rampage, wrecking his research laboratory, erasing all data, and destroying all physical records pertaining to his work. It was rumored he was being pressured by forces within the government to divulge the result of researches which might prove militarily advantageous to the ruling class of his city.*

*Seemingly reduced to an incoherent, semi-catatonic state, Proffit was institutionalized. As a security risk he was made a ward of the state. The name of the institution has been lost. Records for the next six years are scant and consist mainly of semi-annual medical reports, and the institution's financial statements regarding payments made by the state for his care.*

*On a cold Christmas day the institution reported that its patient Proffit, W.A., was missing. Local police and emergency response teams made a search of the area. There were eight inches of snow on the ground and the temperature was 18 degrees F. Proffit had wandered out an unlocked door in the kitchen area of the institution and his footprints lead across new snow on the lawn and out into the nearby street where they were lost to snowplows and traffic.*

*After several hours the search was called off. Authorities notified area shelters, churches, and charities, and a description was broadcast on radio and television and sent to the local papers. A search was resumed the next day. No trace of Proffit was found. Due to the coldness of the weather it was assumed that if he had not obtained shelter, he had perished. Proffit's parents were notified.*

*Two years hence a young reporter for an urban Tribune authored a piece entitled: The Disappearance of William Proffit – Boy Genius. The article ran in three installments, and greatly enhanced the reporter's career, but brought no new information or interest in Proffit's disappearance. It did fire the blood of many a conspiracy theorist.*

*That same year, on a Saturday in July, a man calling himself A. Proffit wandered into the small, unincorporated and nearly deserted, rural, mid-western community of Amagon in the old state of Arkansas. Amagon lay at the intersection of secondary roads twelve miles east of an Intercity Hoverway, on a flat plain extending westward from the foot of a low range of mountains in the central region of a geographic subdivision called "the Ozarks". The area was soggy in winter and spring; hot, dry and dusty during summer and fall. The community consisted of a fuel station/ farm supply and feed store on the southwest corner of the intersection. Diagonally opposite, at the northeast corner stood Kathy's Place, a small cafe set in the middle of a large gravel lot that catered to the locals and the few freight transports that took this back-country route to avoid the regulations imposed on the commercial lanes of traffic. The northwest corner was vacant, except for weeds and rubbish and a couple of abandoned, rusting automobiles. Along the east-west route lay the centuries old remnants of an attempted main street. Small adjoining buildings ran for two blocks, with presumptuous facades of brick work and embossed metal, fronted by cobble stone walks and ornate iron lampposts that had all but been lost to dust and rust and sod. Only an occasional pane of glass still remained in a window or door, and most of the buildings' interiors were now sunlit by day as great, collapsed portions of roof dangled inside. At the eastern end of the town, on the north side of the street shaded by several surviving stunted, windswept trees common to the area stood a slightly off-the-perpendicular, simple white frame church which still drew a small congregation from the surrounding country-side and which boasted a cemetery whose population outnumbered the living and grew as the community died. Several dirt roads crisscrossed behind and beyond the main street and created what might be considered the town's block-grid, with the nearest occupied house belonging the restaurateur Kathy setting just behind the church. Stepping into Amagon was stepping into times long past. Proffit's appearance in the community was first observed by the proprietor of the petrol station, who from the shade of his establishment's doorway saw the disheveled stranger walk in from the east and stop at a corner of the intersection, intently examining what lay up and down the roads.*

*Proffit's appearance was also noted by two old men who sat on a bench, whittling and spitting, at the front of the café. One said to the other, "I wonder who that character is?" The other replied: "Must'uv come down outta the hills."*

*Recollections by a local citizen who was one of the first to encounter Proffit remarked that "though he looked like a "bum, once you talked with 'im, and looked in 'iz eyes, you cud see real quick that he was a real smart fella He had a fire burnin' in his*

*eyes. And when he begun ta' talk religion, why, I
ain't never been the religious type, but he lit a fire
under me!"*

*Apparently satisfied with what he saw, Proffit left
the intersection and proceeded across the gravel
lot to Kathy's Place. His stride was long and
confident and purposeful. He held the Bible to his
chest, clutched in his right hand, and his small
sack of belongs swung rhythmically at the end of
his left arm. As he stepped up and into the shade
of the restaurant's front veranda, he looked both
of his observers directly in the eye, and giving them
a sense that was at once extremely familiar and
comfortable, and yet a bit intrusive and disturbing,
in a strong and well-modulated voice pronounced:
"Good morning, Gentlemen!" Then he lowered
his right hand, and still clutching the Bible, deftly
grabbed the door's knob, pulled the door open,
and disappeared into the cooler, dark recesses of
the restaurant. His bench-sitting commentators
looked at each other quizzically, neither offering
additional remarks, and returned to their whittling
and spitting.*

*Inside the restaurant a buxom, past-forty Kathy
stood at the far end of the counter just serving
breakfast to two drivers whose transports hovered
idling in the gravel lot. Widowed and childless,
she was cook, cashier, and clean-up in this one-
woman operation. She looked up at the sound of
the door and saw the silhouette of a tall, slender
man backlit by the brilliance pouring in from the
large front window. She put down the coffee pot*

*she was holding, wiped her hands on her apron, and shading her eyes with one hand to reduce the glare, stepped to the middle of the counter opposite Proffit. From this vantage she could see plainly the features of the man. Unlike the male observers outside, she did not first notice the tattered clothing and ill-kept overall appearance, but rather first saw the fine, handsomely chiseled face of a man in perhaps his middle thirties, with a rakish abundance of flaxen hair and the most beautiful, penetrating, inviting and yet somehow threatening blue eyes she could ever remember seeing. Her appraisal of him was so absorbing that for a moment she was literally speechless. When she did speak, there was a submission in her voice that was not common to her independent nature. "Can I help you?"*

*Proffit smiled broadly, extending his right hand with its Bible, and his left with its small, ragged sack, and spoke unashamedly. "I'm traveling rather light, as you can see. I was wondering if I could do a little work in exchange for something to eat. Sweep the floor; do some dishes; anything, really. For a bowl of oatmeal and some toast and coffee, maybe?"*

*The man's request was unexpected, and for a moment it did not register. She took a step backwards, to reconsider her first impression of the man. As his greater appearance came into focus, she realized that he was shabbily attired, and none too clean, though the dust did seem only recently accumulated, and not the result of a general lack of hygiene. His beard certainly did not seem to be more than a day's growth. But returning her gaze to meet his eyes, the geniality and good humored honesty they beamed reasserted her initial appraisal.*

*She shook her head and laughing at herself, spoke: "Excuse me! I didn't mean to stare. It's just that, ...well...I was expecting you to order something, or ask for directions, or try to sell me something, or. . . Well, you just didn't strike me as someone that would be asking for a handout. Uh. . .I don't mean handout! I mean. . .you just don't look like someone needing to work for his supper. Oh! You know what I mean!"*

*Proffit laughed heartily, and shrugged.*

*"Sure, sure I can find something for you to do! Sit down and I'll get you something to eat." She smiled at him, and shook her head as she thought: "I can't believe this happening! It's out 'uva movie, for Chris'sake!"*

*Proffit took a seat on one of the stools at the counter. He looked to his left at the two drivers, who sat with forks half way between plate and mouth, their attention turned to Kathy's dialogue with the stranger. Suddenly caught as voyeurs, they reanimated and tried to make the transition unnoticed. Proffit spoke to them. "Hello. You fellows driving the hover rigs out there?"*

*With a gaze stuffed deeply under the brim of his cowboy hat, the nearer driver answered: "Yup."*

*His obvious recalcitrance and the other driver's even deeper retreat under his hat signaled Proffit that they were not interested in his conversation. Proffit took the signal and turned back on his stool just as Kathy set a cup of steaming coffee in front of him. "Oatmeal will take about five minutes."*

*Kathy had noted the abbreviated exchange between Proffit and the drivers. "Big-rig drivers are two kinds – either they are as gregarious as a six month old pup, or as surly as an under-the-porch cur." The smile of understanding which returned from Proffit's face reassured her that her first impression was right. This was a decent man.*

*"I saw the little church at the end of the street. Do they have preacher?"*

*Kathy was not surprised by the question, on account of the Bible. "The Amagon Community Church, you mean? No, no preacher. They don't even have a denomination. Just sort of a mixed bag. Just folks trying to keep a little decency alive, I guess. Mainly it's a social thing. You know - Christmas and Easter and bake sales and picnics and quilt making. I go sometimes just to visit with my neighbors."*

*"It's a good thing, then - this little church." The sincerity in his eyes reached a little more deeply inside her than she expected. She turned away nervously, to fetch his oatmeal and toast.*

*Proffit had his breakfast and spent the morning in chores as payment. He swept the floors and changed a couple of burned-out fluorescent bulbs that had gone wanting for months because Kathy would have had to drag out a ladder and didn't like the idea. He also swept the front porch, around the whittling and spitting of the old men, who only reluctantly succumbed to garrulousness after much good-hearted persuasion from Proffit.*

*Kathy reckoned that the work done compensated excessively for the breakfast given, so as he readied to depart, she slipped him a bag which contained a sandwich and a slice of pie, and a go-cup of coffee. Proffit thanked her, and turning to leave said quite certainly: "See you tomorrow." The woman did not doubt it.*

*For the rest of that day, Proffit could be seen wandering up and down Amagon's main street, examining at length the dilapidated structures that populated it. Occasionally he would sit on the sill of a glassless window front, in the shade provided by the remnant of an awning, his elbows on his knees, hands clasped at his chin as if in prayer, staring. Toward evening he was seen in the churchyard cemetery reading the names on tombstones and sometimes sitting on the grass reading his Bible.*

*No one knew where he spent the night. But most suspected he found refuge in one of the abandoned buildings. When the Amagon Community Church's secretary arrived at precisely 10:30 next morning (as she did every Sunday morning) to unlock the church doors (and to set up the heat in winter, open the windows in spring and fall, or to turn on the rusting and clanking old window air-conditioner in the heat of summer), she found Proffit sitting on the church-house steps. His presence did not surprise her; rumors travel rapidly and constantly in small, isolated communities. What did surprise her was that he appeared to be freshly washed and shaved, and had even managed to shake most of the dust and wrinkles out of his ill-fitting, ragged attire. He rose and greeted her: "Good morning, Ma'm." She acknowledged him with a curt "Mornin'," as she unlocked the doors and disappeared inside.*

*By ten minutes to eleven most of the 25 or so of the church's regular congregation had arrived, and after short and reserved greetings of acknowledgment to the stranger, headed for the cooling interior of the simple frame building. A not-so-regular Kathy showed up dressed as she would be for Christmas or Easter, and shook Proffit's hand before joining the others. When the last of the flock had arrived and the clock's hand rounded up to the hour, Proffit stepped through the church doors. The congregation turned in their pews, looking askance at the stranger; awaiting some indication of intent or action.*

*"I would like to speak to you, if I might," he said, in a tone both plaintive and yet insistent. To a person, the congregation nodded their assent. Proffit walked*

*authoritatively to the front of the church, and placing his Bible on the rostrum, began his sermon. It was a day that changed the course of human history.*

Condo removed the Cap and paused the recording program. The files he had been reviewing were the biographies and personal testimonies of those who had lived in the time of William Proffit - people who had known the man first-hand. They were a part of the accepted legend surrounding Proffit. He wanted to review those files which carried the technical data concerning Proffit's scientific achievements and his own writings and statements regarding his "insanity," and his "conversion," but that would have to wait. It had grown late and Condo felt suddenly overcome by the fatigue that signals the nervous system's need to regenerate its chemical balances, and for the conscious mind to surrender to the unconscious processes which seek truth by avenues other than logic and reason.

CHAPTER 10

S ab'hath officially began at midnight on the advent of seventh yobi. It was a more or less arbitrary designation derived from a synthesis of thousands of years of religious tradition. Of course, in each Habitat there actually occurred 24 such advents as rotation brought each successive longitudinal sector to that time. The meridian for Sab'hath was commensurate with the ancient Prime Meridian on Earth at the raising of New Jerusl'm. An entire department within the Mathematics Division of the Church dedicated itself to nothing but calculating the necessary corrections in orbit and rotation of the Habitats for the proper synchronization of Sab'hath, following the mandate from *The Third Testament:* "Precision is a gift from God."

As the first Habitat sectors rotated into Sab'hath, the message from the Pontimax was transmitted via the  Caps. It was repeated each hour for the 24 hour duration of Sab'hath. The subsidiaries to the Church also transmitted their particular messages during this time, each representing a particular nuance to the Philosophy of Religion that appealed to the intellects and inclinations of it laity. It was the responsibility of the Pontimax, as CEO of Alhumana, to see that a thread of commonality was maintained between these disparate theologies. As it had long ago been determined that morality was the prime ingredient for the social, economic and spiritual health of the Habitats, and of humanity, the Pontimax's efforts then were necessarily to reinforce the notion that above all else, God's commandment to man is – be moral!

An excerpt from a Sermon by the Pontimax (Es'paul Condo *incognitus*):

*"Creatures abound within the Habitats. They are all essential to the fulfillment of the life cycle. They are composed of diverse tissues – muscle, organ, skeleton, membrane and nerve. They possess within their nervous systems potentials to initiate behaviors which promote their survival. The potentials are incited from the surrounding environment or from deeply imbedded biological triggers. These potentials are realized by the sensations of pain or pleasure. The perceptions of these sensations are relative to the state of neurological development of the organism.*

*There is no creature, save man, whether individual, or as part of a social group, which can so willfully behave in a fashion contrary to the instinctive behaviors programmed into its neurology, as to deliberately alter its own physiology for the common good. This is the essence of morality. It is the justification for Excision. . ."*

CHAPTER 11

Upon arriving at his Cell on morg'Mon'yobi, Condo was greeted by the pealing of his secretary. Proceeding to his Console and engaging his back patch, he acknowledged the program's bell and began to review the messages and tasks. Immediately, a marked task caught his attention: "Confirmation of Appointment - Re: Contact Gleaner." Condo called up the text.

*"Your request for an appointment with a representative of the Gleaner community at the Core of Habitat Beta 34 is confirmed. Contact was made in your name with Ho'jin Sada, Elder of the extant community. A meeting is scheduled 1300hr this yobi at the Core, per your instructions. To obtain proper quarantine, please advise Medical of your intent to travel extra-route. Please contact Transportation for routing information."*

Condo acknowledged the message to Medical and Transportation. He indicated a departure time of 1200hr. Then slipping on his Cap, he turned to the business of running a major corporation.

There were meetings of all the department heads to attend: complaints and appeals from the Subsidiaries to review and assign to appropriate Committees on Doctrine; ritual, ethics, semantics, etc.; and most importantly, the usual number of petitions for Audit from various citizens' groups to be researched, reviewed and adjudged. Beyond the moral and spiritual function of Alhumana Corporation, its most important sociological function was the power of Audit it held as a mandate from the populations of the Habitats. As the corporation had evolved as the mechanism of social order next above family, and was the paramount social structure for solitaries, the Audit was the mechanism by which the polity exerted its moral force on these business entities. As every citizen of every Habitat was at least theoretically a voting stock holder in every corporation, a more democratic system could hardly be imagined. In reality, of course, people tended to pursue their own interests, and were active in those corporations which they perceived as most relevant to their individual needs or which operated in areas where the individual possessed particular talents and abilities, and generally paid little attention to the operations of the other corporations. But Alhumana Corporation, as the sole spiritual corporate entity, more nearly focused the interests of human society than any previous social structure or organization, and possessing the power of Audit, it could, if the situation warranted, bring the scrutiny (and political wrath) of the entire society down upon the Board of Directors and management of a corporation that strayed too far from the moral norms. Though fiscally impoverished by the standards of the other corporations, by wielding the moral will of the human race, Alhumana Corporation, Church to the Habitats, was the political behemoth! Even so, by a vote of the stock holders, *it* could be subjected to Audit! Such was the case, then, that the corporate environment within the Habitats was every bit as complex and delicate in its equilibrium as was the biological environment. Everything needed tending all the time! As the Maintenance Corp tended the Habitat, so Alhumana tended the human psyche.

Condo accomplished his abbreviated work day a few minutes before 1200hr and dashed off a quick note to Sar'ha, telling her he might be home late. He had no idea how the meeting with the Gleaner would go, and except for a hunch, did not really know what to expect as a result or how long it might take.

Though lowest on the social scale, the Gleaners were also known as *holy men*. Their station in life was not one inflicted by lowly birth or misfortune, but was chosen. As such, these mendicants were the source of all manner of rumor and legend. Some claimed they were sinners, so burdened by their moral deficiencies that they lived a self-inflicted punishment of exile to the Core Sphagnum. Others claimed that, according to the *Old* and *New Testaments*, they aspired to being the *highest* by being the lowest! Some claimed they were Buddhist monks (or nuns), by virtue of the soiled, saffron sacks they wore for clothing. Still others argued that their philosophy was taken from *The Third Testament*:

"Man cannot know in which direction his future lies if he does not keep one foot in the past."

Condo approached the exit hatch to his Cell just as a van from Medical attached itself. He slipped from the air lock into the van, and was greeted by a nurse. It was a rarity for actual personal contact to occur during the work day, so both were momentarily uncomfortable at this proximity, particularly as encounters of this nature did not allow for anonymity. But human gregariousness does not lie far below the surface and soon asserted itself.

"Uh. . .Hello, Sir." Her nervousness was apparent.

"Just Paul." Condo smiled at her. "And what is your name?"

"Just Mary." She smiled back.

Condo appreciated her use of the Biblical derivative. "Believe it or not, I'm 64 years old and have never ventured below the service levels. Even spent two hitches in the Corps, but I was an arborealist. The only quarantine I know is "workbound" and "homebound." This traveling quarantine is new to me." Condo's talkativeness eased the young woman.

"It's nothing, really. Just a run-up on your antibodies, and then we put a Skin on you. The biologics below the service levels, and particularly at the Core itself are so feculent that one has to be careful not to bring anything back. You'll shed the Skin when you pass back through the service level quarantines." She presented him with the "*I have a question I must ask you*" gaze.

"You may ask your question" Condo acknowledged without speaking.

"Well, it's just that I've never known anyone from management to make a trip like this. Most of our work is to quarantine clergy who are going into an infected sector to minister to the sick and dying."

Condo returned an understanding gaze, and gave this rather obscure reply: "We can never know to what exotic place our quest for truth will lead us."

Immediately, the girl flashed "I don't understand," but suppressed the urge and said: "I am only a nurse, and must have faith." Condo rewarded the girl's tact with an appreciative gleam in his eyes.

A small prick at the back of the hand, and within seconds the analyzer began to disgorge its data on Condo's immune system and antibodies. The nurse nodded her approval. "You're in fine shape. Everything up to standards. Now, if you'll remove your clothes, we'll put a "skin" on you. I should warn you that the membrane makes breathing a little more difficult, but you'll soon get used to it."

Condo slipped out of his Locator and khakis, and momentarily adrift, was immediately encased by the applicator. Suspended by electrostatic charge, he had the sensation of ants crawling all over his body. The nurse responded to his distressed look. "The sensation will pass as soon as the film begins applying."

With that, the air around him suddenly became filled with a mist issuing from nozzles in the applicator's arms. The charge difference set up between Condo and the applicator attracted the mist to Condo, and the material began to deposit itself in a monolayer on the surfaces of his body. "Blink your eyes, so you get a good seal there. And work you jaw and wiggle your tongue. Breathe deeply."

Condo had a hard time not laughing at what he supposed his appearance must be as he followed the nurse's instructions. She smiled and shook her head in response. "Now, don't laugh or we'll have to start all over again," she chastised. The thought sobered him immediately. "There, that's done." The nurse extended his khakis and Locator to him as the applicator withdrew.

Condo felt surrounded – inside and out. "Not so bad, I guess." He noted the slight change in the pitch of his voice. "What's it like getting out of this thing?"

"You don't want to know!" the nurse chimed, with a devilish gleam in her eyes. Condo's sudden downcast countenance won her sympathy. "Not that bad, really!" she offered repentantly.

Finished with quarantine, Condo *say'o'nah*-ed the
nurse and returned to his Cell's airlock. The
Medical van detached and propelled away. Condo
exited the airlock and propelled toward the nearest
down Tube. His transportation instructions would
be waiting for him at the service level port.

As Condo descended the Tube he passed level
after level of Cells suspended like vast
honeycombs between the boles of Forest trees and
crisscrossing girders. As he approached the
Habitat's service level, the radius was sufficiently
diminished that the down Tube intersected another
descending from one of the urban areas that had
grown up along the border between the Forest and
the Hydrofarms. These urban areas consisted of
manufactured housing, stores, theatres, schools –
all the amenities of urban life, stacked one upon
the other from the service level right up to the
canopy and the uppermost terraces of the
Hydrofarms. They represented the frenetic,
densely populated social structures that most of
humanity seemed always to prefer. Condo found
these compactions dehumanizing, intellectually
distracting, and the Ensymphonium they
produced, downright cacophonous. He much
preferred his Pod, and the relative seclusion of
Forest life. Besides, he was certain the seamless,
organic structure of his abode provided superior
protection from infection during the quarantines of
outbreak and epidemic. Still, it was the
tremendous populations of these urban areas, the
greater part of humanity, that were the true purpose

of the Habitats. It was only by their existence that his arboreal life was possible.

The service level was a cylindrical deck that surrounded the Core at a distance of approximately 60 meters. In the Forest areas it was supported by the boles of the living trees; in the farming areas it was supported, or more appropriately "attached," to the Core by girders. Four great Tubes ran longitudinally under the deck at equal distances, and terminated in air locks at the Polar Regions. These eight air locks were the only avenues of egress and ingress to the Habitat. It was here that the extensive quarantine that governed the movement of material – organic and inorganic – into and out of a Habitat was accomplished.

The service level was the mechanical center of the Habitat. The pumps which circulated air through the Ventportation system were located here. All of the technical support for the cells issued from here. The Proffit's Device thrusters located at the Poles and on the Equator, which controlled rotation and orbital position of the Habitat were all controlled from the service level. It was from this platform that the Sweepers and Salvors provided their filtering, reclamation, and recycling functions. Huge Capacitors located regularly across the surface of the level served to regulate the electrical potential between the Core and the Shell, preventing spontaneous discharge, and providing a steady flow of electrical current to meet the lighting and power needs of the population. Wells descending from the Service Level throughout the Core Sphagnum and into the Cylinder Sea gave access to the aqua culture's resources of seaweed, planktons, fishes and crustaceans.

The service level also served as a quarantine zone between the upper biosphere of the Habitat and the Core Sphagnum. Studies in the Maintenance Corps Academy equated the region of the Core Sphagnum beneath the service level with the "soils" of the Earth's extinct biosphere. It was here that the natural processes of decay released nutrients for recycling. Unlike the true soils of ancient Earth, however, very little organic material or associated minerals lay about dormant, as what was released by decay was immediately reincorporated. Here, too, all manner of insect larva and annelids plied the Sphagnum, devouring the vegetation and excreting nutrients for the trees. The giant Worms which served as the principle agent of hygiene for the human habitants were genetically engineered at the service level, the eggs then sent to the Core Sphagnum to incubate and hatch. The adult Worms migrated freely via special Worm holes from the Core Sphagnum to the canopy, providing their cleansing service. Everything that passed between the upper Habitat and the Core Sphagnum passed through the service level. With quantum driven scanners, and the nearly limitless capability of quantum computer-driven quarantine programs, every item, living and otherwise, was inspected down to its last molecule. The region of the Core was such a fecund environment that the evolution and mutation of

Biologicals and Virions was rapid and continuous. The quarantine was essential to prevent unwanted infection of the larger Habitat. Still, on a too regular a basis a bug got through, bacterial or viral, or precursor, which matured in the upper environment. When an infection was discovered, immediately the quarantines of outbreak, and in the worst cases epidemic, were issued.

The down Tube Condo was transiting terminated at a transportation port adjacent to the one of the great filtered intakes of the Ventportation system. Several down Tubes terminated at this port, and though it was of a large volume, the nearness to the circulation pumps created a draft with substantially greater velocity than was generally experienced throughout the system. One had to be ready to maneuver deftly in order to prevent being sucked up against one of the intake grates and floundering there until the Sweepers who maintained the filters made their rounds and dislodged victims along with the other debris which invariably collected.

Condo anticipated the accelerated air stream, and as he was disgorged from the down Tube, called for maximum thrust from his propelletes. Making an adept maneuver, he rounded too, and turning upwind, began a lateral approach to the hatch marked *Transportation Quarantine*. Upon gaining the hatch, he grabbed the handrail that circled it and activated the air lock. Once in the air lock, the hatch closed automatically behind him, and after a short equalization, the far hatch opened, giving him access to the port facilities proper.

The place was a hive of activity. Everywhere the Golem of transportation workers scurried, moving freight into and out of the large freight air locks. The service level provided transport, distribution, and warehouse space for all freight moving within and into and out of the Habitat. From their Cells far above, skilled transportation workers enshrouded in Interfaces controlled the robotic Golem that accomplished the physical aspects of these jobs.

Condo weaved his way cautiously through this maelstrom of activity and made for the opening marked *Personal Transportation*. Once inside he scanned the placards and following the arrows, veered to the right for *Transport - Down*, and then to the right again for *Core -Destinations and Quarantine*. Here he found a large Cell, open at the front, with two actual human beings, back patches engaged to their chairs, busy at consoles which circled the center. As the Cell was oriented outward from the Core, and Condo's direction of travel was toward the Core, his approach was from overhead. A large tetrahedral mirror in the center of the Cell reflected his image to the workers.

"May we help you?" one of the workers queried, upon seeing his reflection in the mirror.

"Yes. Condo, E. With clearance for travel to the Core Sphagnum."

Though anonymity was the desired norm during working hours and secrecy had been requested, the arrival of a man of Condo's stature to the brass tacks realm of the service level did not go unreported or unnoticed. With unmitigated curiosity beaming from their eyes, both workers rolled their heads back on their necks and looked straight 'upwards' at the figure hovering head down above them.

"Yes sir, your Holiness!" one of them stammered. The other, more collectedly said, "Please take a seat," and indicated an empty chair.

Condo settled into the chair and engaged his back patch. He speculated at what rumors would course through the Habitats as word spread that the Pontimax, often affectionately referred to as Ponti Condo, resided in Habitat 34 Beta, and had been seen to visit the Core Sphagnum! He wondered what his Board of Directors would have to say. The more composed worker began matter-of-factly: "You have your blood work and have been fitted with a skin, correct?"

"Yes."

"You understand that if, on your return, you are found to be contaminated, you may be held in quarantine at this facility until the infection is resolved?"

"Yes."

"Your retinal scan please."

Condo opened his eyes wide at the scanner passed in front of his face.

"If you will key your Locator I will download the navigation to your point of rendezvous with one Sada, H., resident of the Core Sphagnum." Condo mentally keyed his Locator and a green light signaled the successful download of course and coordinates.

"Thank you, sir. Your access is through air lock B, across the hall. Have a nice trip." Condo smiled a thank you to the workers, and disengaging his back patch, propelled upward from the chair into the hall. To his right were the airlocks, and he made for the one marked *B*.

He passed into the airlock, and as quickly as the one hatch closed the far hatch opened. As he moved to exit the airlock he was greeted by a wave of heavy, humid, nearly fetid air. Obviously unfiltered and poorly circulated, its odors were so pungent as to affect his taste. The Tube he entered, though made of the same transparent glass as the Tubes above the service level, were opaqued by a greenish/brown scum of algal and fungal growth. A pale greenish light illumined the Tube emanating from its far end, further hued by the growth on the glass.

Very little draft flowed through the Tube, requiring Condo to employ his propelletes for thrust to speed his descent. 30 meters down, the Tube unceremoniously deposited him just above the surface of the Core Sphagnum. Backlit from by the trellis of organoptical fibers within the moss, Condo could make out the movement of all sorts creatures, large and small. Their copious movement through the Sphagnum actually caused the surface to undulate. He actuated his Locator's navigation, and away he propelled, skimming just a meter of so above the surface, in which direction he knew not.

Directly, he entered a stand of the Forest trees. At this level they came very close together, owing to the decreased radius. Their gigantic trunks totally obscured vision ahead, and his Locator began to fly a labyrinthine course that totally confused any sense of direction still remaining to him. Giving up on discovering anything ahead of him, Condo looked down and examined the great tangle of roots and Sphagnum that constituted the Forest floor. He looked up, but in the dim light could not make out where the trees passed through the service level. He knew that the boles of the trees were quarantined at that point, and yet still allowed the movement of various insects, arachnids and Worms, whose reproductive and larval stages spanned the upper and lower Habitat.

Leaving what Condo believed to be the stand of his home Forest, he crossed a considerable expanse of open moss which coincided with one of the agricultural bands above. Entering another stand of trees, he had not gone far when the A-nav of his Locator indicated arrival at his destination. He found himself in a small quadrant of Forest floor formed by the trunks of four great trees. In the middle of this small clearing a round hole several meters in diameter descended into the moss. A burrow. Exposing some of the organoptical fiber of the trellis, the hole was brighter than its surroundings by a small margin. Condo maneuvered over it and peered in.

The burrow was a central shaft that appeared to penetrate all the way to the membrane on the surface of the Cylinder Sea. At regular intervals, smaller openings dotted the sides of the shaft. Silhouetted by the ambient light, Condo could make out a figure approaching him, inverse to his orientation, pulling itself along the mossy surface of the shaft with the toes of its feet. It maintained its body perpendicular to the lay of the shaft, and swung its arms to and fro as it approached. Condo had seen imagery of men in ancient days "walking" on the Earth, struggling against the force of gravity. This was a fair approximation.

## CHAPTER 12

**W**elcome to our humble bog, Holiness. Please, come down."

The face of the Gleaner greeting the man hovering at his burrow's entrance was indeterminable, masked in dark contrast to the green-hued backlighting, but his voice was gentle and breathy, with a hint of lilting singsong. His welcome betrayed neither subservience nor superiority, and though congenial enough, was spoken as if to many instead of one.

Condo rotated to orient with the Gleaner and setting his Locator to maximum neural sensitivity, propelled gently down into the burrow. Stopping just a meter short of his guest, he exchanged gazes with the Gleaner, a myriad of presentations passing between them within an instant.

The Gleaner spoke again, "I am Ho'jin Sada, Elder of the Brotherhood of Gleaners of Habitat 34 Beta." He waited for Condo to present *I understand*," and then continued: "Please, follow me."

The Gleaner turned and began to "walk" down the shaft toward the Core. In the brief interval of their face-to-face meeting, Condo had made several very precise observations. First and foremost was the obvious effect the local environment had on the man. His skin was indeed tanned to a mahogany color except his arms, which when unused were tucked inside the sack. His hair was a flaming orange. Condo had also noted that the man's feet up to the ankles were stained to complete blackness. The saffron-colored sack which was the Gleaner's standard attire, had crude holes cut for the arms and legs and was drawn and tied at the neck with a piece of crude, natural fiber rope, which produced a pleated collar of sorts, roughly trimmed below the face in front, but rising higher at the back of the head.

Condo had been surprised to note the nearly pure genotype Ho'jin Sada's facial features suggested. The great almond shaped eyes, nearly black and inscrutable in their irises and pupils (the rest bloodshot red owing to the environment), with their pronounced epicanthic folds, the flatness of the face, with no bridge to the nose, and the brachycephalic dome of the cranium all indicated a bloodline much more purely Asiatic, that is to say Mongoloid, than the average percentage of the Habitat 34 Beta's population. The original migrations to the first Habitats had brought an admixture of the three Earthly human genotypes. When migration was halted during man's last days on Earth, that admixture became the basis for the general genotypical manifestations of surviving humanity. Asiatics had represented nearly half of those original immigrants, and that genotype expressed itself generally through the population by an oriental cast to the facial features, a reduction in overall stature, reduced primary and secondary hair growth, and extreme reduction in the number and locations of the axillary glands. All in all, the general populations favored the Mongoloid genotype, with each individual Habitat acquiring distinctive characteristics. Yet, never had Condo encountered precisely the characteristics Ho'jin Sada's appearance represented. He did not appear to be a native of Habitat 34 Beta. Condo made a mental note of the fact.

As they descended the shaft, Condo noted that many of the openings in the shaft wall lead into smaller lateral tunnels that disappeared into a distant green glow. Other openings were the portals to small alcoves that were obviously the residences of these monastic mendicants. Stopping briefly before an empty alcove, Condo quickly examined its make-up and content. The structure was obviously created by hollowing out a swelling in one of the succulents. He remembered from the lessons of his Corps days that the roots of trees and succulents attached themselves to the membranes of the Cylinder Sea, and began the great cycle of water through the Habitat. The succulents vined out through the entire of the Core Sphagnum and created a natural irrigation system which the roots of the moss tapped. The moisture thus moved up through the vegetation and trees and was expelled through respiration of the leaves. Excess moisture in the atmosphere produced by this process and by the agriculture of the vast Hydrofarms was then extracted by condensers in the Ventportation system and returned to the Cylinder Sea, where natural purification occurred. It was but one of the many cycles that sustained life in the Habitats.

The interior of the alcove was spartan. A very finely leafed, deeply green colored moss grew parasitically on most of the inner surface of the alcove, creating a lush, natural carpet. Root masses from the Sphagnum and the trees which had penetrated the walls of the alcove had been skillfully woven into the few fixtures the apartment contained. Cocoon-like, they held a Gleaner's few possessions. One particularly large cocoon was obviously used as bedding.

His curiosity satisfied, Condo turned to rejoin his host, who had only gained a few meters on him in the interval. A quick burst from his propelletes made up the distance.

"We live a simple life here, Holiness. Work and Prayer." Ho'jin Sada had noted Condo's examination of the alcove, though he had continued walking. "We are the lowest of men within the Habitats; but our calling is of the highest. We maintain the health of the Core so that the entire Habitat may flourish." Sada stopped before the entrance to an alcove, and turning to exchange gazes with Condo, spoke volumes from the glint in his eyes. With a gesture of his hand, he bade Condo to enter the alcove.

This alcove was much larger than the one Condo had previously examined, and obviously served as a public room. To his surprise Condo noted that it was fitted with several modern conveniences: imbedded LEDs; a ring; several chairs with table; a complete console with Caps and communicator! Noting Condo's surprise, Sada spoke: "We live a simple life, and yet that life cannot be lived entirely separate from our brothers and sisters above. For we are the same body, which must have its lowly parts just as it must have its head. And today the lowest and the highest have found the need to commune."

Sada slipped into one of the larger woven cocoons on the alcove's wall and motioned for Condo to take the chair opposite. Condo maneuvered and engaged his back patch. From a smaller cocoon to his right Sada produced a very old and elegant porcelain tea set, which he attached with Velcro to the table fronting Condo's chair. He deftly filled the tea globe with water and tea from the canisters, and activating the Proffit's Device on the side of the globe, soon had the tea boiling. He dispensed the hot liquid into cups, and passed one to his guest. As Condo brought the cup's drinking tube close to his face, the warm, fragrant steam escaping from the cup wafted to his nostrils.

Sada offered a short prayer: "All that *is* comes from the Creator. Man molds and shapes; only God creates."

Condo took a long, slow draught of the hot, fragrant liquid. He examined the small Velcro patch on the bottom of his cup, and marveled at that ancient and yet terribly clever method of attachment. With it he attached his cup to its patch on the table, and raised his gaze toward Sada. The Gleaner's gaze was already fixed on Condo.

The Gleaner spoke first, in response to Condo's questioning eyes. "It was I who sent the message. I hope the ancient script was not inconvenient. We thought it might serve security." He waited for Condo to display understanding.

"We live a simple life here, but we are not out of touch. We follow with great interest the pursuits of our fellow man. Your interest in finding Amagon and resolving the enigma of William Proffit, has quite captured our attention. As the lowest of men, we are the caretakers of lost memories and buried thoughts. There is much we can tell you of the last days of man on Earth, when the future of mankind was set, and so much of the past was lost."

The eyes of the interlocutors remained fixed on one another, presenting a multitude of unspoken communication. Pleased with Condo's understanding, the Gleaner's eyes smiled.

"We *walk* with our feet so that men may not forget from whence they came. In the grand design of Creation, it was gravity that first brought together the elements of life. And it is against gravity that life has struggled to raise itself. From the ancient seas did life crawl upon the land, and by the Creator's direction, begin its ascent. First did we crawl upon our bellies. And then did we go about on all fours. We were beasts and lived as beasts. We had not yet been given our souls. The eons passed, and struggling upwards, we stood upon our feet, and gaining hands, we began to pray for deliverance from our animal ways. And our hands did the work of the Creator, but of the Destroyer as well, until man came to the brink. All that went before had passed into Extinction. But God saw fit to grant man a morality, by which he might adjudge his actions Good and Evil. And as a fledgling that never leaves the nest must perish, the food of ants and Worms, we were given the choice to fly away, or to die in the nest that nurtured us. And yet, we do not fly so high that we cannot fall back to Earth, to our subhuman, animal ways. And so we walk with our feet so that men may not forget from whence they came, so that men will dedicate the labor of their four limbs to the Creator's purpose."

The Gleaner's account of life's ascent from the sea, to serpent, to quadruped, to biped, to quadraman was quite poignant. Of course, the evolutionary process was not yet complete - the great toe was not as rightly opposed as the thumb; the ankle had not achieved the subtleties of motion obtained in the wrist; and the knee was still a poorly articulated elbow. Yet, even in imagination, Condo had a hard time realizing what a limited existence his earthbound forebears must have suffered, with so much of their ingenuity, and fully half of their dexterity employed in the struggle against gravity. The Gleaner's highly affected "walk," ritualistic and sacrificial though it was, very effectively brought the point home.

Sada spoke again: "Es'paul Condo, you have not come to this place by accident. You come as a part of the Creator's process. The struggle to ever higher forms is God's eternal purpose for man. And in this day, as in every day past, that purpose is under assault by the dark forces of the Destroyer. Entropy will destroy our complexity if it can. Even with the Sacrament of Excision, and its continuing refinement, the animal memory within the genetic code is not expunged. Each day we must pray for reason and morality to prevail. You seek the truth of Amagon and William Proffit and man's last days on Earth in hopes that you will find something missed, some golden age lost. Men today argue against the need for Excision. They rail against the confinement of morality. They question the Creator's purpose. They grow lazy, selfish and self-indulgent. They would become animals again. It was so in the days of the Prophets. It was so in the days of Buddha and Jesus and Mohammed. It was so in the days of William Proffit and Amagon. Your quest will bring

you unpleasant truths. But it will also bring renewed hope. And a reaffirmation of our purpose."

By a process Condo did not detect, Ho'jin Sada caused the console opposite them to come to life. The Communicator blinked its green *ready* light as it accessed the CQC, the central quantum computer. The two Caps slipped from their boxes and by an unseen force, moved to within Condo's and Sada's grasp. Smiling, Sada took his Cap and fitted on his head, and by a nod bade Condo do likewise.

"You, the highest of men, have ventured into the bog to ask questions of the lowest of men. You shall have your answers."

Sada deftly engaged Condo's aural and visual cortexes, and as an Abbot might lead a Novitiate, lead him down the dark and mysterious corridors of ancient compu-synaptic structure, to the inner sancta of Hidden Files.

## CHAPTER 13

From *The Third Testament*: "If Thine Amygdala offend Thee, pluck it out!"

The arguments come as regularly and inevitably as the Worms. Not based in reason, but in instinct. The Worms do not cleanse a man as a purposeful service to the man, but only as a response to the blind, unthinking urge to eat. And when a man's life ends, enshrouded in the milky, translucent belly of a Worm, his remains embark on their solemn descent to the Core Sphagnum. It is with no thought of reverence or dignity on the part of the Worm, though all men whom the Worm passes are touched by such emotions, but instead the Worm and the process are only to harvest the bounty of protein that will then throw the Worm into its reproductive cycle, such that the digested man, save for his bones and ornaments, becomes invested in a clutch of translucent eggs, and the blind, instinctive cycle of life is fulfilled.

This is how the arguments come. From vestiges of instinct that run as filaments of synaptic lace from the lower structures of the brain to the higher. The lower structure can be removed, but the lace remains, so intricately inculcated in the higher structures that complete Excision is not possible. The arguments come and no thinking man should be surprised that so ancient an organ, having for eons

110

defied the edicts of entropy, by trial and error building for itself mechanisms of perpetuation and defense, could easily be destroyed. For the higher structures of the brain, through the Creator's engine of evolution, were crafted by the amygdala and its companion structures. Is it any wonder, then, that so tenacious a collection of neurons should not find a voice? Is it any wonder that this sub-rational ganglia of instinctive urge should not cry out for its own preservation? For its own restoration? And subvert its higher level offspring in the cause? The arguments come not from without, but from within. Each generation anew has to confront this demon, for nothing a father can teach a son, nothing a mother can teach a daughter, nothing Sensei can instill in Gaksei, can totally prepare the younger ones for the rising up of vestigial, instinctive urges which the older others have only in utter loneliness and faith defeated.

This is the great paradox: The will to life is fundamental to the most primitive elements of the innervation, and yet here the phenomenon of life goes unperceived; while the most highly developed elements of the innervation, which do perceive and reflect on life, having evolved in service to the most primitive, are forever challenging the will to life. The Amygdala and its diencephalic partners need no purpose to life; the cerebrum demands a purpose to life, or becomes a likely suicide.

Here is the conundrum: having technologically advanced to the point where total annihilation is a danger, can man permit the evolved, fixed neuronal networks of the amygdala, hypothalamus and hippocampus to remain extant? Fear, anger, aggression, territorial and sexual conquest, which instincts served the species well in primitive times, are now given the destructive power unleashed by human intellectual exploration and exploitation of the natural world. Can such power be entrusted to these thoughtless instincts? Yet, can the species survive without them?

These are the great moral questions occupying the professional life of Es'paul Condo. They are questions that have no answers, only persuasions. And Condo's ascent to the high office of Pontimax has come at a time when the Anti-Excisionists and Anti-Vivisectionists are finding an increasingly sympathetic ear among the populations of the Habitats.

Church doctrine declares that the Sacrament of Excision was revealed to William Proffit through the God-given power of his intellect, as a sacrifice of the flesh for the advancement of the spirit. For ages upon ages men have warred, and women have whored, and the generations have paid a bloody and horrible price. But the time has come when a man driven to aggression by the thoughtless (or deliberate) trespass of another man upon his property or ideas, or by the mindless lust incited by the unconscious, copulatory gaze of an ovulating female, if exercised with the power of atomic bombs (or Proffit's Device!), could wreak as much havoc on the race in minutes or seconds as the ancient pandemics produced in years or decades! Extinction through self-annihilation is the threat! And so Proffit argued, and persuasively in his day, that the Creator had brought this level of understanding to the human mind so that mankind might be spared eternal oblivion.

Condo knew from the Church's historical record that the early days of Excision were constituted of a very crude and blunt procedure. It was little more than wholesale butchery of the basal ganglion. And the results were unpredictable. To be sure, the procedure produced an individual capable of much greater socialization, with little apparent loss of intellectual capability. But it also produced individuals who were difficult to entice into the reproductive act (out of shear lack of interest), and who, deprived of a good sense of fear or panic, were often seen to remain quite calm, even pensive and thoughtfully interested as a piece of errant machinery or a misguided, swinging girder crushed the life out of them. Advancements in knowledge, improvements in procedure, and adaptation and increasingly application of Proffit's Device to the process greatly improved upon the results, however. It was now possible to excise single neuronal pathways manifesting unwanted instinctive responses to stimuli within the ganglion. The procedure had become so exact that it was possible to eliminate the copulatory gaze in the female and its attendant response in the male, while maintaining the rational, procreative desire for sex, and the pleasure of orgasm.

But herein lay the rub. Once the pleasure of sex was returned, and the rewards of endorphin and enkephalin again produced the neuro-narcotic stupor of orgasm, the devils were let to fly from Pandora's Box. Condo knew that the Anti-Excisionist and Anti-Vivisectionist movements were extremely populist, based in the pursuit of physical sensation, not reason, and were not given credence by serious intellectuals. The protestors, however, argued that the Church unreasonably denied the populations the *full enjoyment of Life*. The danger lie in the fact that historically such movements often created hysteria in the masses as reason falls prey to the vestiges of instinct. Now as much as ever, Condo knew that in order to maintain social order, he had to defuse this growing unrest, this stirring of primitive longings, this return to the territorial aggression of the male, and the sexual aggression of the female. He had to produce an argument sufficiently compelling to answer this challenge to the Church's Doctrine. For if the Sacrament of Excision should fall before the common will, then the very fabric of moral society would begin to unravel. And man would find himself no better off in the heavens than he was during his last days on Earth.

There was the economic aspect of it, as well. The market for pleasure thrived as it had in all ages. Though the intellectual prowess of the *true man* had now successfully transplanted the old *status through acquisition and achievement principle* as the measure of an individual's worth and position in the hierarchy of society, in the *pecking order*.

Still, the end of all achievement was the pursuit of reward, though now admittedly more thoughtful than tactile. In this day a man's worth was determined by the strength of his argument. And nothing impoverished a man more quickly than the promotion of an argument found to be false in its premise, or insupportable by the extant evidence. Where once men feared the power of another's money, now they trembled in the face of an irrefutable argument. And as the Virtue of Anonymity was a professed moral principle, (though of course, what the more egoistic individuals practiced stretched the definition of the term to often absurd lengths), even the satisfaction of social recognition was eschewed. But beneath it all lingered the proclivity for pleasure. And where a potential existed, the entrepreneurial spirit sought to exploit it economically.

Such was the circumstance with the sensual pleasures as the procedure of Excision became increasingly refined. Where once a crude procedure admittedly blunted the sensual experience of life, requiring often herculean intellectual efforts to promote and sustain essential behaviors such as procreation and self preservation, advancements had permitted refinement to the point that the warmth of life began a return. And with it, the arguments turned. Just as Church Doctrine declared that the "simple, objective observation indicated that the primary function of life was procreation," so now the "naturalistic holist," the Anti-Excisionists and Anti-Vivisectionists, argued that simple, objective observation indicated that even in so primitive an organism as the amoeba *avoidance* reactions manifested a rudimentary pleasure/pain (anti-pleasure) paradigm from which the active pursuit of pleasure could logically be anticipated; ergo, the pursuit of pleasure was a fundamental property of life. Theologians had a difficult time debunking the argument; entrepreneurs, in defense of the social argument that "a valid economy is one in which the activities and rewards to individuals are based upon the providing of those goods and services which satisfy the verifiable requisites of human life" easily advanced the notion that the pleasure/pain paradigm, as a primordial property of life, was a valid area of economic activity.

These were the arguments which faced the Pontimax and CEO of the Alhumana Corporation, Church to the Habitats as Es'paul Condo put on the Mask of the Pontimax. Condo rightly saw them as the paramount threat to the observed purpose of life and the survival of the species, which faith held as the Creator's *will*. He also realized that the antithetical arguments were gaining increasing support among his brother CEOs at some of the largest economic and financial corporations. The great mass of the populations of the Habitats were little aware, nor greatly cared, that such momentous questions faced humanity. Their intellectual capabilities were sufficiently occupied by the requirements of job and family and hobbies. But the propaganda war which waged along the lines of communication were liable at any moment to sway general opinion, and suddenly spur the masses to action. The only antidote against such herd response was to be prepared with graphic proofs and superior arguments. And it was this preparation that now drove Es'paul Condo in his search for the foundations of the historical and moral certainties from which the truth could be obtained; from which true knowledge would be gained; from which knowledge the faith could be reaffirmed. This was the solemn duty of the Pontimax, defender of the faith, dispeller of doubt, which brought a man of Condo's position and accomplishments into the company of a lowly, disparaged, and often despised Gleaner.

CHAPTER 14

Ho'jin Sada spoke directly to Condo's aural cortex via the Cap.

"You, Es'paul Condo, are by birth right and profession Jesu'tai. I am by the same precepts Buddha'tai. There are also the Mose'tai and Mo'hame'tai. These are the four great theological divisions of human thought. From ancient, anonymous superstitions and fears have we evolved to the point where only the thoughts of true men - as the verifiable product of the Creator's process - are permitted to guide our moral and spiritual lives. We of the faith hold that God speaks to use through the power of our reasoning. As you know, this was not always so. In darker days did men use the gifts of faith and knowledge to advance their personal animal urges. Untruths were foisted upon children and the ignorant to enslave them to the will and desire of other men. Faith and knowledge were declared antithetical. One could not arrive at faith by knowledge; one could not arrive at knowledge by faith. William Proffit taught us that knowledge is the seed from which sprouts the flower of faith."

Condo understood where Sada's monologue was headed. His reference to Proffit referred to excerpts which were believed to have come from the Lost Sermons - Proffit's Revelations. Sada continued:

*"The Third Testament* teaches that these sermons were destroyed by the Amygdalites of Amagon during man's last days on Earth. And yet *The Third Testament* goes on to say that these very sermons shall be heard by men again in times of great travail."

Condo's pulse quickened at the thought. Condo's presentations signaled such urgency that Sada cut his monologue short, and said: "The Lost Sermons are here, among the Hidden Files kept by the Gleaners down through the ages." With that, Ho'jin Sada disengaged Condo's aural cortex, and opening the Files, he let the data flow into Condo's consciousness and understanding.

File type: Encrypt
Security: Maximum
Location: xp176t900a
Authorization: Sada, H.
Open:

***Transcript taken from the digital recording made by W. Proffit of his presentation to the Congregation of the Community Church of Amagon, July XX, 2XXX, representing his initial Revelation to the First of the faithful:***

*"I want to begin by thanking all of you for allowing me to speak to you in your Church. That you should grant a stranger such courtesy speaks highly of your humanity. I hope you don't mind if I record this - I'm really not sure exactly what I am going to say, and I want the record to be straight.*

*I'll begin by introducing myself and telling you a little about myself. My name is William Proffit. Until recently I have not been what you could call a very religious man. In fact, I was educated in the science of Physics, and have always demanded the kinds of "proof" for argument that goes against any notion of faith. And yet, ironically, I have invested my belief in things that are as invisible to the eye as God, and whose only proof lies in the results of unseen forces at work. What better definition of God? An unseen Force at work!*

*'God' isn't a word most scientists like to hear, however. It grates against our egos. We pride ourselves with our ability to solve parts of the puzzle, but are too arrogant to acknowledge the author of that puzzle.*

*But don't misunderstand me. I am as great a skeptic as a good scientist should be. I don't believe in magic; and after much soul searching, I find that I can really only allow for **one** miracle-- the whole of Creation! Every instant of this existence; every breath I take; every sight I see; every sound I hear; each and every one of you here today are a part of the one great Miracle in which I do believe!*

*I didn't come to this understanding easily. I first had to pass through the darkest days a man can know this side of death. And I know there are more dark days ahead. But in the midst of the darkness, a light shined. And with it came an understanding that was not the result of my scientific training; was not the result of any superior intellectual ability I might possess; was not the result of my will. For it is an understanding that comes more readily to simple men and children than it does to one such as myself. But before I could come to that understanding, it was necessary for God to cast upon my shoulders a burden too great to bear. I had to be reduced from my pride and arrogance.*

*(Pause. Footsteps, grating and thumping sounds. A click. Gasps and sounds of surprise from the Congregation.)*

*This* Device *is only a toy - no bigger than a man's shoe. It runs off of batteries. And yet it is creating the light source at the middle of room. I have only to turn the knob a little, and the light gets too bright to look at, and you can feel the heat. If I turned the knob all the way up, we would be burned to ash in an instant.*

*(Murmurings in the Congregation.)*

*This isn't magic. It's no trick. But it isn't a "miracle" either. It is science. It is the result of human intelligence applied to the discovery, understanding and application of the Natural Laws. But you see, I now believe that the Natural Laws are the method by which God rules his Universe. That the Natural Laws ARE God's Laws!*

*(Pause. A click. Footsteps, grating and thumping sounds.)*

*Using the principles employed in this* Device, *I can etch my name on a gnat's eye - or explode the Sun! It is a power so vast that it will either raise man up or be his end.*

*I do not believe that mere chance or accident revealed this power to me. It has always been there, only waiting for man in his cleverness to uncover it. But now that it is found, how will it be used? This is the burden that has crushed all the pride and arrogance out of me.*

*We live in a world that is a series of armed camps. We fight wars for the booty of natural resources. We fight, not for principle, but to maintain a standard of living. The advanced nations rape the lesser states. The lesser states send their patriots as martyrs to avenge the violations. New York and Moscow and London and Paris and Jerusalem and a dozen other cities are radioactive and biological wastelands. The American Empire falls as the empires of the Southern Hemisphere and of Eurasia now rise to prominence. Everywhere the sabers rattle. Each new scientific discovery is quickly appropriated to some nation's arsenal; the military technology increases by leaps and bounds, as the general populations and the infrastructures of society decay. And in the midst of all this, the very power of Creation has been revealed to me!*

*(Pause)*

*My first thought was to blow my brains out; to destroy the tissue whose electrochemical machinations had discovered this piece of the puzzle. I thought it would be better that I die than that such power be set in the hands of such men as rule our world today. But in an instant, humility descended, and I realized that what my mind had been made capable of perceiving would eventually be revealed to other minds as well. To seek solace in death would have been a cowardly act. And yet I became determined not to err in the ways of Einstein and Oppenheimer and Fermi and Teller and a host of others. I would not unlock this Pandora's Box. From that day to this has been an incredible journey. I have feigned insanity, and faked my own death. I left behind a career that promised fame and fortune and all their amenities, and have lived as a homeless vagrant, wandering amid the unfortunate and destitute in search of an answer that science could not provide.*

*I was at my darkest hour, and it was the coldest night of the year. I had been wandering city streets when I came upon a dingy little mission and soup kitchen. I went in for the warmth and the food. I found a lot more.*

*After I had eaten, and the warmth brought me out of my stupor, I found this laying on the table beside me.*

*(Sound of book pages being flipped.)*

*I had never really had any interest in this book. Or books like it. I had always argued that they were no more than the attempts of ancient men to explain phenomena about which they had insufficient knowledge. And that as noble as the cause was, it was in error. And that this error provided for a circular argument which, down through the ages, unsophisticated but ambitious men have used as a hammer for their egos, with which to subjugate others through intimidation and guilt.*

*But it was cold outside, and I really had no place to go, and nothing else to read. So I opened the book. . .*

*(Pause)*

*I found everything I expected to find - men with egos and ambitions, using the art of language to harangue and persuade and subjugate. The book is a historical record of man at his worst-- jealousy, hate, envy, greed, murder, war, and every fleshly debauchery. It is a record of the sexual struggle between male and female; the territorial struggle between brother and brother, and father and son. It is a record of the human race living at the level of its instincts. And yet, it is more. It is also a record of the emergence of human understanding; of the rise of Reason. It is a record of the evolution of the human mind and soul! It is a record of the struggle of man to become more than the animal of clay in which he resides.*

*As I read the marvelous scientific speculations of Genesis; sank into the remorse and despair of Ecclesiastes; sampled the wisdom of Proverbs; was raised up and renewed by the Gospels of Matthew, Mark, Luke and John; and finally was made to consider the future through the Revelations, I found a voice speaking from deep within me: a voice that found no conflict between my rational, deductive mind and the notion, the faith, that something unseen existed, a Force driving man ever upward. And the voice told me that this wondrous book, and the other books like it, in fact are the record of man's God-given gifts of consciousness and reason, turned upon man himself, to finish God's work by freeing the tormented mind, the tortured soul of man from the bondage of animal instincts, and transforming him into the rational, moral creature that is the true child of God.*

*Something else became quite apparent to me as I read. Something that surprised me, really. For I came to understand that the rational move toward morality which these ancient books of religion and wisdom describe is in fact the very process which has brought me before you today. For though my parents were devout enough, I never participated in their rituals. Even at an early age I was much too interested in wonders of "science." And yet this process was going on all around me, in my home, in the neighborhood where I grew up, in the lives of many who taught me in school. And being so surrounded by this uplifting process I was myself lifted up unawares. You see, the moral sense in me, which put me in such a dilemma over my discovery, is not of my own making. It is the result of the thousands of years of human devotion to the betterment of Man, of man looking to God for what he cannot find within himself. The words of a man, a rabbi – Yeshua Ben Joseph, called Jesus, who lived two thousand years ago, have through the subtleties of my education found themselves recorded in the neural networking of my brain. They are an unseen filter, until recently an unrecognized engine of judgment, through which my very Reason operates. I am not here by my own Will; I am here by the Will of all that has come before me – perhaps even by the Will of God!*

*(Amens from the Congregation.)*

*If and when the "people in charge" find out what I have, I will be a wanted man - A HUNTED MAN! No doubt they will use whatever tactics or force necessary. My discovery is of such magnitude that I cannot possibly share it with even my trusted colleagues, for they are men of egos and ambitions, as I once was. They would betray my purpose. I have come to realize that the only way to safeguard the human race from the destructive potential I have unleashed, is to see that it falls into "good" hands first – or no hands at all! And I have agonized, and wandered alone for months, living on handouts and the rummagings from trash bins, searching and trusting no one, until yesterday, when a farmer heading to market gave me a ride and deposited me just down the road a bit. I will not say that it is coincidence that has brought me here. I cannot prove that it is the Will of God. I can only wait and see what tomorrow brings. You will either trust me as I have trusted you, and we shall go forward from here, or you will call the appropriate authorities and have this madman removed from your midst.*

*(Nervous laughter from Proffit and from the Congregation.)*

*Until then, if I could find a little work for my supper and maybe a place to sleep- INDOORS!*

*(Affirmative and congenial responses from the Congregation. Laughter and the shuffling of feet.)*

\*\*\*

File type: Encrypt
Security: Maximum
Location: xp176t901a
Authorization: Sada, H.
Open:

***Transcript taken from the digital recording made by W. Proffit of his presentation to the Congregation of the Community Church of Amagon, August XX, 2XXX, continuing his Revelation to the First of the faithful:***
*I want to thank you all for coming this morning. I guess there must be two hundred of us here. I would certainly be the envy of many a small town preacher if they saw how quickly our Congregation has grown.*

*(Laughter.)*

*I want to thank Kathy for the room, and all of you for the work you've given me, and the support.*

*Some of you have expressed fears about leaving the doors open to everyone. But I tell you we must! If we are going to succeed, we are going to have to grow quickly. If there is to be a Judas among us so be it. We must have faith. Time is of the essence. We must build our numbers quickly and make our organization sufficiently strong so that when the challenge comes, we can withstand it.*

*And it will come. The type of recruiting and fund raising we are going to have to do is going to attract attention. And probably first from the other, established religious organizations. We are going to take some heat. We will be called a Cult; we will be called blasphemers; we may even be called Anti-Christ. So we must harden ourselves, and our resolve. And we must bring as many as we can here to Amagon to begin building a true base of operations.*

*I know many of you still have questions about the* Device *I have shown you. I think it is time I gave you an explanation of how it works. I'll skip all the math and stuff. Some of it seems even quite unbelievable to me anyway! So I'll do this a simply as I can. Please ask questions if I'm not being clear enough.*

*(Acknowledgments from the Congregation.)*

*The Greek philosopher and scientist Democritus once took a clump of Earth in his hand and began to crush it. He theorized that there must come a point where the crushing must stop, where the fundamental make-up of the material existence would be arrived at. He called this fundamental make-up "atmos"- that which cannot be divided. He had no fancy apparatus to prove his theory, no elaborate scientific gadgetry with which to experiment. But he was right, simply by the power of his Reason! Today we have experimental proof of the truth of his theory.*

*I should mention that several times in several different cultures since, this "knowledge" has been lost and rediscovered. In fact, from the time of Democritus until the $19^{th}$ century C.E. before Ascension, his theory languished – actually was suppressed by the Aristotleans!*

*From the example of Democritus' theory, lost for 2000 years, later men argued that if matter is made of atoms, then atoms must be made of something also. And they too were right. A whole host of "particles" was discovered. And the sub-atomic world of quanta was revealed. And proved by experimentation.*

*Parallel with these discoveries runs the science we call Physics. Quite simply, it is the discovery, recording and application of the "rules" that govern how atoms and quanta behave. It all works pretty well, except for the discrepancies that appear when considering different scales of size, or orders of magnitude. Put simply, the rules change when you go from the very large to the very small.*

*These two sets of rules gave rise to two schools of thought, Classical or Newtonian Physics, or physics of the large, and Quantum Physics, or physics of the small. Of course, the two viewpoints have been the source of endless argument. And some of the mathematics and theories advanced to explain this situation have become fantastically complex.*

*To me, this complexity was disturbing. It reminded me too much of the extremes early astronomers and mathematicians had gone to describe a geocentric, or Earth-centered universe. They created equations and even working models to represent what they observed in the heavens, with everything revolving around the Earth! Their achievements were difficult. It was obviously the work of brilliant men. But it was all wrong! Copernicus, Galileo and other risked their very lives in disproving it!*

*Once again following Democritus' lead I have theorized that if matter is made of atoms, and atoms are composed of quanta, then of what are quanta composed? The logical answer is smaller quantities yet. So small in fact as to represent another complete order of magnitude, with another entirely different set of rules! Actually, my idea wasn't a new one, it had been proposed before, but lacking experimental proof was abandoned, even ridiculed. It was the theory of the Luminiferous Ether.*

*A good analogy is to consider what primitive man must have thought of the "air"- nothing he could see or take in his hand, but he could feel and see its effects. He called it "empty." But we know today that it is composed of a sea of atoms of various gases. Far, far from empty. And we have learned to use the properties of the air to produce power and do work.*

*Like the air, the Ether is a sea of particles. It is from the flow of these particles that we see and feel the effects of gravity, momentum and force. It is from these particles that quanta arise, whose presence we experience as energy, and which in turn give rise to atoms, from which we experience matter.*

*The Ether, so rich in particles, is like a rain cloud. It needs only a little disturbance to create precipitation - a downpour. In this case the downpour is quanta. The* Device *I have shown you uses colliding particle beams to crush quanta to the ethereal level, and these particles then disturb the Ether, causing many more quanta to precipitate - like raindrops! The downpour comes according to the amount of disturbance. A little disturbance creates the floating light source you have observed. More disturbance, and the light becomes intense enough to produce heat. A lot of disturbance, and you create more energy than any atom bomb could ever produce!*

*This would seem like the answer to man's current woes. Most of the struggles on the planet are currently based in the acquisition of the resources to produce the energy needed to propel the technological cultures of the advanced nations. Never mind that much if not most of the technology is superfluous. But the sad fact is that this discovery could more easily be used to create weapons for the subjugation of men than to fuel technology to raise mankind up. It would be a matter of "economics." There would be little profit for the greedy in providing a utopian existence for all men.*

*What we must do, what I believe God intends for us to do, is to create an entirely new society, a society prepared to accept this wondrous gift for the benefit of all men, not as just another weapon in the arsenal of men enslaved by the territorial ambition and egoistic elitism that are the manifestations of their basest instincts. We must build this society here, in Amagon. There are two hundred of us now. In a year we must be ten thousand. And a year after that a million. We must appeal to every calling, every talent possessed by men. We must judge a man's (or woman's) intent, and bring them into the fold, or turn them away. And we must find a way to protect our own intentions, our own purity of purpose.*

*I've talked enough for now. Do you have any questions?*

\*\*\*

File type: Encrypt
Security: Maximum
Location: xp176t933a
Authorization: Sada, H.
Open:

***Transcript taken from the digital recording made by W. Proffit of his presentation to the Congregation of the Tabernacle of New Jerusl'm at Amagon, January XX, 2XXX, introducing the Sacrament of Excision:***
*(Symphonic and Choral Prelude.)*
*Brothers and Sisters, we have come a very long way, in a very short while. I see upon this work the Hand of God! Amen!*

*(Amen from the Congregation.)*

*We are set upon by our adversaries from every quarter. Our corporation is fighting in the courts. Our troops stand vigilantly at our perimeter. The American Empire has declared us illegal, and we must hold it at bay with the threat of our power. A great city has grown up outside our gates, profiting mightily from the commerce our mission generates, and yet it is a Gomorrah, filled with sin.*

*Yet here within the walls of New Jerus'lm, we live at peace and in prosperity as we pursue our goal. It is God's blessing! Amen!*

*(Amen from the Congregation.)*

*I am proud to announce the enthusiastic acquisition*

*this week of the Mitsuzuki Corporation of Japan. Their expertise in the design and construction of self-contained Habitats will be a great boon to our efforts.*

*(Applause.)*

*Also, I want to announce the joint venture between New Jerusl'm Corporation and the People's Republic of China's Space and Exploration Agency for the raising of the first pre- populated Habitat by fall of next year.*

*(Applause.)*

*The progress of our expansion into space is nothing less than phenomenal. The current rapid degradation of Earth's environment, accelerated by frantic and desperate demands of unbridled, and amoral capitalistic economies leaves us no alternative but to make this migration. The planet's biosphere in now in such turmoil that its ability to maintain even current human population levels is quickly deteriorating. Surely it is the Hand of God that directs our efforts. Amen.*

*(Amen from the Congregation.)*

*And now Brothers and Sisters, we must broach a topic that has created a firestorm of controversy, both within and without our community. I am talking about Excision of the Amygdala. (Murmuring in the Congregation.)*

*We are people of good hearts and good moral intent. We could not have come this far if it were not so. And yet there is moral strife within us, as individuals, and as a community. With our God-given reason we have examined the problem, and know with certainty that it lies in those behaviors encoded in the neural pathways set down in our long evolutionary past. These behaviors, these pathways, these instincts once served man as the God-given will to survive and to procreate. But that innate will, that blind instinct has been supplanted by a greater gift, our gift of reason. When we were children, we spoke as children. When we were animals we lived as animals. But God has raised us up to be men, and now we must reason as men. We know the source or our sin. We must cast it out! Amen!*

*(Cast it out! Amen from the Congregation.)*

*If thine Amygdala offend thee! Pluck it out!*

*(Pluck it out! Pluck it out! from the Congregation.)*

*Our medical department informs me the procedure can be done on an outpatient basis. The clinics will begin on Tuesday. May God guide your willing feet to this Sacrament. Amen!*

*(Amen from the Congregation.)*

*(Symphonic and Choral Postlude.)*
**End Transcripts**

CHAPTER 15

The sudden cessation of data brought Condo back to awareness of his physical whereabouts. Though the down feed of data was set to correspond with the rate of electrochemical transmission of the human nervous system, still the process progressed much more rapidly compuneurally than it would have if the eyes had been employed for the input. Condo had only been engaged for a couple of moments. But in that time Ho'jin Sada had been joined by two other Gleaners who now occupied cocoons to either side of him and slightly above, and both of the newcomers were enjoying tea. Condo believed the one to the right was a female. He removed his Cap.

"You found the text interesting?" The question came from Sada.

"Yes. The official Church text does not present William Proffit as quite so...so *practical* a man. It would have us believe he was infallible. Yet he seems to have been not certain at all in the beginning. I have never heard such a compelling, and, well...human-sounding account of the founding of his corporation at Amagon, and the beginnings of New Jerusl'm. The Church's account is more divinely directed, to say the least. There is no mention of his vision of an impending catastrophe at all. That seems a strange omission from his sermons." Condo looked to the newcomers who nodded their agreement with his assessment.

"Things are never quite as they seem, Es'paul Condo." This remark came from the Gleaner who Condo supposed was a female by the timbre of her voice. As she turned to face him the swell of her breasts momentarily filled the contour of her robe confirming the fact.

Condo answered: "Yes, Sister, that is so. My presence here today confirms the fact. For having never ventured below the service level, I was left to believe what legends and rumors circulate above concerning you Gleaners. And I find out that the case is actually something quite different."

"Yes, we are quite disparaged from above. And yet it is from above that we all have come. We are not born Gleaners. We become the lowest of the low by choice." The female Gleaner presented a very pronounced interrogatory gaze, to which Condo could only return an uncertain one. She ventured further, "It does not seem reasonable to you that one should leave the rewards and joys of life above to reside in so fetid and infested a place as this. And yet it is in this place where the cycle of life begins. It is to this place that all things organic must come at last. It is here that the Foresters and Gardeners among the Corps cast their detritus. It is here that the Farmers send the straw and chaff, the vines and husks, the stalks and hulls from the Hydrofarms. It is here the Sweepers send the catch from the Ventportation filters and the scraping of excess plaques from the Shell glass. It is here that the insects and arachnids and annelids stir and digest the accumulations and make them accessible as nutrient for the mosses. And it is here that the Worms come, to deposit the products of their daily cleanings, and to digest the corpses of dead men and to lay their eggs and then die themselves. It is we, the Gleaners, who oversee this vast organic process, to see that all is maintained in balance. It is we who sift through it all for the inorganics that might pollute, or which if lost, must be returned to the service level. We monitor and maintain the health of the Core. We gather the bones of the dead, and grind them as food for the moss. We collect the ornaments and clothing of the dead, and sell them to the Salvors so we may buy tea. And we eat the flesh of Worms who have laid their eggs and are dying, so that the cycle between man and Worm is pure and complete." She paused to let all she had said sink into Condo's consciousness.

The Gleaner to Ho'jin Sada's left picked up the chorus: "We who have chosen this life below do so for good reason. For we have come to doubt the purpose of life."

Es'paul Condo could not hide the surprise in his eyes at this revelation! The entire purpose of his career was to dispel doubt, and instill faith in the purpose of Life. Now he stood in consort with those who professed doubt!

Ho'jin Sada, noting Condo's surprise, spoke: "Where would you send a man, or woman, possessed in the sin of doubt? Would you send them to Hell, Holiness? You see, we have come quite of our own accord." He chuckled in self-deprecation.

Confusion was not a state in which Es'paul Condo often found himself. But today was an exception. His mind whirled. He had a strong inclination to put the Cap back on, but knew the answer he sought was not there. He remembered his studies of *The Third Testament* in Seminary. He remembered the history. Great disasters had befallen the Earth in the last days. That much was certain. And man's migration to space in the Habitats had been such a rushed and desperate affair, that the founding records of the corporation were said to have been lost. In the early days just surviving within the Habitats was such an uncertain thing that all energy was expended in that direction. There was no time for the luxury of contemplating history. Hard science and practical technology were the essentials. By the time stability had been achieved, most of what remained on Earth had been destroyed. Legend had it that the Earth had been struck by a great comet, which had ignited the atmosphere, and then plunged most of the planet into a frozen, dry wasteland. *The Third Testament* asserted that William Proffit had seen the coming catastrophe in a vision, and being given by God the secret of the Ether, had built the first great Habitat, and in the last moments before destruction had lifted it into

the Heavens, while the unbelievers of Amagon
assailed the walls of New Jerusl'm.

Condo's mind scrambled to put the pieces together,
to retrace the path that had brought him here. The
path began with his unintended discovery of the
Mitsuzuki Disc. Prior to the discovery all that was
believed to remain as a record of man's last days
on Earth was contained in a collection thought to
be the writings William Proffit's, which the
Church now declared as *The Third Testament.*
Even after the discovery of the Disc, many
theologians argued against its authenticity, or
deemed it allegorical in nature. There was even a
growing element in Theology which argued that
man had never really lived on Earth at all, that it
was all an evil attempt to demean God's greatest
creation.

Condo recalled the images of the first great
Habitat, fully populated, that had lifted from New
Jerusl'm under the slow but incredible thrust of
engines driven by Proffit's Devices. Ring stacked
upon ring, standing on short connecting tube legs,
rising to a height of nearly a mile, and once in orbit
the whole great long cylinder set in rotation to
simulate earthbound gravity. The illustrations
were the classic frontispieces to *The Third
Testament.* But the original Habitat had been
salvaged ages ago, its material incorporated in
newer structures. And only by the slimmest
chance had an ornate box containing the Mitsuzuki
Disc been kept by one of the ancient Salvors as
a memento, and passed through generations of

descendants before anyone had even thought to pry it open to check its contents. Even then, the Disc appeared a valueless thing, except that an antiquities dealer had espied it at a yard sale, and suspecting its technological application had acquired it and sent it to a specialist for examination. This specialist, recognizing the microscopic markings as primitive data recordings, had passed it on to a cousin who was able to retrieve and encode the data in a modern, accessible format. What was retrieved appeared to be a narrative of the preparations for lifting of Habitat 1 Alpha by management level personnel of Mitsuzuki Corporation to superiors at corporate headquarters. It also described the employee's journey to Amagon, and a few remarks about life within New Jerusl'm. On the whole, the narrative seemed so fanciful, and fraught with allegory, that it was deemed a fictional account.

The Disc had come to Condo's attention because of the controversy its discovery had created in one of the subsidiary transactional congregations. Certain remarks contained within the Disc, referring to the "misguided genius of William Proffit," were found to be blasphemous in this fundamentalist congregation. They found this criticism of Proffit offensive. They brought the case to the Pontimax.

Far from being able to resolve the matter, the Pontimax, Es'paul Condo *incognitus* found his own interests piqued. Studying the contents of the Disc, Condo found that his youthful inquisitions were once again aroused. The great mystery of William Proffit, and man's last days on Earth loomed large again. With this new piece to the puzzle his quest had been renewed. He alone had taken the description of the geographic location contained on the Disc as a literal point on the surface of the Earth. By coercing the assistance of experts in various mining and exploration corporations through hints at Audit, Condo had managed to come up with probable coordinates on the ancient, buried surface of the planet. Thus had begun his archaeological quest for Amagon!

Now, as a result, Condo found himself in the company of the "lowest of the low," the Gleaners. He had never imagined that this quest would so fundamentally challenge the very purpose of his life. For it had been the cause of Alhumana Corporation to foster and encourage belief in the myth and mystery of Amagon as the antidote for doubt and to promote the divine origin of William Proffit's revelations, for reason dictated that only this Faith could dispel doubt. As Pontimax, it became the purpose of his life. But now reason dictated that the myth and mystery of Amagon, and of William Proffit and of man's last days on Earth must be revealed. The old faith must be doubted, so that truth might be uncovered. It now appeared that solving the mystery of William Proffit and man's last days on Earth was to be based in the very doubt it was his mission in life to dispel.

Masters in the interpretation of ocular expression and presentation, the Gleaners easily read from Condo's eyes the emotional and moral turmoil that began to boil within as a result of the revelations. Their hearts and minds went out to him. They knew full well the consequences. Ho'jin Sada spoke: "There are enemies of the faith, Es'paul Condo. And I do not refer to mere doubters such as ourselves. But true enemies as lived in ancient days on Earth, who will destroy the Faith to further their own profits and pleasures. They besiege the faith's great gift to man - his morality. They do it incrementally. They do it secretively. They do it seductively. They argue for a remission of the Sacrament of Excision so that they may once again enslave men with their own primitive instincts. Like you, they dredge the waters of the past. But their purpose is not noble; but rather, ignoble. They are pleasure seekers. They are men whose Excisions are suspect. Beware of the man who leads them - Am'riah Redshilt!"

The three Gleaners gracefully extracted themselves from their cocoons, and taking a firm grip of the moss with their toes, exited the alcove and bid Condo follow them out of the burrow. Condo disengaged his back patch, and activating his Locator, propelled abreast of them.

"Brothers and sister, I am afraid my time with you today has raised more questions than it has answered."

Condo's consternation and sincerity were obvious.

Sada answered: "For now it must be so. Continue your excavations at Amagon. And hone your arguments in support of the Sacrament of Excision to their keenest edge. You cannot know anger or fear, it has been cut out of you. But you can know sadness. That living men should desire to return to the unthinking rages and immoral pleasures of instinct must be the sadness that drives you on. And do not deny the *doubt*s that will arise. Nor let those doubts burden any soul but yours. We have today recorded the matrix of your neural pathways, and have entered them into the Authority for access to the Hidden Files. You may at any time further explore the Lost Sermons and other Documents which we hold in our care. The story they tell you will be troubling. But it is the story of man. Blessed be your Anonymity, Pontimax."

Condo and his company of Gleaners had arrived at the entrance to the burrow. The Gleaners nodded a farewell and abruptly turned and began to "walk" back down the tunnel, leaving Condo hovering in uncertainty. But he would be resolved!

Condo keyed his Locator to return and was quickly swept away and up a Tube to the service level quarantine airlock. He was issued instructions for airlock entry and decontamination. True to the nurse's predictions, the removal of the Skin was a very unpleasant affair.

He emerged from the airlock into the upper region, and closed his eyes as he took in a huge lungful of the sweet, light air. He quickly keyed his Locator for home, closed his eyes, and let the sensations of flying release endorphins into the receptors of his brain's pleasure centers. He understood the allure of these sensations. He could not understand how they could destroy a man's ability to reason.

CHAPTER 16

Condo entered the central tube of his home Pod just as Sar'ha and the children were descending from the upper chambers. They swirled down to meet him, and soon all were embraced in affection, their Locators sputtering madly to operate in such a congested environment. These were the sensations he craved. These were the acceptable functions permitted the endorphins after Excision.

Sar'ha backed away to give the brood complete access to their father, and as she hovered above them, Condo's gaze turned to her. He noted as a source of visual pleasure how subtly her feminine form telegraphed through the khaki silk of her clothing. Lust – the copulatory gaze and it sub rational, endorphin-driven response in the male – did not exist in the Excised brain, even for husband and wife. The wiring had been burned out by the very precise surgical application of colliding virtual particles beams from a Device, guided by the precision and speed of the CQC. The neuronal pathways that had previously transmitted the sexual signals below the level of the conscious mind were erased. The only initiation of sexual stimuli lay through the conscious mind; the only course for a response to sexual stimuli was through the conscious mind also. However, the sub rational, endorphin-releasing responses generating the emotions of love, concern, sadness, joy, etc. were encouraged, and even exercised.

At their first glance Sar'ha had detected an inward turmoil brewing in her husband's thoughts. It showed in his eyes as plainly as the pale grey of his irises. Condo answered her silent inquiry: "We'll talk later. It seems the children have plans for us this evening. Tickets to a Handiball game, eh?" The children chorused: "Hurry, hurry, Father! We'll be late!" Condo shrugged, and disengaging the neural output to his Locator, allowed himself to be dragged along by the brood, smiling back at Sar'ha in a mock resignation.

Condo knew the children's enthusiasm was fueled by a host of sensations and motivations no longer in his repertoire. Adolescence would come soon enough to this brood, however, and with it the Sacrament of Excision. But it was held essential that a human being must have some memory of those constructive social interactions and their rewards (as well as the shame and fear of destructive actions and their penalties) in order to be able to effectively experience the proper motivational responses as an adult. It was such a finely tuned and delicate process, this freeing of the human race from the bondage of instinctive behaviors! And now this greatest of human achievements was under assault! Condo put the thoughts from his head as the brood dragged him into a down Tube. They joined the throng of other families from the neighborhood headed for the

Handiball stadium and a match between the teams of this sector's Corps regiments.

Sports, like war, was an activity no longer engaged in by the adult population. The filaments of neural pathway ascending into the cerebral cortex which recorded the vestiges of these impulses, now severed from the basal ganglion, manifested themselves in no more than good repartee, legitimate intellectual debate, impetus for intellectual inquiry, or a good chess match. Territoriality and aggression survived only as the impulses to conquer by understanding. The mysteries and puzzles of existence were the only adversaries. To claim ever more material for incorporation into Habitats and living organisms, and ultimately, man, was the sole motivating force. The rage of emotions and underlying neural chemistry which now flowed through these children had no place in the adult world of the Habitats.

The family exited the Tube, and dissolving into the, crowd approached the Handiball stadium. It was a transparent glass cylinder 50 meters in diameter, and over a 100 meters in length. The interior of the glass surface was marked with metric gradient lines, and at either end a large, funneled, hyperbolic goal was attached by a fixed ring. All around the outside length and circumference of the cylinder row upon row of bleacher back pads stood ready to accept the oncoming spectators.

The scene evoked memories. Condo recalled his days as a pre-adolescent Novitiate in the Corps. He had been a quite enthusiastic and adept Handiball player. The memories elicited pleasurable sensations, but did not approach the nearly ecstatic pandemonium the children experienced. Such emotional pandemonium in an adult was a dangerous and unacceptable circumstance in a closed, well-ordered social and biological structure such as the Habitats represented. But Condo saw this as an opportunity to closely observe his own children, and perhaps to regain some lost insight into the power which pleasure exerted on the un-Excised human organism, and how it subverted the rational mind.

Condo and his family had just found their seats and engaged their back patches when the whistle sounded and the opposing teams filed into the field. They took up their positions, offensively and defensively, and at the second whistle, the ball was introduced into play by the toss winning team's pitcher.

Handiball had evolved naturally from the competitive sports played by all the ancient earthbound civilizations of men (and women). Beyond the limitations of gravity, however, this game was played in three dimensions. And, as the human organism was no longer a tightly musculatured, rigidly skeletonized bi-ped, but instead a highly flexible, quadramanual, free-flying agent, the options for play increased accordingly.

With no frictional surfaces, or gravitational drag to stop the ball, play was continuous until a goal was scored. The players wore sporting Locators capable of much quicker accelerations, and helmets with face masks. Padding was fitted over the areas of extremely vulnerable tissues and organs, and over the nerve plexuses.

The object of the game was to put one's ball in the hyperbolic funnel of the goal defended by the opposing team. The ball was advanced by pitching, batting, throwing, passing, dribbling, banking, hurling, shooting, and even carrying. The most exciting sequences (at least for the pre-Excised spectators) were the prolonged hurling sequences. In these maneuvers the players caught the ball in the hand or foot of an extended limb, and conserved the ball's energy by converting it into angular momentum as they let their bodies rotate, sometimes curling themselves so that the rate of rotation was very fast. Then at a precise instant and angle, the ball was released so that its tangent of departure put it on a course to a teammate or towards the goal.

As play progressed, and the first few goals were scored, the response from the younger spectators became more and more enthusiastic, which in turn seemed to increase the intensity with which the teams played. Condo found himself becoming entranced by the rhythmic, patterned movements of the players within the stadium, and the cadenced, vocal encouragements from the crowd. Increasingly detached, he experienced a sudden welling up of long buried memories. Their intensity was such that aural and olfactory hallucinations were induced. Condo found himself totally empathetic with the young sportsters in the stadium. He could vividly recall the minutest of sensations experienced that long ago time when he had been one of the Handiball players. To his surprise, the memories were sufficiently intense that he actually recalled how the competitiveness had burned within him, even vaguely recalling what he could only term a sense of anger and ill will towards a couple of the players on a long ago team that had proved particularly challenging to him. But the sensations were not supported by his current physiology, so they passed quickly. Still, it left him with a most peculiar taste in his mouth.

He gazed at his children, who had taken back pads on either side of him, the girls to one side with their mother, the boys to the other. The girls' interest in the game was more dignified than that of the boys, though their youthful enthusiasm was well-voiced. But it was obvious they saw the players of the game not as adversaries, but as something else. The boys, on the other hand, by their physical movements, were entirely caught up in the competition of the game. They were obviously possessed of an *us* and *them* mentality, as their cheers for the home team quickly became jeers for the opponents when the ball changed sides.

Condo understood all too well that Excision did not in any way diminish the basic differences between the sexes. It was still oxytocin vs. vasopressin; estrogen vs. testosterone. The X and Y chromosomes manifested themselves as assuredly as ever. It was only the automatic mechanisms which had been disconnected, those mechanisms which predated the evolution of the cerebrum and its higher order functions, mechanisms which came pre-wired in the human brain, and which shunted certain incoming stimuli directly to other limbic or brainstem structures which produced a response with no involvement of the consciousness. If the source of the initial stimuli was itself an unconsciousness mechanism wired into another human brain, a feedback loop was often set up, such that stimuli from one individual induced response at an unconscious level in another, which in turn served as stimuli inducing further response, and on and on, until the individuals were driven to action (all rewarded by the release of endorphins to the pleasure centers of the brain!). If the reactions occurred between male and female, flirtation, seduction and promiscuous sex could be the result. If the reactions occurred between males, competition, anger, aggression and even murder resulted.

As Condo observed his children, he realized this potential resided as a very real force within them. What was so necessary in the infant, and which seemed at times so quaint and cute in the child, became a dangerous, unpredictable and generally destructive potential in the adult. Though perhaps always necessary for existence at the animal level, Condo fully believed that life as a human being required the denial of these potentials. He fully believed that morality and Excision were man's divinely guided struggles to rise up from the clay and become the crown of Creation. He had no doubt that the Excision to which he would subject his children was truly a blessing and a sacrament.

But many now argued otherwise. The blessing was called an imposition; freedom from animalistic urges was called a denial of natural pleasures. Looking out over the crowd, Condo could see that very many of the adults in attendance were imitating, or permitting themselves the same raucous enthusiasm for the game as their children. Even he had to admit that the memories elicited in him by the game were provocative and that the taste left in his mouth was not a bad taste - was in fact, alluring.

Condo looked to Sar'ha, and saw that she had been observing him as intently as he had been observing the children. There was a smile in her eyes, but a questioning and puzzled one. Condo responded with an ocular presentation that reassured her, and yet reinforced her assessment of the gravity of his turmoil. She returned a presentation of patience.

A final whistle, and the roar of children's voices indicated to Condo that the Handiball contest had come to an end. A quick reference to his children's jubilation ascertained that theirs had been the winning team. Taking them by the hand and nodding to Sar'ha, he took the lead this time, and demanding extra thrust from his Locator, steered his brood skillfully through the departing crowd. The sector's Corps Academy and its Handiball stadium lay at the margin of the Forest, just along the edge of an urban area, so that the crowd pressing into the nearest up Tube was substantial. Condo opted to continue free flight with his wife and brood. As they rose above the stadium, they could look out across the large, crystal-like geometry of the urban area which housed all those myriad allures which for ages have attracted humans to huddle in such densely populated megalopolises. Beyond the urban area stretched the great open expanse of terraced Hydrofarms, whose step-like structures were covered in a verdant carpet of vegetation. If they hurried, Condo reckoned they could reach home just before the onset of Ensymphonium. At this moment he could certainly use the emotional exercise and adjustment the music would afford him.

CHAPTER 17

From *The Third Testament:* "He was the most brilliant man of his time. His Power of Reason was unsurpassed; his store of Knowledge was the envy of all. When he was an old man, and lay upon his bed, dying, a young boy asked him: 'Where are you going?" He answered: 'I do not know.' "

The children, worn out from the excitement of the Handiball match and a very intense Ensymphonium, did not resist being sent to bed earlier than usual. They were fast asleep just moments after being tucked into their bedclaves. Brushing a kiss across each tranquil forehead, Condo turned and took his Sar'ha by the hands, pulling them both along the handrail with his feet. As they exited the chamber, the LEDs dimmed and the windeyes closed as the sleeping cycle environment obtained.

Condo craved a little coffee and cake (preferably chocolate!) to temper his nervous chemistry, and some intense conversation with his wife to balance his thoughts on the day's events. Marriage and parenthood were requisite to a position in upper management such as Condo held. The General Council of the Habitats had long ago adopted the principle, as was practiced by several of the religious sects during their earthbound tenure, that for a man to exercise reasonable judgment in matters concerning the human race, he must himself be engaged in its primary function. Condo's exchange with his wife on this evening would be more than mates reinforcing one another during a time of stress, but would in fact be a fulfillment of his obligation as Pontimax and CEO of Alhumana Corp., to seek out and incorporate the feminine perspective in his analysis of the situation and in his course of action. Pulling into the kitchen, he released Sar'ha on a trajectory towards the coffee globe, propelling himself in the direction of the canister cabinets. "You make the coffee; I'll make the cake." His voice was light and adventuresome; romantic.

By the dance in his eyes, Sar'ha could ascertain that her husband was about to share with her the events which had manifested themselves in his earlier presentations of concern, distress, anxiety and uncertainty. He would recite to her what he believed to be the cause of his turmoil, and in return would receive the much-needed female perspective. It would be one of those long evenings that made her marriage to this man the great adventure she believed it would be on the day she had accepted his proposal.

The institution of marriage was not for everyone. The fact was well recorded in the histories of man's existence on Earth, before the advent of Excision - as well as from the histories of the Habitats, after man's Ascent. It seems that once the enticement of sex was removed from the human equation, once the initiation of the act was removed from the subconscious realm and the behaviors leading up to copulation were stripped of their automatic endorphin rewards, a full quarter of the female population was found to be devoid of a self-starting, compelling maternal need. Nearly half the males were found to lack a true paternal need. Condo and his Sar'ha, however, were of that blessed class whose instincts for procreation survived above the level of the amygdala and beyond the mere consequences and pleasures of copulation.

In the first centuries of life within the Habitats marriage had been a socially enforced institution, as it had been in the more conservative, theocratic and moralistic societies of man's earthbound existence. It was necessarily so, in order to at first maintain, and then to increase human populations such that continued existence in Free Space should become viable. As has been true through the eons of life's evolution, success goes to the breeders, clever adaptations and clever technologies aside. Without sufficient numbers the odds are against survival. Now that Mother Earth had become a barren, virtually lifeless rock, the continuation of the great, mysterious organizing force of life was dependent on its adaptation to and flourishing within the Habitats. As life had in very ancient times adapted and evolved to fill the seas and cover the rocky surface of an incidental planet, so now life had to adapt and evolve to fill the vast reaches of Free Space. Where once the thoughtless, irrepressible "logic" of the instincts drove organisms blindly to success, now the carefully reasoned intelligence of conscious minds plotted the course. And marriage was its cleverest device.

Marriage was no longer a socially forced institution within the Habitats, however. As nearly as could be accomplished, the social structure was designed to conform to the "merits" of the individuals within it. It was a system that gave the individual the freedom to choose his or her own prison! If a woman did not feel compelled to procreate, there was no social pressure for her to do so. There was no longer the danger that promiscuity would engender social turmoil, as without an innate, subconscious sexual drive, copulation was an activity not engaged in casually, not even auto-erotically. In a parallel fashion, males who had no interest in fatherhood were not inclined to pursue sex as a pleasurable (and aggressively driven) recreation. The wiring just wasn't there anymore. These individuals were allowed, as drones, to pursue those socially beneficial activities for which their native talents best suited them.

Es'paul Condo and his wife Sar'ha were persons whose desire to procreate had through some natural evolution separated itself entirely from the hard-wired programs of the basal ganglion. It had its origin high in the gray matter, perhaps as some of the vestigial "lace" of neuronal pathways that had their origin in the amygdala or the hypothalamus or the hippocampus, those ancient structures from which the first gray matter evolved.

Whatever the case, as Breeders, the obligation to carry on the race fell heavily on them. They had not only to replace themselves, but in order to keep up the momentum of expansion which was the pronounced purpose of Life (From *The Third Testament:* "Go forth, and fill the Universe!), Condo and his wife had to produce young to replace the non-breeding males and females. Condo and Sar'ha accepted this burden willingly, with great honor and anticipation, and a true need. Mar'oi, Beth'ha, Io'suf and Io'zak were the second brood of four. Their first brood had matured and migrated to other, newer Habitats, and were all successful breeders, now raising broods of their own. Sar'ha, being still in the second quarter of her life could produce yet another brood. It was something she and Condo had talked about. They would talk about it again, when this brood was raised.

But now the children slept. And the quiet within the Pod was only disturbed by the murmuring of the coffee globe, as it brewed it elixir, and the gentle clatter of canisters as Condo prepared his confection. The matters that Condo and Sar'ha would share in this intimate interlude would go far beyond the simply domestic. Condo was about to embark on an adventure that would challenge the very fabric of his faith, an adventure that would leave him filled with doubt that would cause him to question the very purpose of life! It was absolutely essential that he incorporate the female perspective in the decisions he would be called upon to make. For just as every whole is composed of two halves, so the whole of human experience can only be obtained by the addition of the two halves of the race, man and woman. Condo contemplated these matters as he prepared the cake. It was a late night specialty of his, and Sar'ha relished it so!

Such a melding of minds was not easily if ever achieved before the advent of the Sacrament of Excision. It is true that some of the more mystical and hypnotic theologies created nirvanic states in which a truly high level of communication could take place between the sexes. But the circumstance was rare, very rare, and maybe only the stuff of legend and myth. For morality and reason seldom won the fight, struggling against the unseen, unheard, unconscious stimuli elicited in the amygdala, and the subsequent, undetected and often irresistible neural chemistries that produced the instinctive behaviors. Even the intellect, the conscious power of reason was so often and so subtly subverted, that morality itself was demeaned and lowered without the practitioner even being aware until some objective observer hurled the epithet: "Hypocrite!" at them. So it was of old, when men and women tried to communicate in reasonable fashion that the undercurrents of stimuli sent forth unawares from the ancient cranial organs forever confused and entangled the pursuit of truth with the fulfillment of primordial, instinctive urges.

Condo was well-read in matters concerning human behavior, particularly those works of earthly origin.

Excised at the onset of adolescence, he had never personally experienced the intense, inexorable sexual attraction that had played between his earthbound ancestors. He often tried to imagine how it must have been to be so overwhelmed by involuntary neural chemistry and function as to be rendered incapable of rational thought. He found it as inscrutable as ancient man's much referenced "fear of falling." It was something that lay entirely outside his realm of experience, though in extremely acute, subjective moments he imagined it must be something like the dread and yet fascination all children of the Habitats know, the fear of being "outside" the Habitat, alone in space, with no living thing to see or touch or hold or smell. Helpless and alone. He remembered as a child going to the canopy with his father, nearing the Shell, and feeling the darkness beyond calling to him, pulling him, so that he feared he would suddenly and uncontrollably be propelled through the Shell, the glass shattering, and he suddenly, terrifyingly, and yet ecstatically being swallowed by all that great and vast blackness.

He tried to imagine how it must have been for women before the advent of Excision. How subtle must have been the nuances of the copulatory gaze. Given without thought, the presentation would elicit in the on-looking male (or on-looking males!) an endorphin response which in turn would stimulate neuronal pathways in the primitive ganglion that entirely bypassed the higher functions, sending instead impulses directly to the limbics, causing arousal and movement toward the female. In the culturally or intellectually unrestrained male, any challenge to this movement brought immediate and thoughtless aggressive responses. (Sadly, even the most culturally and intellectually restrained males often fell prey to these primitive responses, the edifices of their morality collapsing totally before the greater power of the instincts.) Often, the elicited aggression resulted in violence against the female herself, an unintended and tragic result of such thoughtless motivation.

Condo marveled at the protestations of innocence by females which abounded in the ancient literature. Could it truly have been that they did not consciously understand the power they had wielded over men? Or had they practiced an incredible deception, so complete they themselves were deluded by it? This very topic had occupied many a late night talk between Sar'ha and Condo. She, too, marveled at the claimed ignorance of her earthbound predecessors. How could such power have been exercised unawares? She claimed to be incapable of imagining such circumstances, having been, like all females in the Habitats, Excised before the onset of menses. And yet, even now, when Sar'ha and other females made such claims, a certain, inscrutable presentation came to their eyes, verging on the fallacious, and yet not a lie, but a secret!

The delicious fragrance of warm chocolate wafted from the oven as the cake completed baking. Condo had whipped up an excessive amount of rich, dark icing for the modest loaf and spread it liberally. Small globules of the stuff broke free from his creation as the still too warm cake melted the edges of the icing. Condo intercepted a few of these with his fingers as they drifted towards the kitchen's collector, and put them to his tongue and lips, rolling his eyes in a mock ecstasy, much to Sar'ha's delight.

"Chocolate and caffeine! Oh, what sinners we are!" he chortled.

Sar'ha laughed aloud and set the cups and coffee globe on the table. The two engaged the back pads of adjacent chairs, and as Sar'ha dispensed the coffee into the cups, Condo broke off a piece of the cake and with his hand fed it playfully to his wife. She accepted his offering, and then mischievously bit his finger. He feigned shock and injury! She laughed again.

Then, as sudden as the frivolity was spontaneous, the mood sobered. Sar'ha presented: "*You have something to tell me.*"

Condo presented in return: *I have something I must ask you.* "Tell me, dear wife, what is the purpose of this life?"

Sar'ha understood from the extremely obtuse nature of this initial question that her husband's intent was to align their thought processes before directly addressing the real matters at hand. It was a little mental exercise intended to stimulate the parallel neural pathways; a catechism of the Church used to prepare the mind to contemplate the fundamentals of existence. She understood that her husband was not simply inquiring as to the opinion of his wife, but was instead seeking from her a thoughtful presentation representative of the female of the species. For all its apparent intimacy, this was to be a very formal communication. She appreciated that he kept it so friendly. She responded by rote: "Reason reveals that the function of life is self-perpetuation. Faith instructs that the purpose of life is to beget life. Man has not the power to discern function from purpose. In this, then, do reason and faith agree."

"And what of doubt?"

"Doubt is the Great Destroyer. Whosoever doubts the power of reason cannot understand the Creation. Whosoever doubts the power of faith cannot know the Creator."

Condo's eyes smiled at his wife's accuracy. "Always such the splendid pupil," he teased.

Condo continued: "You know that doubts have been raised as to the need to continue the Sacrament of Excision. The arguments come mainly from the commercial sector, the investment and entrepreneurial guilds and associations being the most vocal. One Am'riah Redshilt, an investment banker and an Abbot in the Association of Innovative Investment Strategists and Market

Development Specialists seems the principal antagonist. It seems that the vestiges of greed and ambition are more pronounced in some individuals than others, and like all Similars, they tend to form their own congregations. That is to be expected. But what is bothersome is that their unrelenting advertisements and informational propagandas are starting to have a marked effect on some in the academic and theological sectors. There seems to be a subtle but deliberate effort to incite latent potentials within these populations to advance the influence and social standing of the commercial sector. Of course, the greatest opponent to the theological sector and to the Church has always resided within this group. These are men who measure the success of their lives by the number of atoms they garner under their control, and not by the number of ideas they dispense to lift up the minds and hearts of their fellow creatures. It is an ancient selfishness, which even Excision at its current level of precision fails to remove entirely."

As a pediatric physician, and board-certified Excisionist, Sar'ha understood completely the intricate nature of the situation her husband expounded. The medical art of Excision had come a long way from it crude origins. During man's last days on Earth, Excision was so primitive as to consist of gross surgical removal of amygdalic and other associated basal and limbic tissues. Though done on a nearly microscopic level, still much harmless and even beneficial tissue was removed to achieve the desired effect. With certain individuals the process sometimes resulted in lethargy and dullness. With the great refinements in technology and technique, and particularly with the adaptation of Proffit's Device and its incredible powers of accuracy, however, it was now possible to map the specific neural pathways involved in a given stimulation and response paradigm, and to effectively target for division just those synapses critical to the unwanted, automatic, sub-rational behavior. The complications arose from the fact that long ago it had been rationally and morally determined that Excision should not be performed on the organism until the determined onset of adolescence. Early on it was proven that until the mental faculties had reached a certain threshold, the endorphin-driven, pleasure-rewarding mechanisms of the instinctive behaviors were essential motivation for the survival of the human young. Robbed of reward, too many infants languished and died, even under ideal environmental parameters. The endorphin release stimulated by human touch, the sound of a mother's voice, the sights and smells of siblings were all requisite to initiate the will of the organism to survive and to stimulate its development, physically, mentally, psychologically and spiritually. But by the time these developments were achieved, those neural pathways which came inherently "pre-wired" in the basal ganglion and produced the instinctive behaviors had already affected the learned behaviors, and as divergent neural pathways ascended from the proto-gray matter atop the amygdala, the hypothalamus and hippocampus far into the upper reaches of the cerebrum. As most of the pathways served many different functions, it would be impossible to disconnect every offending circuit without destroying the "mind" of the individual.

This, then, was the perpetual battle. Though the old, subconscious, sub-rational behaviors were cut off at their trunk, but not before they manifested themselves ever so subtly within the very frame work of the conscious, rational mind. It often seemed the ancient, instinctive structures had planted in the conscious mind the seeds of their own return as an incessant infiltration of the logic with a longing for the old ways. The rational mind ought to readily see that mechanisms evolved to insure the survival of primitive organisms in a thoughtless, predatory world had no place in a well-ordered, rational environment. Yet, the lure of the endorphins seemed always an enticement back to those predatory times.

All of this seemed so evident to Es'paul Condo as to be *a priori*. Yet he understood it was not so for all men. Am'riah Redshilt, for one. He did believe, however briefly acquainted, that Ho'jin Sada surely saw the world as he did. He wondered if women perceived the situation as he did. It was his purpose for talking with Sar'ha. As defender of the faith, and dispeller of *doubt*, it was absolutely essential that he understood the problem from every angle, in its every facet. It was the historical aspect that had lead him to his archaeological search for Amagon. It was the nascent, evolutionary aspect of the here and now that demanded that he understand the problem from the female perspective. A problem half-solved could be more dangerous than one let alone.

"And what does woman think of Excision? Having excised a brood of your own offspring, do you see it as an unreasonable imposition or as a blessing?" Condo's question was point blank.

Sar'ha thought carefully before she spoke. "Excision does not heal the great divide between man and woman. They remain two halves of the whole. No half, alone, though it increase its size and scope to infinity, is ever the whole. As reason reveals the distinct functions of male and female, so faith instructs their different purposes."

Condo nodded appreciatively at his wife's quotation from *The Third Testament.*

Sar'ha continued: "I cannot imagine the lives of my ancient sisters. Possessed of the power of reason and capable of such great understanding, yet the very function and purpose of their existence were subject to a set of neurological stimuli and responses over which they had no conscious control. How often it must have seemed like a renegade hand, forever plunging a dagger into its own heart."

Sar'ha was well-read in the ancient literature. She understood, as did her husband, what a lamentable record of the struggle between reason and instinct it contained. Such great tragedies as befell the human race before the advent of Excision and man's Ascent from his earthbound prison, if they were not the result of the vagaries of an unmarshalled planetary environment, were invariably the result of the unmarshalled behaviors elicited by the primitive stimulus/response mechanisms encoded in the instincts. The subconscious sexual aggression of the female incited the territorial aggression of the male (which often needed little assistance!), and the stories told of the warring and the whoring, and the human misery that resulted left one to wonder that man had avoided his earthly demise sufficiently long enough to survive the Stone Age!

"History records that the mind of woman turns its energies to nurturing the flesh. It is the great and wondrous gift of motherhood! It is not the edict of man; nor is it the conscious choice of woman. It is the nature of the Creation. Faith and reason agree that it must therefore be the will of the Creator." Again Sar'ha quoted *The Third Testament* precisely.

Condo responded: "Likewise, the mind of man is turned upon the Creation, to discover and to use as tools Laws of Nature to make a suitable home for his wife and children. This too, is the will of the Creator."

Sar'ha rejoined: "Before the advent of Excision, sin was the natural course, and virtue the agonizingly unattainable. Now virtue comes as naturally as the breathing of air, while sin must find its converts only among the Unfortunates and the Sociopaths"

Condo conclude with a passage from the Excision rite: "With the Sacrament of Excision do we bless our children with the higher purpose of God's intent."

Condo gazed at his Sar'ha with a presentation of profound and appreciative understanding. Then he asked her: "As a medical professional, do you also find the practice of Excision to be justifiable?"

Sar'ha thought a moment, and then responded: "Cancer cells are living tissue. They possess the same organizing force as do all living cells. And yet they are primitive, and undifferentiated. They represent a stage when life was not organized beyond the cellular level, each cell an individual, uncooperative, self-serving entity, mindless of its interactions. Such a cell adrift in an ancient, primordial sea had its place; in the highly specialized, interdependent structure of the human organism it is a deadly disease. The cancer must be cut out or otherwise destroyed or it invades and corrupts the higher tissues, and brings death. So it is now with the instincts. Though once they served a purpose, when man yet existed at the selfish, predatory, individualistic animal level. Yet now, with the interdependence of the human race rationally understood and faithfully accepted, such selfish, animalistic individualism is as a cancer. It destroys the fabric of the social network, and would bring death to the human race here, as it did so long ago on Earth. Excision is the physician's healing art applied to this disease."

Condo had closed his eyes as he listened to Sar'ha's impassioned response. As her words entered his consciousness, they fired down the synaptic circuits of his own thoughts on the matter, aligning so perfectly as to bring a great reinforcement of those neural pathways, and a subsequent release of endorphins that washed over him as a warm and comforting tranquility.

Condo opened his eyes, smiled at Sar'ha, and presented a gaze of deep understanding and gratitude. He had come to her seeking a reaffirmation of the female perspective and he had found it. Now he could dispense with the rational formalism and indulge in a little speculation and "gossip" with his wife. He broke another piece of the chocolate delight from his concoction and fed it to Sar'ha. She too broke off a piece of the cake and fed it to her husband. They laughed.

Condo spoke more casually. "Am'riah Redshilt presents a problem."

Sar'ha's only "proper" knowledge of Redshilt was the corporate database entries that listed his various management positions and seats upon boards of directors. The Virtue of Anonymity declared that if you knew a man's name and face, you could not know his occupation or Habitat. Likewise, if you knew a man's name and occupation, you could not know his Habitat or face. And so on. But like all ideals, the practical reality fell well short of the intended. And particularly with men like Redshilt, who not so subtly made sure that the strictures of the virtue did not effectively obtain. He was a man forever making himself known. Sar'ha knew his reputation.

Condo continued: "Redshilt's behavior borders on the sociopathic, though he does provide great service to the Habitats. But he is an Accumulator and like the Similars of that accord, he is not driven by a rational understanding of the social consequences of his actions, but by a sub-rational need to accumulate and control. We are only fortunate that to this point his talents have proven quite valuable to our proliferation. But I fear that as he ages, these urges exert a greater influence over his rational thought processes."

Sar'ha knew that the speculations her husband now shared with her could not be voiced in any public forum.

"He is a brilliant innovator and manipulator. His skills in managing the commercial flow have provided the needed resources for many an inventor and entrepreneur to bring their products and services to market. He is a formidable force in helping to create the diversity in the various aspects of human existence that make life interesting. And yet there is something sinister about him. It is manifested in his need to be in control. And it often goes dangerously beyond the meritocratic."

Here was Condo's greatest criticism, and deepest fear. For on principle, the Habitats existed solely by the exercise of the strictest meritocracy. The developing mental abilities of every inhabitant of every Habitat was closely monitored and recorded. Talents were allowed to develop naturally, according to the genetic disposition of the individual. And the individual was allowed to pursue any (and in the case of truly exceptional individuals, *all*) of the occupations for which those talents suited the individual. No attempt was made to force development in an area beyond the basic essentials needed to make a well-rounded, socially adaptable citizen among those devoid of talents. There were certain genetic strains, however, that had the tendency to resist this socially stabilizing practice by surreptitiously schooling its offspring to conform to certain occupations, whether native talents existed or not. It was this remnant of gene pool preservation that Excision did not successfully eliminate. It was prevalent in certain lineages, one of those being the Redshilt.

In the modern sense, this is a purely sociopathic tendency – daddy was a banker; and so must junior be, though the one be a genius and the other an idiot! But as no society in  human history has actually attained Utopian ideals, such imperfections are necessarily tolerated. It is even argued by some that such resistance to absolute conformity is the very fundamental force of evolution, *ergo* variety within a species is always the first step towards new speciation. But in the case of the Redshilts, where this marked sociopathic tendency to resist conformity was coupled with a proclivity for accumulation and control, Condo feared that a true threat existed to the fundamental morality upon which the governance and survival of Habitat society depended.

"Redshilt has also made certain statements directly related to the character and moral uprightness of William Proffit. He has insinuated that the Ascent, as described to us in *The Third Testament*, may not be correct. His blasphemies have created a stir in some academic circles and have incited emotional outbursts from some of the fundamentalist theologians and their congregations. There have been some calls for Audits of Redshilt's business ventures."

In the company of his wife, and the privacy of his home, Condo wandered into speculations and admissions that would be unthinkable elsewhere, given his position – except, perhaps in the presence of Ho'jin Sada.

CHAPTER 18

From *The Third Testament:* "So that no man shall cast stones, we shall all live in glass houses."

If Condo was to prevent the devolution which he believed Redshilt's challenge represented, he knew that he must understand totally the forces which had instigated man's evolution from a planet-bound, instinctive organism, to a reason-directed life force existing in Free Space.

Condo recalled from his days at Seminary: "It is very often the case that more than one set of theoretical processes can successfully explain the phenomena of the observed physical reality. Our reason cannot with certainty determine which of these theories is the *absolute* truth. It is the great (and humbling) limit set upon human knowledge. Yet we do believe that truth exists. It is the foundation of the Faith."

Proffit's Theory of the Ether proved no exception. The man himself stated in *The Third Testament:* "No creature of the Quantum Realm can have certain Knowledge of Ethereal Things. We can by faith alone reach out and touch the Essence of God's Creation."

In fact, Proffit avoided ever claiming "to know" anything about the subject of his Theory, but always began his remarks with: "I believe. . ." All children in their first year in the Maintenance Corps were introduced to Proffit's lay interpretation of his Ethereal Theory:

*"Democritus began it all with his Theory of the Atom. He proposed that Things are not what they seem, but in fact are made up of Lesser Things. His notion that a clump of dirt, crumbled in his hand, was in fact a collection of "parts" that were the "essence" of dirt was the idea that set man on his path of inquiring into the "essence" of all things.*

*And what have we done since that day but crush Democritus' clump of dirt into smaller and smaller bits. For each new bit we have discovered, we find that it too is made of bits, of "particles." Even the illusion of "wave theory" does not interrupt our descent, as we determine that particles are made of "waves of lesser particles." And so it goes until we arrive at the notion of a 'quantum,' the very essence of perceivable reality, the stuff we call energy!*

*And here we encounter a barrier, a threshold. We see nothing beyond but a vacuum. And yet our logic does not like to be stopped so abruptly. In our further inquiries it becomes evident that something lies just below this threshold of our perceptions. Something undetectable from the quantum level, detectable only by the power of our minds. Into this realm only imagination and faith can proceed. We sense a "virtual" existence, a sea of potential – a nascent reality.*

*I believe my Theory is simple enough. I believe that the structure of "particles made of waves of particles" descends to the infinitesimal. In such a place, particles would become infinitely small, yet infinite in number, such that the distances between them would also become infinitely small, as viewed from the quantum level. In this place it would appear that all particles would then be infinitely near each other, such that interactions or events would seem to occur at infinitely small intervals of time. Observed from the quantum level, it would appear that all events occur immediately adjacent to one another, and simultaneously. Time and distance, as quantum perceptions, would be meaningless. Only direction would be relevant. I also believe that this "sea of particles," this Ether, is saturated, always on the verge of precipitating the larger particles we perceive as quanta, or energy. Smashing an extant quantum into its ethereal bits and seeding the "virtual particles" nascent in the Ether, these particles that only require the smallest perturbation in order to precipitate into reality, such "seeding" ought then to precipitate an upwelling of energy--of quanta! That is precisely what my "Device" accomplishes.*

*Further, I believe this vast Ether interacts continuously with the Quantum Realm, which collective interactions we perceive as mass, gravitation, acceleration, momentum. . ."*

It had been many years since Condo had reviewed Proffit's Theory of the Ether. With the assistance of his Cap he quickly accessed the great list of Devices whose operation was based on the creation and manipulation of ethereal particles to precipitate quanta. The first was the incredibly powerful Ethereal Induction Engine, which created such a tremendous precipitation of quanta that thrust at any power level and for any duration is easily achieved. It had been this great Device that had lifted the first Habitats from their subterranean shafts slowly, gracefully, and seemingly effortlessly, with no need for tremendous accelerations with their consequent g-forces. Second came the micro-Devices, which could disintegrate existing quanta into ethereal particles, allowing the destruction of bits of matter without releasing uncontrolled nuclear energies, or which could "tweak" the Ether in digital code, so that communications could be accomplished instantaneously across any distance. Such micro-Devices were also used in the delicate Excision procedures, annihilating specific synaptic bonds, thereby eliminating specific neuronal pathways within the basal ganglion and their consequent instinctive behaviors. A modification of the Excision Devices was used in the process of psychological cleansing, whereby Unfortunates could eliminate from their own minds the disturbing and debilitating thoughts that caused their various neuroses, psychopathologies and socio-pathologies.(These individuals became known as Unfortunates, because generally by the time mental pathologies progressed to the point that treatment was sought, the individual usually ended up destroying so many neuronal pathways as to be reduced to nearly a vegetative state.) More highly refined, the derivatives of these Devices made possible the technology of the Caps, whereby streams of ethereal particles were used to scan the most intricate neuronal networks and to detect the firing and sequence of individual neurons, so that the actual physiology of human thought could be detected and transmitted. Conversely, this technology permitted the stimulation of neurons upon specific neuronal pathways such that information and functions stored within the databases of the CQC could be transmitted directly into conscious human thought.

It was the revelation of this theory and the full weight of its technological implications which had created the great moral struggle within the young Proffit. He knew that it was only a matter of time before some like-minded scientific inquirer would also make this discovery. It was the power of Creation and Annihilation given into the hand of man. But the young scientist believed that man had not yet evolved to a level to handle such power without destroying himself. So he came to the conclusion that man must be made to fit the new paradigm. To him the truth had become a singularity, the function of the universe as understood by man's reason was the same as the purpose of God's Creation as professed by man's faith – life was to beget life; to expand ever outward, raising the inanimate to the animate and sentient. And if some greater purpose than this existed its revelation lay yet in the most future reaches of this human expansion. For now, the job at hand was the observed function of life: to procreate; and by all human ingenuity to ever expand the conditions which permitted the success of this endeavor! If it required the altering of man to make him suitable to this purpose, then so be it! Thus began the young scientist's crusade to remake man into a rational, moral creature, fit to possess the knowledge of the Ether and the vast powers that lie within.

## CHAPTER 19

Am'riah Redshilt's home was a rather resplendent cubicle perched at the summit of one of the urban partitions separating Forest from agricultural center within Habitat 61 Gamma. The partitions served as breaks designed to help regulate exposure to solar radiation as the Habitat executed its 24 hours rotation cycle. As with all things within the Habitat, multiple functions were employed where structure was required. And as natural housing could never accommodate the dense population within a Habitat, these partitions doubled as the great urban centers of population and commerce.

Each Habitat contained at least four such structures, which in their social function mimicked the ancient earthbound cities. As has been the habit and inclination of the species throughout the recorded millennia, such social aggregations as these partitions represented are the preferred condition of existence for the greater percentage of the human race. So it was in the Habitats, with an average of 75% of a Habitat's population residing in these urban centers. And, as has been the human circumstance since time immemorial, where people gathered, a hierarchy naturally developed. The play of genetics cares nothing for democracy, so that no matter how carefully and rationally a society is planned, the great and untamable force of evolution will not be contained. Some men (and women) *are* better than others. This hierarchy does not bend to reason. All virtues aside, with the exception of philosophers, mendicants and mystics, the cream of Habitat society inhabited the uppermost tiers of the partition's cubicles, just as ancient aristocracies inhabited the palaces upon the hills.

Though both the Church and the social ideology professed adherence to the Virtues of Anonymity and Humility, as with all human systems, the practical reality held little resemblance to the idealized one. Am'riah Redshilt's residence was the perfect example. Though in its basic structure it differed little from the thousands of other cubicles stacked one upon the other which made up the great body of the partitions, by its location at the summit and the obviously, even ostentatiously-applied effects of exterior ornamentation, it was apparent this was the abode of no ordinary citizen. Golden filigree laced the windeyes of the cubicle's lesser compartments, and the hexagonal portal that gave access to the cubicle's central corridor was decorated with a monogram and heraldic coat of arms.

It was a given within Habitat society that persons existed with motivations and talents of such value to the whole that individual license had to be granted. The Redshilt Clan was a collection of such persons. It had been the earthbound ancestors of Am'riah Redshilt who had provided much of the financing that had allowed the proselytizing

Proffit to gain credibility within a culture and society that was crumbling morally, ideologically, and economically. With this credibility Proffit was able gain the means and the people to construct his New Jerusl'm, and within its confines to create the human paradigm that would at last free man from a dark and irrational past of instincts and thoughtless urges and propel him into the heavens, a creature of such rational purpose as to be worthy to inhabit God's domain. Am'riah Redshilt was proud of this heritage; the part his family had played in bringing about the great Ascent of humanity. And it was in this pride that he often found resentment towards the likes of Es'paul Condo, who would presume to impose the social restrictions of ordinary men upon a man like himself.

Am'riah Redshilt considered himself a moral man. He was a good father, even doting, and the early successes of his third brood attested to the good genetics and good environment he provided his offspring. His wife, Re'kaba, was also from one of the *old families*, and in most regards concurred with her husband's sentiments. Re'kaba ran a very precise household; Am'riah handled the family business with an exquisite precision.

There was an aspect to Am'riah's make-up which escaped an appropriate accounting whenever he engaged in self-appraisal, however. It was a characteristic he shared with the men of his caliber down through the ages. It was an attribute (or a flaw, depending on the perspective of the appraiser) that compelled men to rise above their peers – to not only live their own lives, but to lead the lives of others. It was a drive to control; it was a will to power. It could manifest itself in the guise of a noble ambition, or it could descend into the sociopathic machinations of a megalomaniac.

Am'riah's ambition was not the only unaccounted flaw in his character, however. There existed a deeper flaw, a more profound inconsistency between the truth of his nature and the self-image he maintained. Am'riah Redshilt tended toward an unconfessed reversion to instinctive urges, emanating from his cerebral cortex and descending to the remnants of his basal ganglion. The higher functions of his brain were possessed with the irrational intent to re-establish those now diminished organs to their past and primitive grandeur. It was a satyric impulse of such intensity that it twisted and turned his very powers of logic and reason, and unbeknownst to his own conscious processes, every minute of every hour of every day subtly subverted his every action and turned those actions from the noble pursuits of truth and reason to the primal pursuit of pleasure. Am'riah Redshilt was possessed of a sociopathic lust, a satyriasis so fundamental to his make-up that it went unrecognized, or at least denied by his conscious self.

Most evenings after Ensymphonium and the family meal, having seen his brood of children to their bedclaves and retired from his wife's company to the privacy of his study to catch up on some business, the darkness that descended over Redshilt's Quadrant in the Habitat descended as well over his mental processes. Ensconced in the privacy and security of his study, however sincere were his intentions, after a few moments, in the certainty that he would not be disturbed, Am'riah Redshilt would go to and open a cleverly disguised compartment within his console, and from it extract a Cap. But this was no ordinary Cap, for by its very design, the purpose of its creation, it was not intended to Interface with the CQC for the purpose of expanding human intellectual potential, but was instead designed to simulate in the mind of the wearer those primitive structures of the basal ganglion, the amygdala, the hypothalamus, the hippocampus, in their most primitive completeness, and give to the person the full range of every primitive urge and pleasure that men had ever known. It was an illicit possession, this Cap – its very existence antithetical. This night, like so many nights, Am'riah Redshilt slipped the supple Cap over the great rise of his cranial bulbs, and activated its Devices. Shortly, the light of humanity faded from his eyes. In his mind thought was replaced by sensation; action was replaced by reaction; the addiction of unlimited endorphin poured such pleasure through his veins that even life itself seemed a valueless commodity in comparison.

A cause had arisen around the creation and dissemination of these illicit Caps; a cause whose adherents spanned the entire of the social spectrum.

And the Cause, as it was increasingly and secretively called, had now grown to such numbers that a subtle, deteriorating influence began to infuse the social structures of the Habitats. It was this deteriorating influence that Redshilt's nemesis Es'paul Condo now so fiercely battled from the moral bastion of Alhumana Corporation. Though rumors abounded, it was not clear whether Condo lent them sufficient credence to recognize his enemies by their purported association with this Cause, or even whether he truly believed the Cause existed. He certainly had no direct knowledge of the illicit Caps. A battle was joined, however, and it found Redshilt and Condo in opposite camps.

The great philosophical separation between the camps lay in their perceptions of the purpose of life. The moral argument espoused from Condo's camp based its argument in the reasonable observation that all life seemed, in fact, was provably directed to procreation and continuation. This function was held to be the only perceivable purpose given the current state of knowledge. In the other camp, Redshilt's camp, a different conclusion was reached using the same reasonable observation of life; namely that all life was provably directed to the pursuit of pleasurable experience and the avoidance of the unpleasurable or painful experience. The first corollary to this principle was that the absence of pleasurable experience in fact constituted in itself an unpleasurable experience and was therefore to be avoided. On this point Redshilt's camp, albeit anonymously, had begun to increasingly criticize and condemn the practice of Excision as a barbaric, totally unnecessary procedure intended to deny pleasurable experience, the ensuing malaise used as an agent of control over the masses.

Very often before descending into his wanton pursuits of primitiveness, Redshilt would take several minutes to review these moral arguments, always finding his way round to a rational justification for his actions. This night, as on so many nights, Am'riah Redshilt put his moral qualms to rest, and engaging the entire of his security apparatus to prevent detection, with trembling hands slipped on the illicit Cap, and plunged into the electric sensations of primitive fears, desires, pleasures and rages. There was no primitive act that the Cause had not faithfully and meticulously recreated in the Cap's programming, such that the experience was almost as tactile and real as the beating of his own heart. Redshilt always emerged from these sessions so mentally and emotionally drained, that he, like other members of the Cause, was certain a great purge had occurred, a renewing catharsis, such that he was in fact a better human for the experience. In fact, he only emerged further addicted to the lure of his own endorphins. On this night, as Redshilt downloaded and executed a particularly orgiastic cannibal ritual, the swirl of endorphins in his blood caused his head to loll and roll in uncontrolled, orgiastic stupor.

CHAPTER 20

From *The Third Testament:* "The last days of man on Earth were days of turmoil and destruction. The primitive, instinctual urges emanating from the basal and limbic organs had so overpowered the rational functioning of the mind of un-Excised Man  that he descended into an uncontrolled orgy of rage and rapaciousness that led to his ultimate destruction."

By his third visit to the Core, Es'paul Condo was aware that a security apparatus was in place, and that the now familiar faces of the nurse and the personnel at Quarantine were the result of someone making sure that these trips were assisted and observed by as few persons as possible. Condo doubted these participants were aware of the fact that they were being manipulated. He was also not yet sure who was doing the manipulating. But since his first trip to the Core and his initial encounter with Ho'jin Sada, there had been a subtle but detectable change in the circumstances of his profession.

Security apparatuses abounded in the societies of the Habitats. It was generally held that this near obsession with security was the manifestation of the territorial instinct as it had mapped itself into the higher cortex prior to Excision. Unlike the raw demand for physical territory that had plagued Earthbound man, or the desired accumulation of those tokens which represented physical space or objects (ancient men had called these tokens *money*), the Excised man of the Habitats dealt in a rational world of ideas. It was the ideas, the particular thought processes and resultant conclusions of an individual's reasoning ability, which now elicited the remnants of the old instinct. For a man's ability to reason was the currency of his wealth in the meritocracy of the Habitats, and the Virtue of Anonymity aside, a man's wealth of ideas promoted him through the ranks, bought for him the additional shares in a corporation that brought the reward of control. And although the meritocratic principle which guided social structure within the Habitats declared that individuals were subservient to the collective, still humans had not yet evolved beyond a need for motivation – a motivation pure reason alone did not yet provide. They still required some tangible evidence of achievement, some measurable reward for their efforts. Consequently, each individual, and to a greater degree, each corporate structure jealously guarded its intellectual properties. Alhumana Corporation was no exception. It was a subtle shift in the patterns of the security apparatuses through which Es'paul Condo operated and communicated within the corporate world and through which he interacted via the Cap with the CQC which now made itself apparent at the periphery of his awareness. He was certain he was being observed.

But Condo had no time to dwell on such matters at the moment. A crisis was brewing within the General Council of the Habitats. A delegation led by none other than Am'riah Redshilt had approached the Council and upon the preliminary findings from Condo's own investigation at Amagon, had challenged the moral foundation upon which Alhumana Corporation based its social legitimacy: the divine inspiration attributed to William Proffit's discovery of Ethereal Mechanics; the subsequent raising of the first Habitats; the inspiration revealed in the text of *The Third Testament*. On the virtue of this doubt they were calling for an Audit of Alhumana Corporation, and its Pontimax and CEO.

As Condo exited the down Tube from Quarantine and hovered, he was surprised to be met this time on the surface of the Core Sphagnum by Ho'jin Sada and a cadre of other Gleaners, all stained, orange of hair, red of eye, clothed in their saffron yellow sacks, and all clinging by their feet to the surface of the moss. Sada spoke.

"Your Eminence, we are again blessed with your presence. We of the Brethren. . ." (with a sweep of his right arm Sada indicated that he spoke for all present.) "We of the Brethren are well aware of the spiritual and moral conflict which now arises regarding William Proffit and *The Third Testament*, and that Excision and the moral foundation of Alhumana Corporation are now under attack from several quarters."

Ho'jin Sada turned away from Condo, and began to "walk" towards the entrance to the burrow. His fellow mendicants lined up single file behind him, and beginning a quiet, melancholy chant, followed with heads bowed. Over his shoulder, Sada looked directly into Condo's hovering gaze, and with an unexpected command to his voice said: "It is time for revelation!"

Taken somewhat by surprise at the Gleaner's sudden forcefulness and the glaring *I have something I must tell you* presentation, Es'paul Condo let the procession gain some distance on him before he flexed his propelletes and slowly followed them into the burrow. His mind occupied by Sada's reference to "revelation," Condo hovered behind the entourage, his Locator A-cav set to auto. He did not notice they were descending further into the burrow than he had ever been before, and only when the dance of refracted light upon the burrow's inner surface indicated that water was near did he focus on what lay ahead. He saw that they were approaching a great, crystalline portal opening into a large, transparent Cell that protruded into the Cylinder Sea. The prisms at either end of the sea and the abundant growth of the sponge-like organisms whose fibers possessed natural optical transmission properties carried the light to the Sea's greatest depths, by no accident refracting light into the blue wavelengths. It was homage paid to the Mother Earth. What now bathed Condo's visual cortex and soothed his nervous chemistry was the green halo of the burrow's interior surrounding the liquid, glowing azure of the life-giving waters. The mix of colors and light emoted an irresistible tranquility. Abandoning his ruminations, Condo began to take in the visual data and noted with some surprise and consternation that the interior compartments of the glass Cell were lined with consoles for operating Golem, for communications, and for access to the CQC. At each console sat a Gleaner, the back patch of a Locator firmly attached to his chair. Each wore a Cap, and was so engrossed in his labors they paid no attention as the portal's lens receded and Sada and his entourage let go of their hold on the moss, each grabbing a Locator hanging ready at the entrance. Deftly fitting the devices, they propelled across the open space of the Cell's central shaft to a compartment at the far end. Confused and bemused, Condo followed without a word. Sada and his flock settled on a table ring which occupied the center of the terminal compartment and each took his place in orderly fashion, engaging their Locators' back patches to the table's seat pads. A chair was left open directly opposite of Ho'jin Sada, obviously intended for Condo. He maneuvered into position with a flutter of propellete flings and engaged his patch.

This end compartment protruded furthermost into the Cylinder Sea and its hemispheric shape descended around the table ring so that looking outward in any direction, a seated person was greeted by the blue depths. The glowing waters revealed a great tumult of life, kinetic and varied.

Though Condo had often traveled to the Poles to swim and fish, he had never before viewed the sea at these depths. He marveled at the diversity of forms that inhabited it.

Directly, Ho'jin Sada clapped his hands and a handful of novitiates in their white sacks appeared with tea globes and cups. They set a cup before each of the table's occupants, and dispensed the hot tea into them, small puffs of fragrant steam escaping from the drinking tubes. When all were served, and the novitiates withdrawn, Sada began: "Let us pray. . . "The mysteries of life remain unsolved. For each piece of the puzzle solved, a dozen more are revealed. The Creator has given us life so that we may wonder and revel in these mysteries. In His time, and not in man's, shall all things be revealed. Until that day, we follow his Commandments, as revealed to William Proffit, made known to us through the gifts of Reason and Faith. Amen."

"Amen!"

As soon as the prayer was finished, the novices reappeared with trays of bread and meat. Condo recognized through their transparent packaging that the meat was the roasted flesh of Worms. He was immediately repulsed, and yet surprised by its appetizing aroma, yet the knowledge of it caused a gorge to rise in his throat and discouraged any temptation he might have harbored for sampling the fare. Their guest's reluctance to dine did not inhibit the  gathered Brothers from ravenously attacking the menu. Not a word was spoken during the meal. When the Brothers had finished, the novitiates returned to gather up the dirty dishes and to sweep the surrounding bread crumbs and the small globules of congealed fat from the roasted Worm flesh that had escaped the enthusiastic maws and drifted in the space around their now sated forms.

When the task was accomplished and the clatter subsided with the departing novitiates, Sada spoke again: "Eminence, I see that you have refrained from partaking of the Worm's flesh. It is understandable. It is hard for a man without the deepest of understanding to consume what must one day consume him, or has possibly previously consumed one whom he loved. But it is the way of life. *The Third Testament* tells us that "From its simplest origins, life must consume itself, and in each consumption, manifest itself into ever higher form. It is the path to the Creator." Condo presented understanding with his eyes.

Sada detached from his chair, and hovering, bid Condo to follow him. He soared to the zenith of the dome and turned to greet Condo's approach. "From here, deep within the sea, we are undetectable. That first message I transmitted to you gave away its general location in the Core only at my purpose, to entice you here by curiosity. Any more deliberate a contact would have been discovered and noted. Even your trips through Quarantine are so heavily masked by deceptive transmissions that only a most resourceful and purposeful detective would see through our ruse." Again Condo presented understanding with his eyes.

"Things are never as they seem. And only by ever increasing the power of his senses to perceive and the power of his reason to understand does man slowly strip away the veils which conceal the ultimate truth. In a day long past men fashioned lenses of glass and revealed the universes that lay below and above the power of their natural vision. And the truth was changed. In a later day, men created in silicon, and then in the very life-giving waters, the intricate circuits by which nerves produce conscious and rational thought. And new universes of perception and calculation were again opened. Particularly, with the advent of the quantum computer William Proffit possessed the power to precisely calculate and control the collision of particles so as to be able to crush the very quanta that lay at the foundation of our existence. And another veil was stripped away. What was uncovered, however, was and is as great a mystery as any before. It puts into the hand of man the very power of Creation. And yet its true nature escapes him. He is like an ancient child

playing with fire. He knows not its workings and yet it warms him and gives him light. Yet, as fire in the hands of a child, it contains the possibility of horrible destruction."

None of this was revelation to Condo. He understood that Ho'jin Sada's purpose in reiterating this standard fare was to synchronize their thought processes and prepare him for what came next, what he now anxiously anticipated- *a revelation*!

"We are told in *The Third Testament*, in the words of William Proffit, that the day of the Ascent of Man came at that moment when the unExcised men of Earth who inhabited Amagon, the vast Amygdalite city that had grown up outside the walls of New Jerusl'm, attempted to breach those walls. In this they were in concert with all of the other unExcised men of Earth. For a great envy had grown up among the Amygdalites, whose dissolute ways had brought them disease and famine and war and misery. They saw the great wealth and power of New Jerusl'm and marveled at the stories of paradise that lay within its walls. And yet they had no thought to convert – to accept Excision – but instead thought by armed struggle to conquer. They did not know what great power William Proffit possessed."

Sada stopped his narration momentarily to examine more closely a most peculiar looking lifeform that approached the glass from deep within the sea. It was not a creature that Condo recognized. Nor was it immediately apparent if the creature was fish or otherwise. Sada tapped at the glass with a finger and the startled creature fled again into the depths. With a bemused smile, he looked at Condo and shrugged.

"Actually, there was no single day of conflict. As New Jerusl'm grew in wealth and power, it was inevitable that it should become embroiled in the geopolitical struggles of the day. The planet had gone through nearly a century of uninterrupted warfare, and the social apparatus had devolved to a handful of feudal, corporate states. At street level, radical religious and other ideological sects were encouraged and financed to keep the great populations in confusion and turmoil, while high in the fortified board rooms of the corporate citadels the great egos of corporate warlords played out their games for world dominion."In fact, there were several 'small' nuclear wars, as the old states, and particularly the American Empire slid into decline. The democratic institutions collapsed under excessive diversity and were replaced by oligarchies. Ideological and religious terrorists detonated nuclear devices in most of the principle cities of the old civilization – New York, Chicago, Los Angeles, London, Paris, Moscow, Tel Aviv, Tokyo, even Beijing"

Sada looked to Condo for confirmation that the Pontimax of Alhumana was presenting an understanding gaze, signaling the adequacy of his historical knowledge. He was.

"It was in this climate of decay that for forty years William Proffit gathered the faithful to New Jerusl'm. When he contracted with Mitsuzuki Corporation to construct certain vast underground Habitats within the walls of his city so that its inhabitants might survive the increasingly hostile and polluted environment, the perpetual conflict and pursuit of wealth engaged in by the oligarchies – he found also a race of men who were more than ready, morally, emotionally, and intellectually, to pursue the radical 'new civilization' that New Jerusl'm and its Excised citizens represented. But all of this is known to you."

Ho'jin Sada made a beckoning gesture over Condo's right shoulder and with a gentle whirl of his propellete's flings the Pontimax turned to see to whom the Gleaner signaled. What he espied was a procession of Novitiates rising slowly from the compartment's entry hatch, propelling between them a very ancient apparatus attached to two long, parallel poles which the white-clad novices grasped, thus forming two columns with the apparatus in their midst. As they came closer Es'paul Condo recognized the great square apparatus atop the affair as an antique plasma screen viewer sitting atop a cabinet containing several slots. With a whir of flings the procession came to a halt, and the foremost novice handed Sada a metal box from which he removed a flat, circular, silver disc. He inserted the disc into one of the cabinet's slots. Directly, with a crackle and hiss of electrical charge, the ancient screen began to glow, its excited gases emitting photons, which, when taken into the eye produced an image on the retinas. As the image cleared and became recognizable, Condo realized he was viewing a representation of a very aged William Proffit. The man was dressed in a saffron robe, which the force of gravity held tightly down to his shoulders, and from the collar extended the short neck and smallish head with it terrible expanse of untamed, superfluous hair – unmistakably an image of the author of *The Third Testament* and the promulgator of the Ascent of Man. As Condo looked on, the image began to speak. . .

CHAPTER 21

S ar'ha Kier was the first daughter of the second brood born to Hans'ra and Ra'kael Kier. From the moment of her birth the exquisite symmetry of her form and her significant cranial capacity attracted notice. Though so many factors come into play in the development of the child after birth, the proud parents held out every hope given these auspicious beginnings.

The process of birthing within the Habitats held little semblance to the tortured process which had existed on Earth. As Hans'ra had looked on, his second brood swam into the world with the impetus of only the mildest of contractions. Never subjected to the force of gravity, the human skeleton no longer calcified, but remained a flexible, collagen matrix, so that the female pelvis was sufficiently elastic that not only did birth occur with little effort, but also permitted the passage of larger crania. This was perhaps the most accelerated of evolutionary changes which life in Free Space instigated. It had manifested itself prominently in Sar'ha.

As Sar'ha and her siblings floated freely at the end of umbilical cords, Ra'kael looked on in peaceful ecstasy, the great sack of her distended belly gently undulating under the uterine contractions which sought to dispel the four placentae. Hans'ra took each child in turn and inspected it for the appropriate number of limbs and digits and eyes and ears and such. He lingered with Sar'ha, with her striking symmetry of features and flawless cranial globe, who even in her infancy promised to advance the human race to new heights of perfection.

And Sar'ha did not disappoint. By her eighth year an intense interest in the procreative sciences and pronounced displays of maternal ability as directed to her siblings marked her as a Breeder. At 16 her achievements were such that she became a candidate for the Executive Breeding program. She left the Corps and entered the Convent, where her preparation for the appropriate mating began. Devoid of the automatic neuronal responses which time and evolution had constructed in the basal ganglion, human procreation had become a largely conscious and reasoned activity. Spontaneous excitation leading to copulation no longer existed between male and female. The female's unconscious signaling of ovulation and its subsequent elicitation in the male of pursuit and conquest behaviors was short-circuited by Excision. However, ovulation still produced hormonal changes within the female that affected the higher brain functions. The breeding programs of the Habitats were founded on the degree and type of mental aberration these hormonal changes produced in the individual females.

A majority of females experienced a mild to moderate urge to nurture at ovulation. This was sufficient motivation for the females to have themselves inseminated and for them to successfully gestate. This did not necessarily imply an urge to rear the child. So shortly after birth the social structure of the individual Habitats assumed a communal care for the infants and for their rearing and education to functional levels commensurate to their native abilities. Parenting became a communal business activity. For a select few females, however, the hormonal changes induced thought processes which went far beyond the motivation to seek impregnation, and included speculative and philosophical lines of reasoning directed to the probable development of the child and probable outcomes based on alternative rearing practices. Herein lay the seeds of social evolution, and as social evolution was as necessary a sustaining force as physiological evolution, these females were enrolled in an Executive Breeding program – a program where the female intuition was permitted to exercise its prerogatives. Here, as in the time before Excision, the female selected her mate, though not by unconsciously triggering aggressive behaviors in potential mates, but instead by studied, calculated, and intuitive examination of the potential outcomes of specific genetic admixtures. Of course, this tendency in a female had a very strong genetic content so that as Sar'ha's mother had been an Executive Breeder it was no surprise that she should also prove to be one. And as Sar'ha's mother had once joined the select few chosen for the Convent, so had Sar'ha followed in those footsteps.

The Convent was nestled among the upper branches of the canopy, just at the Forest's edge, so that from its windeyes one could look out across the great, green carpet of tree tops, filled with the various arboreal horticultural and husbandry activities, or into the vast open space of a hydroponic Quadrant, divided by its gigantic urban partitions, which from this distance looked every bit like a toy castle swarming with ants.

Though the great overview of the Habitat's interior afforded by the Convent's lofty offices was a result of deliberate location intended to spur the young females into philosophical reflections on the human condition, more importantly, and much more deliberate an outcome of this arboreal nunnery was the vista afforded each and every novitiate each evening as their Quadrant rotated antipodal to Sol, and the plaques of the Shell clarified to reveal a vast, dark, and mysterious Cosmos.

The natural progression of Sar'ha's education, befitting her coming station within the Habitats, led her to medicine in general, and the pediatric sciences in particular. Now the professional realm of the female, the medical schools were housed within the Convent, operated by the Sisterhood, with only the occasional presence of a male research scientist whose particular area impacted upon the practice of medicine. It was here that the medical art of Excision was taught.

Early in her medical studies, Sar'ha focused her attention on the study of the neural physiology, and particularly those pathways ascending from basal ganglia to cortex, and those descending from cortex to basal ganglia. As the science behind the procedure of Excision advanced, it became increasingly clear how complex the integration of the primitive brain and the modern brain had become. The old theory of the triune brain had long ago been abandoned for this notion of integration, of course. Human neurophysiology was much too complex to be so easily compartmentalized. And yet, it also became increasingly clear that among this tangle were distinct pathways dedicated to instinctual behavior, whose Excision freed the higher functions of the cortex from unconscious interference.

One of the most startling discoveries, occurring during the course of Sar'ha's studies was the apparent existence of pathways within the cortex whose purpose appeared to be the survival of the basal ganglia and limbic structures! As cortex and ganglia had integrated, the primitive structures had provided for their own preservation by casting filaments deep into the cortex, whose function was to coax conscious thought away from such notions as Excision. It also appeared that among the mass of humanity their existed a small minority whose power of mind was such that even these subtle nudgings could be recognized and suppressed. Sar'ha belonged to that minority.

Given such a complex integration of intelligence and instinct, sorting among the pathways to determine which were permissible, then, and which required Excision raised the practice from science to art. And Sar'ha was to prove one of its most adept practitioners.

Upon matriculation Sar'ha became a Sister of the Order, and a bride candidate. As such, it was incumbent upon her to choose an appropriate mate, one that would complement her genetics, maximizing the potential for favorable evolution. It was an obligation she took very seriously, and so it was with consummate care that she prepared her resume and selected its recipients.

In the same year Sar'ha matriculated the Convent, Es'paul Condo finished Seminary. As a designated Breeder, he also immediately began accepting bride resumes, undertaking the arduous task of determining who among the bride candidates were appropriate to his profession and likely ascendance in the corporation. He was meticulous in his examination of prospective brides, carefully tracing genetic lines in order to nuance those most subtle of characteristics – mentally, physically, emotionally, and spiritually – unique to every bloodline. Once he had narrowed the prospects to a half dozen candidates, he began the interviewing process.

Condo was well aware that although Excision would spare both he and the candidates any excessive sense of rejection, he must be very careful in each interview to find as much fault and failure in himself regarding a possible match as with the interviewee. Then, when the final decision was made, those not chosen could be comforted by the notion that it was their superiority that was the deciding factor. For even with Excision, an inexplicable  element of female vanity remained.

Condo exerted every bit of the intellectual rigor in his assessment of the bride candidates as he had ever expended in the most difficult of Seminary studies. He realized that the choice he made would have ramifications well beyond his (or her) personal lives. Assignment to the executive breeding program carried with it the responsibility of promulgating old executive bloodlines, or establishing entirely new ones. Such responsibility could not be taken lightly by an individual of Condo's faith and convictions. He spent many an hour referencing and cross referencing observations and data regarding each candidate as the interviews progressed. He spared no mental energy, applying every element of reason and logic of which he was capable in assessing the sufficiency, or lack thereof, of each succeeding young female. Finally, there was but one interview remaining. Condo would as carefully examine this final candidate as he had the first, allowing no prejudice due to fatigue, or impressions made by previous candidates. He would give this interviewee as clean a slate as he had the first. Examining her resume prior to the interview, he noted her success at Convent, and her current pediatric internship, with specialty in Excision. He also noted that her interview had been postponed twice, with no specific reasons given.

Condo arrived early to his Cell on the day of the last interview. It was his intention to conduct this final interview, make his assessment, make his final comparisons and analyses, and have his decision made by the end of the work day. With his interrogation ready, he attached to his desk, and donned his Cap. The interviewee, located at some distant and unknown point, prepared herself by disrobing before the bank of interview cameras. Her images would be transmitted directly to Condo's visual cortex, where he would begin his analysis by a physical examination of the candidate, to assess phenotype, symmetry, and overall physiological compatibility.

As the transponders in the Cap synchronized with Condo's synapses, the image of this final candidate came into view. As had been first noted by her father, Condo was immediately by the exquisite symmetry of the young woman's form. Each gentle curve, each rising and falling of the flesh on the one side perfectly mirrored on the other. Her cranium, with its high temples and generous and rising frontal bones, and everywhere closely covered by the silken, nearly gossamer, tightly curled golden hair, crowned improbably delicate sculptures of brow, nose, cheek, and chin. It was the type of beauty ancient artist's had coaxed from stone and clay, but seldom if ever existed in reality. The young woman, in modesty, kept her eyes turned down during this initial inspection, though eyescreens above each camera displayed Condo's intent gaze. Meanwhile, Condo struggled to maintain his perspective as this image of living art slowly rotated in his mind. At last, coming full round, and having inspected every physical aspect, it came time for their gazes to meet. As Condo focused his attention on the images from the front-most camera, Sar'ha Kier raised her pale blue eyes to him. In that instant all reason left Condo; logic failed him utterly; the mental processes by which he measured and prided himself fell aside. In that instant he understood, however improbable, however opposed to the functions of intellect – he would be making no decisions this day! For in one great rush of sensation, coming from whence he knew not, he realized *he* had been chosen by *her!*

CHAPTER 22

From *The Third Testament*: "We do not confuse what we *must* do for what we *could* do; for the one shows moral courage, while the other only weakness."

Ho'jin Sada paused the image on the screen, and turned to Condo: "These images exist only in this ancient form for a reason. Though access to the CQC is highly regulated and monitored, still hackers and others are able to trespass into restricted zones. The information contained here is for select eyes only. Its effect on the general populations would be disastrous at least, if not cataclysmic, even among those who are not truly believers." Sada waited a moment until Condo's presentations settled, and then resumed the display.

Condo found the 2-dimensional nature of the imagery a bit peculiar at first, but as his attention was drawn to the intense gaze of the speaker and the insistent and urgent quality of his voice, the lack of 3-dimensional representation, such as resulted from direct transmission to the visual cortex, became less and less noticeable. He became transfixed by the aged and now haggard countenance of William Proffit. Satisfied Condo had successfully adjusted to the unfamiliar medium, Sada allowed the presentation to continue.

*"This will be my final communication with you, my Brethren. You must remember what I say here, and forever keep its secret from the innocent. I have made you, my Brethren, the keepers of all that is to come. I lay the future of man into your hands. I have also set among the corporations one who shall lead the Church. When judgment is required – and I fear those times will be so often as to make you weary – you must seek the counsel of the one who leads the Church, for he alone, in his love for man, shall have the right to judge. Listen wisely to his words, so that what we have here initiated will not become the bane of man, but instead his eternal salvation.*

(The image of William Proffit turned its gaze from the camera and consulted a myriad of papers laid out before him, clutching an obviously offensive one his hand.)

*I have remained here on Earth to do what it is only mine to do; what I have always known would one day be necessary. I have before me reports that leave me no alternative but to act. Everywhere governments and corporations assail us. We are condemned as heretics, as lunatics – as a dangerous and powerful Cult. We are condemned for withholding from men the source to immeasurable wealth and power. We daily exhaust ourselves fending off assaults: from hackers; from military adventures; from attempts at infiltration. The masses are now so enamored of their hysteria that they cry: Anti-Christ; Armageddon; Judgment Day. They call down the powers of their deities against us. And now the atmosphere is so virulent that if there remain among them those who would follow us they fear to approach, knowing they will be set upon and destroyed by the mob.*

(The image returned its gaze to the camera, now more weary and saddened than before.)

*They, who would not lose their passions, their desires, and join us, now live in a fear and torment of their own making. The men whose counsel they admire, incite them in hopes of gaining some advantage against us by their numbers. Or perhaps they think we will shrink from our resolve by some misguided humanity. They are wrong.*

*From the day we engineered innocence by the Sacrament of Excision, we created a dangerous imbalance. Now we must set the scales aright. For innocence, by its nature, cannot survive in a world where thoughtless avarice obtains. We, the herders, cannot abandon our lambs to wolves. We must deny the wolf its existence!*

*We of the Brethren, who remain unExcised, chosen by the power of our minds, have taken upon ourselves the burdens of man. We decide what is good and what is evil, by the grace of God, or the tenacity of our own human arrogance. But our justice is vindicated because we have judged ourselves also. We take into ourselves the device of our own destruction. On the day we pledged ourselves, it was implanted in our cortex, an impartial measure of our neuronal activity, making our innermost thoughts known to all Brethren. And when we have fallen short, we have not hesitated to judge one another, even to judge ourselves! Now we must administer that same judgment upon the masses of unExcised!*

(Proffit calmed himself before continuing.)

*When the power of the Ether was revealed to me, I thought it was by the power of my mind alone. The Ego reveled in its accomplishment; the Id lurked in its dark recesses, and imagined the adulation; the Super-ego imagined the salvation of man. In the end, it was the Super-ego that triumphed, but not as I expected. It examined its own impulse, and with the help of Ego, and apprehension of the Id, determined my discovery was not the salvation of man, but his certain destruction! My ensuing and much publicized madness was only partly fabricated, in order to escape the consequences of what I had achieved. Only in my lonely wanderings did the solution appear – that man in his current state was not fit to wield such power; that he must somehow be made fit.*

*Another, greater truth was revealed to me also – that the accomplishment was not mine alone. Every human mind that had pondered existence, and sought to understand it had left its mark upon my consciousness, by however circuitous a route – be it mathematician, musician, physicist, philosopher, theologian, conjurer or astrologer! Every book ever read; every work of art; every theory explored – all coalesced as neuronal pathways within my cortex. I was not an individual phenomenon, but a summation of all that had come before. Mine was not a single intellect, but a collective – the unavoidable product of all previous human cognition. The only question that remained was: What shall I do with what has been given me?*

*The world that exists today is the answer to that question. You, my Brethren, there, high in the heavens, removed from the torment and turmoil of Earthly existence, hold in your hand's the new infancy of man – born again, not of Earth, but of Heaven. By our vows we stand guard over that new infancy.*

*I have been given the power to pass judgment on the men of Earth, or I have taken it. I does not matter which. The end result must be the same. It is the evolution of the species as has been ordained by the Creator, or as it has been imagined within my collective intellect, or as likely, as a collection of chance occurrences. Again, it does not matter which is the case. And God himself, whether omnipresent, omnipotent, or imagination; prime mover or original quantum fluctuation, has by the virtue of existence itself ordained this day! The butterfly's wing, in a single delicate flutter, gave birth to the vortex within which we now swirl toward our destiny.*

(Proffit halted, letting his head fall forward slightly, his forehead propped against his gathered fingers, which massaged in small circular motions the bulbs of his cranium's frontal bone, as if to relieve some pain there, or to coax from the underlying cortex some as yet unexplored option.)

*It is clear that they will not cease in their attempts to bring us down. They become ever more ingenious in their assaults; we spend increasingly more time and energy in defense. Eventually, they too will discover what is known to us, if we do not act – if I do not act!*

(Proffit raised his head, and spoke as if to someone else in the room.)

*Already the missionary modules ascend to you, with the last of the converts. As quickly as they begin their ascent, the armies of the nations set upon them with every available weapon. Here, in Amagon, the walls of New Jerusl'm glow from the constant bombardment. Everywhere, unExcised propagandists broadcast to their flocks that the final battle against evil has begun. How little do they realize the truth of what they say! Great congregations have gathered in the hallowed places, where the meek – those innocent through ignorance – now fervently pray for deliverance. They dream of a salvation from above, from one who will open the sky and rain down fire on the misery of their existence, and carry away their delivered souls to paradise. . .*

(His voice trailed off. Suddenly, Proffit once again

looked directly into the camera. His eyes burned
with the fire of a zealot!)

*I shall give them what they most desire!*

*The quantum entanglements which the energies of
their lives have produced will persist, and disperse
into the Ether – that undiscovered land to which
all our souls must eventually journey. They only
precede us to that place. The only question to be
answered is if the path now taken will free man
from the curse of his particular place among the
living things in the Cosmos. Given the capacity to
engineer his own destruction, or to prevent his own
extinction – has the proper choice been made?
Only time will tell.*

*In the end, I am just a man: as small and
insignificant as any. Yet I wield the power of life
and death over all my fellows. In the arrogance of
my certainty I administer this judgment; in the
depth of my agony, I turn the blade upon myself.*

*Keep my secret well, Brothers. For only faith, and
the absence of doubt, will guarantee the success of
this experiment. When the last module from New
Jerusl'm has reached a safe distance, I will open
the sky for them – and the fire of redemption shall
rain down upon them, and wash away their sins!*

*May God have mercy on my soul!*

## CHAPTER 23

Ho'jin Sada waved his hand and a Novitiate quickly terminated the power to the plasma screen. The now frozen image of William Proffit faded to black, a ghostly negative persisting for some seconds, either as residual charge in the ionized gases of the screen or a persistence of vision resulting from the reactions of the photo sensitive chemicals in the retinae of his eyes. Unused to such visual presentation, Condo did not know which.

As the visual image dissipated, the mental images proliferated in Condo's consciousness. Proffit's final, haunted, desperate, yet determined presentation stared down upon every corner of Condo's psyche. Wave after wave of impulse transited his cortex, as the existing neuronal structure tried to assimilate the new information; struggled to find the correct categories, the correct compartments, the appropriate departments to which this new information could be successfully consigned. It was an unsuccessful effort.

Condo's internal turmoil was so obviously reflected in his external presentation that Sada reached out a gnarled, tannin stained paw to caress the Pontimax's suddenly feverish brow. Condo surrendered to the sensation, accepting its invitation to retreat to the safety of Prayer. Still attached by his back patch, Condo curled his body in Prayer, as his mind curled upon itself.

After several minutes of REM Condo began to re-emerge into consciousness. The journey seemed a long one, ascending as he was from a deeper, darker chasm than his psyche had ever before descended. In these few minutes of Prayer, Condo had revisited to entire of his sentient life, from earliest childhood memories, to most recent revelations. So violent and circuitous a journey engendered a sense of vertigo such as he had not known before. It was difficult to suppress the sensation of motion as he opened his eyes once again to the conscious world. He turned to Sada, yet began a conversation with himself: "No Armageddon! No salvation! The Earth was 10 billion souls when man made the Ascent! Only a billion in the first Habitats! 9 billion souls erased in an instant!"

Sada expected Condo's reaction. He had seen it before. He would not feed the panic, but sought to re-establish reason. He spoke quietly, but firmly:
"It is a matter of fact that major extinction events have generally resulted in the loss of upwards of 90% of species, and often 90% of the individuals within species that do survive are lost. Only the fittest continue."

Sada's words initially bounced off Condo's confusion. He repeated himself until the distance in Condo's gaze began to lessen. Finally, the Pontimax's presentations cleared, and his signal was unmistakable: *I have a question I must ask you!*

Sada began his narrative slowly and precisely, just as it had been taught to him: "Who are we to know whether it is by the hand of God or the vagaries of chance that we exist? We know only that we *do* exist. How are we to know if the future is pre-ordained or if each new quantum fluctuation leads us into an unanticipated future? We can only know what *is*, not what *will be*. Yet from these simple things, with reason and faith, can we build the future history of man."

Sada paused to see that Condo was focused on his words, and then continued: "Whether Proffit was an agent of the Creator – or a madman! – does not matter now. It is written in *The Third Testament*: What I *was* matters not; what you have *become* is the only truth."

Stunned and disoriented, Condo began a self-searching monologue. Sada did not interfere. He had been witness to more than one Pontimax finding himself suddenly cast into a strange and new reality.

"All of my life I have inquired into the nature of things. I have left no stone unturned in my pursuit of truth. I have studied and learned. I have read all that has been written. I have used every facet of my reason to compare and to analyze. And in the end, all things added up; their appeared to be one truth – and it gave me faith!"

Condo's presentation became more pleading. But Sada, well versed in the drama of such revelation, remained aloof, and returned only a steady, opaque presentation. Condo continued: "I defeated doubt! Referenced and cross-referenced; examined and re-examined. Yet, never an indication that I possessed anything but the truth! Only the mystery surrounding William Proffit. . ."

Condo turned an accusative eye toward Ho'jin Sada. It was a presentation he had not known before. He immediately realized by the tautness of brow, the constriction of iris, the narrowing of lids, that a response had been elicited from him that was unfamiliar, that was called up from someplace deep within a subconscious he did not know existed until this moment.

"I have been lied to!" Condo knew the word by its historical definition, but he had never used it other than colloquially – had in fact never made such an accusation.

"No. Merely denied the whole truth." Sada's presentation remained a blank.

Condo's mind raced. He recalled the innumerous times he had traced arguments to their logical ends, only to find some passage in *The Third Testament* that stated the result more succinctly.

Had it all been a trap? Was it an intentional misdirection? Why had the pieces fit so neatly together? Had he been intentionally misguided since youth, destined to be a pawn in some twisted man's delusions? The arguments and uncertainties raced through his mind. Had he been capable of rage, it would certainly have erupted. As it was, only doubt, the destroyer, the great dark enveloper of faith, now threatened to engulf him.

"As you have seen and heard, it was his secret. It has been our pledge to him." Sada waited an instant for his words to extract Condo from his own, internal dialogue.

"The records were not lost; the mystery surrounding Proffit and man's last days on Earth were not misplaced during some great human struggle. Mankind's instincts did not lead him to destruction in some great, final, animalistic struggle. Armageddon was the act of a single man, prosecuted in a single instant. Proffit pushed a button, and his Device ignited the atmosphere. Unwilling to question the rightness or wrongness of his actions, he remained on Earth, counting himself one of the unworthy, and the judgment he meted upon those hapless billions, he passed upon himself as well." Sada's dialogue was delivered without a hint of emotion. He saw that it had a calming effect on Condo.

"Was it the will of God? We do not know. Was Proffit a singularly brilliant madman, or the agent of the divine? We don't know. Could events have taken a different course? We know that they did not!" Sada paused, almost reflectively, and then continued:

"We only know that we are here now. We have been cast from the cradle, and cannot return. The embrace of our Mother Earth would now result only in a crushing, suffocating death. And yet here we have prospered, to the trillions. You have witnessed it from the canopy, looking into the night sky, Habitats in the millions, a sparkling ring stretching as far as the eye can see, bathed in the reflected light of the distant Sun."

Though Condo's mind wanted to once again retreat to the haven of Prayer, Sada's words, in their blunt but reasonable account of the circumstances appealed to reasoning circuits in the Pontimax's cortex. The rational functioning of his mind began to dispel the confusion, and what had been a whirl of uncontrolled synaptic activity once again fell under his conscious control. As Sada began to speak again, he focused his attention narrowly.

"You are not the first to have gone digging." Sada let his remark sink in.

Condo felt the impact of the statement drive deeply into his consciousness, clearing away the debris of confusion as it bored. He turned suddenly to the Novitiate that hovered silently at Ho'jin Sada's side. His gaze seemed somehow familiar, and yet cast in other tones. Consciously, he lightened the skin, and removed the red from the eyes. How had he not seen it?! In whispered surprise he queried:

"Hersh'ma? Hersh'ma Krulic?"

"Yes, it is I." Hersh'ma attempted a grin.

Sada interjected: "Your archeological assistant, in the flesh! Sent to you by the Academy, yes?"

The Gleaner let the revelation settle in for a moment, and then continued just as Condo presented *I have a question for you*: "The dig is actually quite old. Commissioned in the eighth century after the Ascent by one of your predecessors. We have maintained it ever since. It has proven quite a useful tool in our work."

Again confusion attempted to overwhelm Condo's conscious mental functions. This time the questions flowed without hesitation. "Your work? Your WORK! What is your *work*?!" For the first time Condo's voice carried the authority of his office.

"Your Eminence...your Holiness...Pontimax." Sada's serial address carried not the slightest hint of arrogance, derision, or ridicule. He continued with obvious solemnity: "Our *work,* the work of the Brethren is as has been revealed to you – to keep the *secret*, and to access the deeds of men. And, as commanded by Proffit, to defer to the head of the Church for final judgment. We bring you into our confidence now, as we have time and again brought your predecessors, because the deeds of men require your judgment. You must stand in their defense, or submit them to justice, as you choose."

Condo suddenly recalled the sudden change in demeanor and unexpected death of his predecessor. Sada noted the growing awareness in Condo's presentation. He countered the Pontimax's query before it was presented.

"Do you truly believe that life within the Habitats can be naturally so idyllic? Does a garden grow only flowers, or does it require tending by the gardener, who plucks the weeds from amongst the blossoms? We, the Brethren, are the gardeners who tend this *Eden* of yours." Sada noted the rising rebellion in Condo's presentation. It was not an immature rebellion, confronting authority, but an intellectual rebellion at least, fighting to preserve past beliefs, past truths. It was to be expected.

"You must leave us now, Es'paul Condo, Pontimax and CEO of Alhumana Corporation, Church to the Habitats. Go, and look upon your world with these new eyes. For soon you must pass a judgment upon these men."

CHAPTER 24

Es'paul Condo was at first oblivious to his surroundings. His Locator, with its A- nav set to *auto* and destination *home*, carried him along as a debate between the two halves of his consciousness – Faith and Reason – raged in herculean form! But as he emerged from the Core and passed through Quarantine and into the upper levels of the Habitat his awarenes returned, yielding an experience as profound as birth! Like a babe first opening its eyes, the forms and motions and colors flooded his synapses with stimuli strange and new. And like a babe, he was without speech, for the vocabulary by which his mind now communicated had no available syllabic or syntactic form. He was seeing his world for the first time through a new lens, and for an instant he empathized with the schizophrenic, as common objects seemed to take on uncommon form, and the colors of things appeared to shift freely across the spectrum.

As he exited a Tube and rose slowly upon propelletes to his home Pod he felt very much like an insect rising to pollinate a flower in a well-kept garden, with this exception – he alone among the colonies knew their world was a garden, tended by unseen hands.

Because he was behind schedule (Ensymphonium had passed, and the eight hours of leisure well begun), Sar'ha anticipated some complication had befallen Condo. Also aware of his clandestine trips to the Core, she was doubly apprehensive. As a Sister of the Convent she knew more about the Gleaners than she had ever shared with her husband. During her cloister she had taken her instruction in the Sacrament of Excision, and in learning to read the neuronal map of a human brain, she had been taught to be ever on the look-out for certain abnormalities. When such abnormalities were encountered the candidate for Excision was referred by the Sisterhood to a member of the Brethren of Gleaners. Generally these individuals lacked the natural abundance of pathways connecting the cortex with the basal ganglion. Sar'ha and her colleagues speculated among themselves that perhaps a secret breeding program existed or that some other sequestered purpose was found for these individuals as they were never returned for Excision.

On this evening, Sar'ha busied herself around the blossom end of the Pod, spuriously tending to the collection of arboreal orchids surrounding the portal. She noticed Condo's ascent long before he became aware of her presence. She particularly noted his distraction, as the direction of his gaze was not the direction of his travel, and he gesticulated as if engaged in ardent conversation with an unseen hearer. Only when his A-cav sensed the nearness of objects and the gossamer flings of his propelletes suddenly reversed their thrust like frantic fairies' wings was he delivered from his dark reverie, and in raising his head made eye contact with his wife.

The sensation that washed over Sar'ha as their gazes met was very nearly alarm. She believed that she saw terror in his eyes, a presentation seldom if ever encountenanced by one past infancy! But quickly her strong, maternal networking took charge, avoiding any sudden discharge of adrenalin, any tendency to panic, and instead releasing endorphins into the empathetic centers of her brain. The resulting response was like that felt when an injured child turns its pleading eyes to a parent, signaling pain and fear and hope, and questioning why, and the parent, oblivious of all else, embraces the child, giving comfort and solace.

## CHAPTER 25

E s'Paul Condo studied the list projected before him slowly, methodically, only advancing to the next individual after he had consciously pronounced the name and carefully considered each fact included in the biography; had gazed deeply at the eye-screen records from which retinal patterns could be read holographically. Most of the names found no registry in his memory though he now deliberately worked at placing them there. And though the list ran to millions, more than he could ever manage or hope to account, he did not hurry. Yet, as he struggled to maintain his focus, the one name known to him, the one individual with whom he had discoursed, argued, and sometimes pleaded, kept writing itself upon his thoughts. A man with whom he had shared many a contention, and yet for whom he held not a single malicious thought; a colleague who, like himself, held a place of leadership and trust among the Habitats; whose intelligence and dedication had advanced the human cause by solving many of the mundane practicalities that human economies always entail. Again and again he returned to that particular listing, to review the data, to again gaze into the ocular image, trying to find some clue as to origin of the malignancy. In leadership circles, where the principle of anonymity was a ritual practiced only superficially, the name Am'riah Redshilt was as familiar as his own. It was not possible or practical for human personalities to successfully interact at such an important level without some level of intimate intelligence. As had always been the case, and most likely always would be, what held as necessary for the masses was excepted for the hierarchs.

Yet, for all the familiarity with biographical and biometrical data, and immediate recognition of his eye-screen, Condo had never seen the man in flesh; the man whose fate he now held in his hands. The eye-screen, whose image Condo now conjured as easily and recognizably as his Sar'ha's face, was intended to serve the principle of anonymity, of course. But as with all things perceived, the fewer the details provided, the more detail was found. If a hundred eye-screens were suddenly presented Condo would have no more difficulty in recognizing Redshilt than he would in recognizing his own children. Yet, if suddenly presented with the physical man, less his eyes, Es'paul Condo would not know him from Adam.

Even more disconcerting than this sudden confrontation with the realities of anonymity, Condo suffered a terrifying vertigo as the intellectual, emotional, and spiritual balance of his existence was suddenly knocked off its axis by Ho'jin Sada's revelations: he and the other CEOs of the Habitat Corporate Structure were not truly the ruling body; William Proffit had not saved the faithful from mankind's mindless self-destruction, but in fact had passed judgment on those who did not conform to his standards, and annihilated them; the ultimate purpose of the Pontimax was not to dispel Doubt, but to pass mortal judgment on his fellow men.

Condo dimmed the projection, and tuning his Cap, reviewed the memories of his last visit to the Core. Immediately Ho'jin Sada's mahogany countenance appeared before him, topped by its flaming orange hair, and framed by the pleated saffron collar of his sack. The eyes of the visage sparkled intensely as auditory hallucination replayed his dialogue: *"It is not unreasonable to imagine that the primitive structures of the brain – the reptilian and limbic structures – should inculcate strategies for survival into the developing neocortex of the embryo, eventually penetrating to the highest functions. These structures, after all, were the only conduit of communication with the outside world through the sensess. Prior to the invention of the Cap, they were the gatekeepers to human experience. It is also not unreasonable to assume that Excision, for all its modern precision, cannot identify and eliminate every unwanted axon and dendrite."*

Condo knew that Excision, being a human exercise, was imperfect. He had never considered these implications, however. He returned to his recollections, his visual cortex once again focusing on Sada's face. *"It is these survival mechanisms that again manifest themselves in a growing population, the problem being that once they are "discovered" and activated in an individual, their neuronal pathways quickly substantiate, and the survival impulse begins to subvert conscious activity. Like an infection, there is contagion as communication with the infected individual activates the pathways in others, subtly, unconsciously, undetectably."*

Condo compared these revelations to the purpose of his office, and the understanding became complete. As CEO and Pontimax of Alhumana, he strove daily to quell doubt wherever it appeared. He full well understood its infectious nature. Though he preached to the masses, he was ever alert to individuals manifesting doubt, and singly pursued their rehabilitation through persuasion, indoctrination, or monastic isolation. But here, much more was required of him – to pass judgment on the right to life of the afflicted. The hallucinations resumed. *"Those behaviors that permitted man's Ascent from the primordial do not permit his existence in the heavens." The absoluteness of this axiom manifested itself in the recollected visage of Ho'jin Sada's piercing gaze. "And evolution has yet to make dominant the diminished amygdala and basal ganglia that are the deficiencies by which I and my brethren are chosen."*

In recalling, Condo was stung again by the depth of his ignorance. He knew that certain children went unExcised, and were referred to the Brethren of Gleaners. How could he not have understood the implications? He returned to his memories. *"Because we are deficient, we do not "love" mankind.*

*Of course, our intellects tell us that the purpose of life is to beget life, but we do not "love" life."*

The remembered indifference that sounded in Sada's voice was itself a revelation. *"It is part of Proffit's genius that he commanded that we of the Brethren may decide what is "right" or "wrong", but we may not pass judgment on men. That must be reserved for one who loves mankind. Only then is justice done."*

As after to original experience, Condo retreated into Prayer after the recalling. He curled, and surrendered his consciousness to Prayer.

CHAPTER 26

As after every excursion Am'riah Redshilt emerged invigorated, motivated and slightly intoxicated. The sense of being alive was never so intense. And with each excursion the rational certainty of his position became more acute. What had passed for life before held no comparison to the sense of living he now experienced. Am'riah folded his Cap and returned it to its secret place.

With increasing certainty Redshilt's inclination toward action intensified and his confidence of success increased. Long an anonymous supporter of the Anti-Excisionist movement, his position in upper-management finance precluded a more active participation. But now, with increasing support and encouragement from the Cause, he began a campaign, albeit surreptitiously, to recruit acolytes. His intellect now fully engaged in pursuing the resurrection of lost delights, he and his confederates had even taken to referring to their cause as *redeeming the forbidden fruits*. To disparage the moral precepts of Excision they labeled it *the castration of humanity*. As the apolaustic appetites of the Cause members grew, their proselytizing activities infringed upon their economic productivity, and their illicit debaucheries began to fill their leisure and family hours. Redshilt, like the others of his ilk, rationalized these impingements as the necessary sacrifices to a worthy cause – *the freeing of the human race from moral bondage.*

Most people confronted with Redshilt's argument found it hard to dispel. Once foisted upon their conscious processes, it began to play upon long dormant impulses only vaguely traced in the cortex, but once activate, susceptible to self-innervation. Herein lie the mechanism by which Am'riah Redshilt and his cohorts intended to gain the support and participation, or at least the acquiescence, of Habitat management. The subsequent financial advantage would be the hammer needed to break the irons of moral restraint imposed upon the masses by the Church. Without the financial support of the other corporate sectors Alhumana Corporation would languish; would lose the means to sustain it indoctrination.

Still tingling from the rewards of sated urges, the sharp edge of instinct cutting deeply into the fabric of his consciousness, Redshilt felt as vivid and aware as at any moment in his life. He believed these were moments of true inspiration denied the bound, Excised spirit. And he believed it was at these moments that his clarity of thought brought to him solutions otherwise unattainable. In these moments he authored the best of his propaganda:
*"We come into this world as separate and unique organisms, requiring no other heart than our own to beat; no other lungs to breathe; no other eyes to see; no other mind to perceive the world. We are*

*whole, and complete, and indivisible."* Redshilt quickly donned his traditional Cap, to capture his enlightened and brilliant narration.

*"Just as we exist alone, a consciousness contained within our brain only, so we die alone. At our death, the only light extinguished is our light; the enveloping darkness swallows not the multitude, but only our single, sentient spark. What right has another, or any other, to demand more from us than this solitude?"* Endorphins and neural-opiates flowed as the afterglow of instinctual structure imposed by the illicit Cap continued to demand its rewards. The persistence of these reaction networks after removal of the Cap prolonged with each excursion. Consequently, the metabolites that excreted to the surface of skin became a beacon to any marauding Worms. One approached him now through a windeye, and already enamored of pleasure, he quickly doffed his tailored tunic, inviting the Worm's cleansing instincts. The creature hesitated at the presence of the Cap, but Redshilt quickly suppressed its reluctance by pulling its gaping maw over his head and shoulders. His mind continued to race as the additional stimulation of the Worm's cilia titillated nerve endings already made vivid by the evenings adventures. Thus enveloped, he continued his narrations: *"What do we have in the interim – the time between birth and death? There are the necessary functions required to obtain sustenance, of course. Certainly these are accomplished in concert more easily than alone. But isn't that a transaction balanced on its face? Do we owe any*

*more than is owed to us? And when the essentials are accomplished – for self; for community; for family – what of the life lived between times? Do we close down our senses? Does our consciousness hibernate until needed again? No! We hunger for pleasure, for sensation, for purpose, so these moments do not go unaccounted in our life's ledger."*

The Worm disgorged the now sanitized advocate, whose further stimulation evoked greater heights of hedonistic philosophy: *"Are we to live only the necessary life, settling for the small pleasures it affords, with eternal oblivion our reward? Haven't we the right, as keepers of our own souls, to fill those empty moments with pleasure when we can? What if death is tomorrow's destiny? Am I to idle into its embrace? I cannot spare my brother his death, nor can he spare me mine. Why must the prison he chooses for himself be imposed upon me as well?"*

Am'riah Redshilt hurriedly returned to his console, afire with the certainty of his rhetoric, wanting to broadcast it to the Cause while its passions still seethed, intent on seeing the infection of his genius spread to masses. He quickly transferred his narrations to the secret network established by the Cause's hierarchy, and as quickly as the task was accomplished, succumbed suddenly to an intense but delightful fatigue. The lights of his study dimmed as he exited and made his way hazily to his bedclave, where once ensconced, he fell into the dreamless sleep of the bacchanalian.

CHAPTER 27

Sar'ha sensed that life altering circumstances were evolving. Their second brood would soon be leaving for the Corps, and thoughts and intimate conversations should turn to preparations for a third. But day after day now Es'paul Condo returned home distracted, often muttering to himself, sometimes forgetting to disengage his Locator so that only the sudden deployment of propelletes by the A-cav stopped him crashing into the Pod's blossom end. She would find him there, disoriented and disheveled, the look of a lost child on his face.

To see her husband in such turmoil incited the great empathic urges within her. But the teachings of the Convent, and the obligations incumbent upon her as a member of the Sisterhood and a designated Breeder moderated her behavior. She would not, could not, inquire too deeply into the nature of his torment. And just as adamant was the Order's dictate to never reveal the extent of Excision's success, or its inadequacies – matters she knew lay at the heart of his troubles. She drew emotional and intellectual comfort from *The Third Testament*: "It is better one man bleeds than a hundred. For in the immeasurable vastness of the Cosmos, our only worth is in our numbers. Alone, we are but wastrels, squandering time and resource without cause."

Sar'ha understood the tribulation now assailing Es'paul Condo was the result of his office and his obligation to it. She knew full well that his oath demanded he put the good of all before the good of any one, even himself. She knew that the well-being of a trillions of souls now rested on his shoulders.

Oaths and pledges accounted, it was impossible for a mated couple to exist next to one another without seeking some comfort. So, avoiding the direct, Sar'ha engaged her distracted husband in banter and philosophical balms. One particular evening she found him near the Pod's blossom end, slowly revolving head over nether parts at the point where his Locator's A-cav had abruptly stopped him. Totally absorbed with some internal dialogue, he was oblivious to place and circumstance. The sight of him engendered a tearful smile.

So as not to startle him, Sar'ha set herself into a rotational motion parallel to his, and slowly advanced into his field of view. Directly, their eyes met. Condo extracted himself from his musings, and smiling to see her familiar countenance, made excuse for his tardiness.

"Sorry, darling. I didn't see you there. I, uh . . ."

Condo's gaze slid from Sar'ha's eyes to a point just over her left shoulder. Bemusement knitted his brow as he noted the changing scenery behind her. Quickly turning his glance right and then left, he was surprised to note their current state of motion.

"How long have I been…?"

"Not long, dear"

Sar'ha reached out, grasping Condo's shoulders, and using her propelletes, stopped their rotation. Taking his hands in hers, and embracing him with her feet and legs, she propelled them both upward into the Pod. Her arms sensed no resistance. Condo surrendered totally to her direction, as an infant surrenders to sleep in the certain safety of its mother's arms.

There was little conversation during supper, and afterwards, as the children prepared for their bedclaves. Once the familial duties were accomplished, Sar'ha again took charge, removing Condo's khakis and undergarment. The day's stresses had produced metabolites that signaled a nearby Worm that a cleansing was needed. It descended through its portal, engulfing the pliant and distracted Pontimax. Once disgorged, Sar'ha proffered his night silks, and at the lack of response, took him as a mother takes a sleeping child, manipulating each supple and unresistive limb into its proper sleeve. Sar'ha did not forget her obligations, but once surrounded by the bedclave's familiar embrace, she began her gentle query, hoping by his responses to find that point at which she could offer him comfort.

"Do you remember when we first met? I was just leaving the Convent, and you just finishing Seminary. We were both so full of purpose, so certain in our obligations; committed to our vows. I was designated an Executive Breeder! You were bound for the Church hierarchy! We were all formulas and formalities; purpose, protocol and determination! And then the unexpected happened. We found something we were not looking for – something unaccounted, unanticipated, unnecessary to our cause. We found a blending of spirit, a union making what had once been two into a single thing."

Condo sighed deeply, soulfully. She knew that he had followed her through each memory, reliving each sensation, relishing each emotion. She continued. "By chance, or by Divine intent, we have known and shared what is denied to the multitude. It wasn't necessary to our purpose. Certainly we would have accomplished no less without it. It was a gift, given by chance or by a Creator's charge. But it is no prize to be valued for itself."

Sar'ha chose her words carefully, monitoring the slightest of responses in her doleful and dreamy mate. Though she could provide him no revelation by quoting *The Third Testament* – he better than she understood its profounder meanings - she knew the euphony of its words would resonate in his musings.

"*The Third Testament* tells us: No man who holds a pen is an author, but merely a scribe, recording what is revealed in the Creation. And no man can understand the meaning of Life who cannot forget himself – every nerve, muscle, organ, and bone – and in so doing becoming only sight, gazing upon the vastness of Creation as seen from the Creator's eyes."

A slight twitch, followed by slow, easy breathing told Sar'ha her husband had surrendered to sleep. She hoped her words had comforted and conveyed the intended meaning. She knew the changes that lay ahead would separate them; that Condo's obligations to his office would supersede the family. She knew from her teachings at the Convent that such a union as hers came with this possibility. She had accepted the fact. She wanted him to know she understood and did not challenge his greater obligations. Still, the powers of Excision did not spare the ache now growing in her heart. In the confines of the bedclave she embraced him with all of her parts, wondering if this would be the last time.

## CHAPTER 28

The fear of the Audit was more imagined than tangible. The Church could point its accusatory finger at the slothful and avaricious, inciting investors. But the actual sanctions it could enforce were limited and easily circumvented by clever management. Am'riah Redshilt had long exploited this weakness in the system. Particularly since the Pontimax's wooden performance at the last Ecumenical Board meeting. He had seemed like a puppet, delivering staged lines, totally absent the usual contentiousness toward the Financial Sector. It was this very circumstance, however, that emboldened Redshilt in his cause.

With the chance of Audit apparently diminished, little chance existed for Am'riah to be called on the carpet for neglecting many of his fiduciary responsibilities. He reasoned that the cause of personal freedom, as manifested by the doctrine of the Cause, far surpassed any economic anomalies that might occur as a result of his truancy. What was the economic inconvenience or deprivation of a few when the individual might emerge as paramount to the mindless masses?

Redshilt was now all but estranged from his family, another justifiable sacrifice by his estimation. He spent most of his days in consort with other members of the cult, either strategizing new avenues of proselytization, or participating in joint excursions into the realm of instinct and its feral inspiration.

The most recent simulation had been the fabled battle at Thermopylae, where the 300 Spartans had faced the armies of Xerxes on long ago Earth. Now using Interfaces to enhance the simulations, the rage and fear and exaltation of battle was enhanced with a physical sense of muscle mass and strength; the smell of blood was synchronized with searing pain as sword and arrow, spear and lance tore at flesh and bone. It was agony and terror, ecstasy and transmigration – from mere mortal to god!

The participants in the simulation experienced such intensity that none minded the agreed upon time limits. Redshilt was the last to extract himself, as the last of the dying Spartans. He emerged from the Interface drenched in the metabolic exudations of several days. He was immediately set upon by half a dozen Worms, the intensity of the exudates seeming to signall the presence of multiple individuals to the creatures' primitive senses. Am'riah Redshilt guffawed heartily at the realization that the stench of battle proved so permeating. He felt more the man for it!

CHAPTER 29


Ho'jin Sada's emotionless gaze gave no hint of inner feelings, if he even possessed them. It seemed Es'paul Condo's education would continue in this stoic manner. He had come to this meeting a bit feisty, believing he had in his possession an argument that the Brethren had not fully accounted. He had reminded Sada of his letters to the Board of Directors pleading for archeological funds, and subsequent letters describing his finds. He even made note of Am'riah Redshilt's objections. The response he got set his mind and emotions reeling.

"Do you believe that the Brethren, who have hidden from the eyes of the masses unnecessary truths, who have engineered your discoveries, and who now guide you in your purpose, would be so inept as to permit such a circumstance?" Sada's slightly raised eyebrows gave him a bemused look.

"Though you may have authored and posted them, no letters were received by the Board of Directors."

Condo quickly contested: "But the meetings…there were meetings! I looked these men in the eyes!"

"Into their eyes, Pontimax? Or into images of their eyes?" Ho'jin Sada cocked his head like an inquisitive bird. As a stone falls albeit slowly in the microgravity of the Habitats, so Es'paul Condo's understanding descended to reality. Deception upon deception! But to what cause! Indignation drove the question:

"Why? Why all of the lies! What purpose in setting a man to live by lies, only to murder him with the truth?"

Ho'jin Sada closed his eyes, and began to recite from the Brethren's Dialogue: *But what if the original Truth is no truth at all, only something hoped for or imagined; a speculation in the quest for meaning and purpose; a dream of universal goodness? And what if the dreamers were truly lovers of mankind, willing to sacrifice themselves? Is this not a noble cause? Can its secret not give purpose to our lives?*

Sada opened his eyes and met Condo's with a penetrating and yet amorphous stare.

"We have confessed our sin to you, Pontimax. We are doubters. We do not see in the vastness of the Cosmos any necessity for humankind's existence, nor God's. Nor do we see that it serves any particular purpose. It appears to us only a chance happening; a chance permutation of the elements. In a past age we might have been the emotionless psychopath, as calmly taking a human life as smashing an insect. And yet in this time, because our intellects have been honed to sharpness upon the philosopher's stone, we are not bound by probabilities, but must endlessly consider all possibilities. And it is *possible* that Life is itself the purpose of all things. To that end it is now our purpose to see that you fulfill yours."

Condo could not tell if he detected a note of emotion in Sada's delivery. He could not deny the palpable sense of determination in the Gleaner's pronouncements. But again the revelations set his thoughts into a spin, vortices of anguish and elation and despair and hope. The impact on his nervous system was so great it induced an involuntary response from some deep ceded survival instinct lying beyond Excision's reach. He curled into Prayer.

For three days the Gleaners monitored Condo's vital signs and body chemistry, watching for signs of evolving pathology – neurological or otherwise. There were records of men in Condo's position who had retreated into a persistent catatonic state as a defense against unfaceable reality. Ho'jin Sada believed his execution of the revelations had been well within the limits of Condo's tolerances, however, and did not doubt his recovery.

Condo was restrained by a fine, silken web while his Prayer endured. The gossamer caress of its threads now stimulated the back of his neck as he swam from incredible depth to ever bluer waters. As is often the case as the conscious mind is restored, he began to question the nature of returning sensation. He detected something familiar in the undulating intensity of the light. He was aware of the blueness before he was aware of his closed eyelids. He was trying to remember something of great importance, realized clearly in the darkness, but now fading in the increasing light. And then his eyes were open, and before him lay the depth of the Cylinder Sea, awash in the light transmitted by thousands organoptic fibers. Still held by his silken web at the center of a great glass bubble protruding into the Sea, Condo's mind raced to digest a universe of data, both internal and external. His strongest recollection was as of a battle, with demons from Hades to Halphas, always standing in defense of man. It was from this recollection of struggle that the memories of events prior to his Prayer found their way to him. But now, instead of confusion, they presented an orderly argument to be considered. He was relaxed and clear headed; ready to proceed. As he contemplated escape from his silken chains a familiar figure entered his field of view. It proceeded to the bubble's wall, and there examined a small, undulating creature of unidentifiable specie. A finger's tap sent the creature scurrying to the water's depths. The figure turned toward Condo and shrugged.

"Evolution at work!" Ho'jin Sada countenanced one of his rare smiles. "I see our petitioner has returned! All is well in the land of dreams?"

Condo returned the smile, and acknowledging his neophytic state, inquired: "Where to now, Sensei?"

"There is the true history of the Brethren; the

records of the great plagues; more to know about our noble Worms than you might imagine."

Though generally emotionless, the Gleaner's eyes seemed to sparkle in delight at this opportunity to share more of the secret. It was infectious, causing Condo's mind to obscure the darker aspects of his circumstance in favor of the joys of learning.

"Shall we begin?" Sada helped Condo pull away the silken webs, and with a firm grip on his protégé, used his Locator to steer them to the nearest console. On their approach, its user quickly evacuated, leaving his Locator and Back Patch in place for Condo. Once secured, Sada rescheduled the console so that its screen displayed the beginning text of the Brethren's Dialogue.

Es'paul Condo was aware of the existence of the Dialogue, and even occasionally encountered esoteric excerpts. But it had never been a subject of his scholarly interests. He now wondered why. As Condo perused the text, Ho'jin Sada began a narrative.

"All those who worked with William Proffit did not feel his moral imperative. Many were men of science who saw his solution not as THE answer, but as the lesser of extant evils. They did not see a moral side to Proffit's final action and self-immolation. They saw it as only the most recent, massive, and probably not final, interspecific homicide resulting from the old Malthusian tenets.

It was this group of agnostics whose skills Proffit required in order to raise his New Jerusl'm that entered into contract, as non-believers, to support the technological base of the Habitats and to monitor the psychologies of the inhabitants for reversions or deviations that threatened health, stability, or survival of the Habitats. Of course, these were not amoral men, only of a different cast. They understood the implications of the monitoring and refused to serve as the grim reaper of aberrant souls. William Proffit well understood their reservations, and settled their objections: "I do not ask you to serve as executioners, but merely indicators. You have only to point the finger and lay the accusations. Cry "witch!"- and the truly faithful will know how to proceed."

Condo's mind turned in ways it had never known. And yet every word Sada uttered echoed passages from *The Third Testament*: "Let those whose live apart, and view from a distance the journey's path, advise us of our needs" now took on a very practical aspect. "Let he who accuses accept the judgment of holier men" was not some abstract parable to be interpreted a hundred ways, but was, in fact, a precise procedure ensuring that not only reason, but compassion would be a man's jury.

When Condo's focus returned, Ho'jin Sada, the lowly Gleaner continued: "A contract was written and signed by both parties, the collection of scientists and William Proffit, setting the conditions. As a scientist himself, Proffit reminded his colleagues that honesty and integrity were all a man without faith can command. Their names upon the contract pledged these before their peers, with solemn oath, to shun unto death any who failed in their obligations. They also understood that their pre-ordained place in the heavens was the lowliest of the low, Gleaners of the refuse of Man. But for this pledge they would be permitted the pursuit of their scientific passions to the utmost – every need provided; every resource available; and upon peer approval, application of their discovered principles within or without the Habitats – with this one caveat – all must be sanctioned by the Pontimax."

Another burst of light in Es'paul Condo's eyes indicated further understanding. The endless stream of reports from the "Scientific Societies", always anonymous, always a surprise and delight to the technological Brotherhoods when delivered from the Office of the Pontimax. Not evidence of divine inspiration, but the product of life-long researches done surreptitiously." When he was satisfied that Condo had "gotten the picture", Sada continued: "*The Dialogue between The Brethren and William Proffit* is our contract. Its most important part is its beginning –

*William Proffit: Mine was a life of science, driven to despair by the prostitution of great minds, seeking resource for their scientific inquiries by servicing the avaricious and malicious desires of men not fully human. Is there one among you who is not in some small way stained by this sad truth?*

*The Brethren: It is true.*

*William Proffit: Those of our colleagues not with us today, who yet serve the enemies of true men, though they have abilities, lack human intelligence. Those ancient structures in the brain, through which all data from the senses must pass, and through which all utterances from the higher functions must negotiate, still rule their lives. They are clever apes, and no more. Only when the higher powers have evolved sufficiently, so that the senses may not deceive us to satisfy the wants of the flesh, and our utterances are not corrupted to serve those same wants, are we truly human.*

*The Brethren: It is true.*

*William Proffit: I confess to you that I remain the skeptical scientist, always in want of proof. But I also confess to you that I have glimpsed something far larger than myself – only vaguely, and at a distance – that has given me a faith I did not have before. A faith that Life is its own purpose, the purpose of all things. And that whosoever or whatsoever authored Life authored all things. My worship of this great mystery is the practice of my science. Though I shall not know it, I believe Life will one day know its author. The Preservation of Life until that Day, then, is the one commandment we can know.*

*The Brethren: It is true.*

Ho'jin Sada had given his little dissertation with his eyes closed. Condo had watched his countenance closely, and had noted the serenity and surrender the mantra had worked upon the Gleaner. When their eyes next met, Sada made no attempt to disguise his emotion. It was his religious experience – dedication to something greater than oneself – that was the bond of humanity between lowly Gleaner and the lofty Pontimax.

CHAPTER 30

Am'riah Redshilt had come from a long line of ambitious and prosperous men. Their fortunes were recorded early in the written histories of men. But as the last days of man on Earth approached, and conflict became universal, the opportunities to profit, and more importantly to protect that profit, became ever more difficult. When the prosperity and evident invincibility of Proffit's New Jerus'lm became apparent, the family don declared that the clan would convert en masse and immigrate to Arkansas in what remained of the United States of America. They would later consider how to overcome the inconveniences their new-found "religion" might impose upon them.

Redshilt's ancestors had guessed correctly that all systems, whether rational or mystic, had areas of weakness; vulnerabilities that could be exploited without wholesale violation of the rules. History had taught them that systems, particularly human systems, were willing to compromise in order to guarantee survival. And they prided themselves, and justified their means in the fact that their machinations generally proved useful to the prosperity and continuance of their hosts. When such was not the case, they blamed it on the basic inferiority of the others.

Of all the lineages represented in the Habitats, it was the houses of finance, and the families they represented, that kept the best accounting of historical transactions – monetary, political, and ideological (along with impeccable family genealogies) from man's earliest attempt at civilization to his present life in Free Space. Unlike most who inhabited the current realm, for whom memories of Earth existed only in the tales from the holy books, Am'riah Redshilt carried in his head and heart a record of the talents and accomplishments of his people from earliest times. And it was this extensive record of nearly constant successes that gave him confidence in his current endeavors. If it was the product of a Redshilt mind, it must be true and right!

Certainty aside, Am'riah Redshilt did not abandon the eternal caution of his kind. He continually examined pragmatic models to better understand the consequences of what would be immensely reorganizing forces in the society of man. He ran economic models to determine the productive and profitable parameters of such social changes. And above all, he considered the profound impact it would have on the Redshilt legacy – legitimizing the primacy of the individual, and the bloodline that had sired it. In Redshilt's innermost model of the world, competition was not the vestige of hardwired, pre-nescient behaviors, but the *divine* impetus that had raised man from poverty and bestial existence to this life in the heavens.

It is not surprising that he held a particular though well camouflaged contempt for Es'paul Condo. Chief among Am'riah Redshilt's tenets was the unshakable belief that all else being equal (i.e. born with a fully formed brain, viable senses, and four good limbs) a man's station in society should be determined by his accomplishments, not by some arbitrary set of ideals. Because Condo had been "chosen" for his position due to the chance alignment between his personal dispositions and the philosophy in force at the time and not because his mettle had been tested in any real way, Redshilt considered him to be at least an interloper, and at worst a charlatan. That such a one should suppose the right to impose upon a true participant in the eternal struggle for existence constraints to individuality and all its entitlements was outrage beyond measure! But, like his ancestors and the wisdom their DNA imparted to him, he first guaranteed the survival of his lineage, only then to turn to these other matters. And the Redshilt's had taken care of that primary business on their first visit with William Proffit. Am'riah knew this part of the family history well. As a representative of the 12 families, Don Redshilt had approached Proffit's representatives and requested a meeting, which was granted. The meeting was held within the protective walls of the original New Jerusl'im compound, in Amagon, Arkansas. The family archives contain this transcript: *Don Redshilt: I come as the representative of the 12 families, to negotiate a position in your regime.*

*William Proffit: Mine is not a regime, but only an idea whose time has come.*

*Don Redshilt: Be that as it may, our interests converge in the midst of the present turmoil. You have need of resources to complete your projects; we have or control those resources.*

*William Proffit: If you come wishing to barter goods for power, you are mistaken.*

*Don Redshilt: I am not mistaken. I come not seeking power, but a place for the 12 families among you. Like you, we see that man has degenerated beyond redemption, and will soon annihilate himself. And this would be true whether you and your idea had come to pass or not. Like you, we also believe man cannot escape his ages old competition unless there is sufficient space for all. And, like you, we believe there does exist a force in the universe compelling us ever forward, both in number and ability. Though the paths to our realizations may not be the same, you see that our goals are.*

*William Proffit: There are requirements, you understand, that are not negotiable. Excision is the path that joins us, nothing less.*

*Don Redshilt: I fully understand, as do all the elders of the twelve families. But you see, we also believe we have been chosen over the ages for our abilities, now deeply encoded in our genetics, which will remain undiminished by the absence of a few instinctive urges. We ask only to manage our own procreative destinies.*

*William Proffit: All well said, Don Redshilt. But if you have come to bargain, there is another side to this coin.*

*Don Redshilt: Yes . . . It is this: Should you find no place for us, the result will be our total withdrawal from the current processes. As the majority of nations have now turned against you, and intend to prevent you from succeeding, without our help your only method of procurement will be slaughter, for none will give to you willingly, at any price. And then how are you better than any past megalomaniac using force to impose your will? If you are the man of compassion you pretend, you will show it by diminishing the suffering of those who will not follow, and making a place for us.*

*William Proffit: It is done.*

*It was by the very hand of William Proffit that the 12 families, among them the Redshilts, were given their destinies. Am'riah Redshilt could not reconcile that history with the present circumstance in which the metaphysical meanderings of unchallenged philosophers and mystics fettered the talents of men of action.*

CHAPTER 31

Es'Paul Condo was also aware of the contract between Proffit and the 12 families. But to him it presented a different argument altogether, not the least because Proffit had penned a note in the margin of the official document: "Even Noah made a place on the ark for the serpent that had been responsible for man's exile from Eden."

Proffit's obvious note of caution engendered in Condo no prejudice against the financial houses, nor any specific animosity towards the special place they held within the Habitats. He accepted the differences among men as inevitable, even desirable. For were each man and woman a mere copy of every other, there could be no true consciousness, no independent self-awareness. No distinction could be made between individuals, so no sense of individuality could arise. Human existence would take on the flatness of the amoebic world. In all truth, the Pontimax admired the talents of Am'riah Redshilt, and marveled at his ability to provide the rights fruits for the right labors, so that men and women prospered and multiplied within the Habitats.

CHAPTER 32

Ho'jin Sada early accounted differences between himself and his classmates at the Corps. It occurred to him that his sense of separateness was an "abnormality." He often sat apart, quietly observing his companions as if they were a quite separate and interesting species. He found there predilection for play and sport nearly incomprehensible; their repetitive and often meaningless behavior a mystery He early learned that trying to communicate these thoughts to others brought looks of bemusement, sometimes even contempt, however. So he withdrew to his philosopher's perch and turned his thoughts to the really interesting things around him – numbers and relationships and systems and interactions and invisible forces – the very fabric of existence!

The young Sada, a quick study in mathematics, chemistry, and physics, soon fixed on the notion that no combination of processes from these disciplines combined to provide a reasonably sufficient explanation for the phenomena of consciousness; the sense of self-awareness; the sense of "me-ness" that even he in his most abstracted moments could not escape. The more deeply he considered the matter, the more diligently he studied the old masters to find some good starting point, the more he concluded that the old Descartian adage had it backwards: not *"Cogito ergo sum*", but rather "*Ego sum ergo cogito*", which led to the inevitable question: *WHY* am I?

All these things had jelled in the young Corpsman's mind before the advent of his tenth year. And with these "peculiarities" of mind had come a certain suppression of other neural activities, particularly in the limbic regions. So neglected were these ancient synaptic pathways that they had actually begun to suffer and atrophy. In a single decade this singular individual had acquired enough data to keep the cortical synapses occupied, with little or no need for input or desire for output. The senses and their communion with the outer universe were often all but ignored in favor of the internal universe. Often the boy lapsed into extended periods of catatonia, only to revive as if nothing extraordinary had occurred.

The principle external manifestation of Ho'jin Sada's neuronal nuances was an apparent lack of emotion. Unlike his peers, who had mastered and begun to individualize the presentation of the five primary states, Sada presented only an *interested* gaze. His classmates often squirmed under its scrutiny, feeling like specimens under the lens of a microscope. As a result, the young Ho'jin made no friends, which didn't matter, because he didn't need them.

When given the pre-Excision examination in his thirteenth year, such self-induced modifications to the regions of interest had occurred that no intervention was necessary. In fact, none yet existed that could improve upon the pruning accomplished. By edict he was immediately referred to the Brethren of Gleaners. He was appropriately bundled and without farewells to parents or peers, and showing not the least apprehension or separation anxiety, but only a haunting hunger for the as yet unexperienced, he was dispatched by Ventportation courier to the Core Sphagnum.

CHAPTER 33

Ho'jin Sada was greeted by the Headmaster
of the Brethren's School upon his arrival
at the Core. Both the man before him and
the environment of Core were absolutely foreign
to him, yet he felt no apprehension, only the
greatest curiosity. When their eyes met there was
no exchange of primaries, no sense of acceptance
or rejection, no attraction or repulsion, only the
intensity one might expect of one universe
inspecting another.

The Headmaster began the mantra immediately.
He waited for no reply from the novitiate. He knew
the boy would not speak for days, perhaps weeks
or months – on the rare occasion, never. It was of
no consequence. He was where he belonged, and
that was the only necessary thing.

Chanting in wavering tones, he began:

*We are of the mind alone;*
*Chosen by that which is hidden from us*
*In some future place and some future time.*

*We are of the mind alone;*
*The soul that seeks to know the unknowable,*
*The sentient dust cast upon the void by mother*
*stars.*

*We are of the mind alone;*
*But the body is our fortress and dome*
*So we must tend it well so that Life may know its*
*source.*

*We are of the mind alone;*
*So we must chant our hymns and verses without*
*fail*
*Lest we neglect that which breathes and gives us*
*form.*

*We are of the mind alone;*
*And must outlive the farthest star and furthest time*
*Until the light of the universe shines from Life*
*itself.*

Sada and the Headmaster had descended one of the long, backlit tunnels into the Sphagnum as the verses were chanted. The Headmaster ceased his chant as they arrived at the first alcove. A fellow Gleaner approached the pair, in his hands the traditional saffron sack. The novitiate was quickly relieved of his Corpsman's uniform, and the sack installed and tied securely at the throat. He offered no resistance, nor any other response.

"This is your mentor, Ba'tul Samon. He will instruct you in all things." Abruptly, the Headmaster turned and exited the alcove, his darkened feet clasping and tugging at the moss to propel him on his way. The mentor took the docile Sada by the shoulders and maneuvered him into a nearby cocoon. As docious and pliable as an infant,only the intensity of Sada's focus betrayed the great neuronal explosion occurring behind his eyes. The mentor settled into an adjacent cocoon and began to chant:

*We are of the mind alone;*
*But must feed and quench our fleshly abode*
*For thought proceeds from the tissue and organs.*

*We are of the mind alone;*
*But can only succeed upon the great wave of humanity*
*Set adrift among the stars as waifs in need of care.*

*We are of the mind alone;*
*But have no source and substance except what others provide*
*And in recourse entwine our fortune with their blessed ignorance.*

*We are of the mind alone…*

CHAPTER 34

From his vantage high upon the Partition Am'riah Redshilt looked across the vast bowl of the Quadrant, its great basin a patchwork shade of greens and all the other hues created by expanses of Hydrofarms both vertical and horizontal. As the levels tiered upwards, great verdant terraces alternated with the glistening glass and steel of partition structures, dedicated first to industry and commerce, then to domiciles for the laboring masses. The purely agricultural terraces gave way to natural spaces and recreational areas higher up, and industry and commerce gave way to finance and culture. Ever smaller terraces became decorative gardens, and at the pinnacles, referred to colloquially as the "penthouses", were the domiciles of bankers, moguls, and politicians. At this level the partition were a scant 50 meters across, so that Am'riah's cubiculure estate provided overlooks on adjacent Quadrants - on one side a great agricultural center; on the other a great Forest. From this vantage point, Am'riah Redshilt surveyed what he considered to be *his* creation. He was not entirely incorrect in his assessment.

It is an historical truth that in the conduct of human affairs individuals participate at levels commensurate to their intrinsic interests. For most this means that the level of reward is secondary to the gratification received by accomplishing the task itself. Of course, such interests must necessarily include a task such as acquisition – of power; of money; of control. Very often when acquisition is the activity of interest, power, money, and control become an inseparable and inevitable consequence. Am'riah Redshilt, and the genetic dynasty to which he belonged had through generations of selected breeding captured the genetic essence of acquisitiveness. And those genetically garnered talents had served the clan well, from the distant past to the present day, resulting in an abundance of power and money and control. But the thing acquired was not as important as the acquiring, so that as long as some new or novel thing appeared within range of view, it too must be acquired.

So it was with Am'riah Redshilt. As he gazed across the vast Quadrant he saw his mark; his imprint upon all. Every idea that manifested itself in some physical reality in this Habitat was at his bidding. Ideas were financed and prospered or were denied and faded, not on their merit, but upon his attention or neglect. And the result lay before him, a Habitat both abundant and secure, functioning with businesslike precision, its every part there by his good graces.

Of course, what Redshilt did not understand, did not perceive, would be incapable of understanding, was the unseen hand of the Brethren. For those ideas from which he harvested his results were in fact seeded by none other than the lowly Gleaners, who by manipulation of curriculum were able to transmit their ideas surreptitiously to the pliable young minds of the Corps, upon which fertile soil they bloomed, each and every one a precious flower, so that any bouquet assembled was predestined a successful arrangement. Redshilt's necessity, and that of the others of his caste, lie in the fact that the Brethren could not be bothered with mere gardening when it was the essence of the garden itself they sought.

Oblivious to these greater truths, primarily because they did not fall into his field of view, Am'riah inhaled deeply of his success. The titillation of endorphins quickly turned his mind from his acquired success to those success yet to be obtained. Retiring to his study he secured the hatch and removing the illicit Cap from its covert compartment quickly engaged his back patch to the desk chair. Donning the unholy helmet, he began to tremble with licentious anticipation. His fingers and toes sought to input codes to the most recently contrived and every increasingly profligate adventure. Like all ideas that fell within his interest, his financial support increasingly favored the output of the unseen and unknown authors of these proscribed pleasures. Little did he suspect that his current escapades fell beyond the pale of his necessity.

## CHAPTER 35

The young Ho'jin Sada had adapted instantaneously to his new surroundings – or perhaps more accurately - needed no adaptation whatsoever. Life at the Core among the Gleaners was the life he was meant to lead. He had understood it as clearly as he understood he must breathe to live. For here he knew his peculiarities were no peculiarities at all, but the merely the common urge to *know all* shared by every Gleaner, from Novitiate to Abbot.

A much aged Ho'jin Sada now reflected upon those long past experiences. It seemed that even the life of pure intellect, with its infinite possibilities for discovery and understanding, took on a certain staleness as the now withered and well-stained Abbot sojourned deep into his second century. The involuntarily stoic and dispassionate youth who had arrived at the Core so long ago, uncaring but eager to know and understand, had managed, through the years of chanting the mantras, to rejuvenate certain regions of his deficient limbic structures wherein resided the impulses for compassion and caring. No, he had not come to love man, but as a man himself, became empathetic to man's most mature need – the need to find peace when life's questions remained unanswered.

Even Excision did not expunge from man a certain fear of death, particularly when confronted with it at a premature or unexpected moment. It was one thing to drift into the eternal night when life had been so long that the mind no longer made clear distinction between the world within and the world without. It was quite another to contemplate the process while in full possession of one's faculties. The Brethren had long ago decreed that when possible, death should come as a warm, reassuring embrace, not a violent rending of soul from substance. To that end the Brethren had through the generations bred a particular class of Worms to tend particularly to the hospice of the aged and infirm. Sensitive to those metabolites produced and exuded by failing flesh and organs, these Mortuary Worms could be seen lingering in the vicinity of the abodes of the Habitat's most ancient citizens. When the final throes sent forth their chemical signals, the Worms descended, and long before pain and panic could ensue, engulfed the dying, dispensed soothing, narcotic potions and ecstatic hallucinogens with their cilia. Never was a struggle seen, only a gentle surrender, as an infant falling asleep in a loving mother's arms. Sada thought it one of the nobler achievements of his kind. It guaranteed that no one should die except they were at peace. And all was confirmed by remote temporal scan of the brain as its functions ceased.

At his last meeting with the Pontimax, Sada had revealed another use to which these Worms were employed – as Assassins. Already beleaguered with the chore of deciding the fate of offending citizens, perhaps in the millions, Sada witnessed the weighting, palpable resignation that now cloaked Es'paul Condo. He did not envy him his task. But it was now as it had been for the 500 generations since the Ascent – humanity existed now in glass houses, where no stone throwing could be permitted.

Sada had also revealed to Condo the complete and complex story of the Brethren, from the original contract signed by those scientists who had helped to create New Jerusl'm and the first Habitats yet could not compromise their objectivity by openly subscribing to Proffit's mysticism, or tolerate an Excision that might in any way reduce their mental faculties. They accepted a place apart from the masses, to support, maintain, and innovate the technology needed, and in return would receive all maintenance, sustenance, and resources required and desired, so long as they did not directly interfere with the broader social machine. Their knowledge would be appreciated; their opinions would be welcome; their direct participation would never be tolerated. It was written in *The Third Testament*: "And if in a future day the lowly shall presume to rise above their station and talk of reason without faith, then men shall on that day cast them in their entirety into the void." Not a prospect the Brethren were likely to test. Of course, many who signed that original contract found a change of heart once the Ascent was realized. The spartan, challenging conditions of the first Habitats wanted a sense of community found lacking in the machinery rooms and laboratories of the Core that were the assigned domain of the scientists. Many later opted to accept Excision and take the chance, rather than live apart from their fellows. There were those, however, and they were many, who were steadfast. It was from these remaining that the Brethren and their lowly station as Gleaners evolved, with all of their rituals and traditions born of necessities.

The first and most immediate adaptation these remaining scientists required was some method of self maintenance. The living conditions within the machinery and laboratory spaces rapidly deteriorated. These men of intellect often lost themselves within their work, going days without sleep or nourishment. And being generally antisocial by nature, they paid little attention to the conditions of their fellows. But, being men of intelligence, they did not remain unaware of these circumstances, and in cool and reasoned fashion addressed them. After several meetings and draft proposals, a solution was settled upon. A routine must be established the provided for those deficiencies in behavior that were detrimental, even life-threatening. The wisest among them, who would become the first Abbot had studied eastern philosophies and religions as a neurophysiologist, and had determined that repetitive behaviors produce real differences in brain structure. He recommended that mantras be used to reinforce those limbic regions associated with survival. Simply put, a small ritual should be employed to remind everyone to eat and sleep.

And so the first mantra was penned:

*We live the life of thought.*
*It is the mind that thinks.*
*It is the brain that provides the substance of the*
*mind.*

*The brain must live for the mind to think.*
*The body feeds the brain.*
*The body must live for brain think.*
*We must feed the body.*

*We live the life of thought.*
*It is the mind that thinks.*
*It is the brain that provides the substance of the*
*mind.*

*The brain must live for the mind to think.*
*The body protects the brain.*
*The body must live for brain to think.*
*We must protect the body.*

Almost infantile in its simplicity, a schedule was set for this first mantra. It would be recited in unison every eight hours by the clock, signaled by a gong. From this modest but necessary beginning had evolved the intricate multitude of rituals which Ho'jin Sada's generation of Gleaners practiced, each behavioral deficiency compensated by a mantra, a prayer, or a song. The Gleaners prospered under the regimen.

Of course, there was the one fatal flaw to the plan. The natural monasticism of the Gleaners, male and female alike, did not provide for continuity. Their lack of normal human appetites extended to sex and procreation. As none seemed inclined to resurrect or reinforce these behaviors, a deal was struck with Proffit's representatives, forerunners to Alhumana's corporate population, that during preExcision examination, individuals meeting certain criteria would be referred to the scientists for assimilation.

CHAPTER 36

L ike mothers everywhere and always, the Sisterhood sensed the coming crisis. It was not the first crisis, of course, nor would it be the last. But they knew another great sadness lie ahead. Particularly for Sar'ha, wife of the Pontimax and the Mat'ushka, the sense of impending doom took on a personal note.

The Sisterhood was ever aware of the imperfection of Excision. The human brain was just too complex a system to accurately map. Add to the complexity the fact that it was a self-altering organ, so that each new input impacted the entire of the neural network to greater or lesser degree, so that from moment to moment the conscious mind literally became something entirely new. The general structures and functions remained intact, of course, but the subtle (or not so subtle) changes in the network of synapses could not be precisely associated or accurately mapped. Even in the unconscious state the mind self-modifies. Since the purpose of Excision was to remove very precise synaptic structures that might change between analysis and procedure, the process was only generally successful. Yet, its practice had so diminished those behaviors that had plagued man's tenure on Earth that the few millions who had escaped had multiplied to the tens of trillions that now populated the Habitats. As the generations had passed and aggression no longer played an active role in survival of the species, those individuals born deficient in that native talent survived, prospered, and reproduced as well as those whose placidity was accomplished only by Excision. In fact, it was the executive breeding program imposed by the Sisterhood that was intended to one day compensate for Excision's inadequacies, or even to render the process unnecessary. Unlike breeding programs imposed in antiquity by earthly despots, or lesser species, where dominant males or females set the agenda, all within the Habitats were free to reproduce, or not, except those whose genetic dispositions minimized or negated the need for Excision. If those traits marked for Excision were reduced or absent by virtue of genetic make-up, those individuals were sent to seminary or convent, and prepared to fulfill their social duty. *The Third Testament* declares: "If your seed is one of peace and humility, then you shall be mankind's plowman and handmaid."

An important part of Sar'ha's education at the convent, in preparation for her impending motherhood and career as an Excisionist, was the study of the historical remedies for Excision's inadequacies. Early on the only alternative had been multiple Excisions, sometimes to the point of effective lobotomy. Most tenacious of the problems was the afterglow of instinctual behavior that managed to impress itself upon the higher regions of the brain before Excision occurred, however. But Excisions given too early noticeably reduced an individual's development and functional capacity.

So the inadequacies were tolerated and compensated by other means, primary among them social interaction and pressure. But now that same social pressure and interaction was proving itself a problem, as likely to stimulate unwanted neural pathways as to suppress them. With the populations of the Habitats numbering in the tens of trillions, with no sign the exponential nature of the increase would diminish, outbreaks of unwanted behaviors could quickly induce behavior modifications in multitudes.

Added to the increasing challenge of Excision's limitations was a growing social argument surrounding what constituted acceptable behavior. It represented the very *doubt* that Sar'ha's husband worked so diligently to assuage. No matter the vast amount of historical and empirical data available; no matter the documented cases of failed Habitats, where highly organized, sentient life reduced to primordial slimes in the course of but few generations; no matter a social and educational structure designed specifically to inculcate in the citizens the highest principles – still the outbreaks occurred and had to be dealt with.

One thing Sar'ha was not familiar with was the exact nature of the remedies applied to past outbreaks of aberrant behavior. Though information flowed freely within and between the Habitats, that information was primarily of a pragmatic nature –new technologies or processes; corporate reports; census information; educational assets – but nothing of what had been once called "news." For one thing, the general level of education being equal, people now demanded fact, not speculation; truth not conjecture. The last of the old style "journals" had been hounded out of business shortly after the foundation of the first Habitats. Any of the forms of information made available to the general public were only issued after intensive peer review and approval. And no bylines were permitted. The cults of personality that had so dominated, and contaminated the flow of information in antiquity were eliminated at their source. As a result, the resolution of past crises was only evident in the return to normality. Yet, Sar'ha sensed, and by sensing knew, that extreme measures were often required. She also believed that the resolutions emanated from the highest offices within the corporations, if not from the highest office of all – the Pontimax!

That something was afoot could easily be gleaned from the daily flow of information, without interpretation by some agenda driven interloper as had happened on Earth. The indicators presented themselves like the symptoms of a disease – census reports indicated declining birth rates; essential productivity diminished, while non-essential demands increased; people's activities, both physical and neural became more isolated and congregated; and for the most discerning ears, Ensymphonium took on a muted tone – all beyond the normal variations that constituted a stable, harmonic balance. Only small variations beyond the norm appear at first, but every prediction model indicated that even mild initial perturbations amplified if left undamped, resulting in extreme and destructive oscillations. Sar'ha accepted that Pontimax Es'paul Condo, father to her broods, would be maestro to the great retuning of society; she did not know how the symphony would end.

CHAPTER 37

At the same moment Am'riah Redshilt stood at his window surveying his realm, Es'paul Condo hovered at a windeye of his Pod surveying the depths of the Forest beyond. Streams of solar photons penetrated the canopy in places creating great crepuscular rays as small particles in the air refracted the photons at angles that intercepted Condo's field of vision. The photons entering his eyes stuck light-sensitive molecules in the retina, exciting electrical charges which traversed the optic nerves to arrive as impulses at the visual cortex creating in his mind the illusion of sunbeams. Condo understood every process involved. The understanding increased the beauty of what he beheld. Now and then larger particles drifted through the stream of photons, their intense reflections and refractions appearing as flashes and sparkles. And now a bird, its great cape of iridescent feathers producing a spectacular undulating rainbow as it swam lazily through the beam. All of this a visual poem such as men have attempted to capture in words, and yet must always fall short. The Pontimax breathed slowly, deeply, contentedly. What he knew and believed were one: man is not the Creator.

He turned reluctantly from his reverie, and snatching a handrail propelled himself upwards, into his study. The tranquility he had so recently partaken of retreated as fog before the wind. The task at hand had nothing of tranquility about it; peace and mercy and compassion where hard to implicate in its calculus. What had fallen to him found no precedent in his life's experience. All of his faith and belief withered before this assault on his reality. He had built the entire fortress of his being upon the principle that goodness would win out, that he would never raise his hand against his fellow man, that he would be an agent for healing and rebirth. Instead he had now been cast as the avenging angel in a play whose author he now questioned and whose final act he did not yet know.

Settling in at his desk brought his console to life. He called up the list, but lost focus as it began to scroll, his thoughts turning to his most recent meeting with Abbot Sada. His arguments had been so reasonable and yet his conclusion antithetical to all he thought he knew. The drone of Ho'jin Sada's most recent monologue began to play audibly in his mind: *It is true that we Brethren pursue all things by reason alone, and the facts and evidence such pursuits produce. You might be surprised by our conclusion. We, who apply the laws of mathematics and physics and logic to all things, have taken a measure of this universe of ours; we manipulate its matter and energy and forces; we probe at the underlying ether and use it properties, though it remains largely a mystery. We can understand every process from the nascent particle teetering on the cusp of reality to the apparent singularity of the black-hole. By the power of our*

*minds we can discern the patterns that reveal
tomorrow's consequences of today's actions. And
when we put it all together and take an accounting,
we are left with this: ALL of the processes by
which the universe obtains culminate in a single,
preeminent product – life! So we are left with this
single, philosophical consideration: If life is the
ultimate produce of all that is, is the purpose of all
that is life? It seems that our science and your
religion beg the same question.*

Condo had not found that segment of Sada's
monologue particularly enlightening or
encouraging, though he had certainly detected an
element of satisfaction in the Abbot's demeanor at
its close. He closed his eyes and continued to play
his memory's recording. What came next was the
part he wanted to ingest more fully and digest more
completely. Ho'jin Sada's voice returned: *By
whatever route we take, our cause is common. We
of the Brethren, who seek understanding, reason
that the preservation of life is the path to greater
understanding, that future men will find the answers
to the questions we pose. But we men of mind have
little talent for our own survival. In a sense we are
parasites on the fecund mother of humanity and
must forever feed at her breast. As we have no
pride, it is an easy fate to accept. What is more
difficult is protecting our source of nourishment
from the innumerable maladies. It is here that we
conspire with you to cure the disease.*

Es'paul Condo recalled the bitterness that had
risen in his throat at Sada's remark. He recalled his

outburst: "Why was I not told?! Why was I deceived?!" He remembered the Abbot's cool reply: *If you had known from the beginning that the power of life and death was in your hands, would you have remained the pure and upright soul that you are? If you had been told from the beginning that the prosperity of the Habitats rested not on divine blessing, but upon the actions of men who had the will to sacrifice the few for the good of many, would you have worked so faithfully and effectively to dispel the doubt which grows now even after your best effort?*

Condo opened his eyes and the voice faded. He focused on the names scrolling by on his screen. They certainly numbered in the millions, though he could not bring himself to call up a count. He laid his hand upon the screen and the list faded. He fetched his Cap from its cradle, pulling it down snuggly over the great bulbs of his cranium. He would try again by persuasion to succeed where he had to this point failed. He invoked Alhumana's network, and began a general communique.

*10036.12.22.6 Ano Ascensu*
*Es'paul Condo*
*Pmx/CEO*
*Alhumana Corp.*

*To: Locus omni*
*God has given us life. God has given us purpose. May it ever be so. Amen.*

*Brothers and Sisters all – Our Faith has given us peace, prosperity, and increase. May it ever be so. Amen.*

*The data tells us all. For the numbers are the script of the Natural Law, and the Natural Law is God's Law. May it ever be so. Amen.*

*Brothers and Sisters all – the data now tells us all is not well. The forces of Doubt perturb our harmony, leading us ever further from the middle path. May the power of our Faith prove the stabilizing force. May it ever be so. Amen.*

The short communique was instantly presented on every screen, and for those in their Caps, currently connected to the network, impressed upon their visual cortex, while an accompanying audio was fed to the auditory cortex. For those in the sleeping Quadrants, the communique would be presented with morning vespers.

Condo knew that the simple communique was no remedy. He did believe that it would put the general population on alert for any new and unusual information, setting their radars to scan and consider more closely its nature, serving as an inoculation against further spread of the disease.

## CHAPTER 38

Am'riah Redshilt drifted up from his latest illicit emprise sweating and exhausted, still tingling with residual sensations and yet ecstatically revivified. As usual a Worm lurked nearby, having sensed at considerable distance the excessive metabolites he exuded. Am'riah removed and secured the illegal Cap, quickly shed his soggy suit and prepared for the Worm's embrace. With such heightened sensitivity even the Worm's work became a new and extraordinary experience.

Once disgorged, Am'riah propelled himself toward a cabinet to get clean, dry clothing. Sliding his arms and legs into their sleeves, he closed the center seam and tugged at the fabric until its back patch was properly centered. Pushing off the cabinet, he drifted towards the hatch, noticing that its hailing light was lit. Obviously Re'kaba or one of the children had returned home prematurely and seeing his office occupancy light aglow had hailed him. Deep in the stupor of debauchery, with the illicit Cap not connected to the normal networks, he had not received the hail. He wondered how much time had passed.

Apprehensively he opened the hatch and grasping a handrail with his feet propelled himself down the long corridor to the common living area.

As he approached, the strains of an old ballad played on the harp ukuleles began to reverberate on the air. It was Re'kaba. Though just a recreation, her playing was masterful. It was her *modus contemplatio*, which only added to his apprehension. They had become increasingly distant in recent years, only rarely sharing familial or connubial pursuits. How many times had they passed one another, he going while she was coming; she always presenting: *I have questions*; he always verbalizing his response: "Sorry, darling. I haven't time now. I must…"

Redshilt stopped short of entering the great common space. Near its center, just to the right of the immense blue column of the family aquaria, Re'kaba was back-patched to stool, embracing her harp ukuleles, her head swaying rhythmically to the beat of the music. Oblivious to all, he could see that she presently inhabited a space not defined by the laws of this universe. Recalling the sweetness of the bond that had once flourished between them, a momentary sentiment flowed through him, but gave way quickly to concerns. What was it that had her in such a contemplative mood in the middle of day?

Not wanting to startle her, he produced a deliberately audible thud as he propelled from the corridor handrail toward the aquaria. On target, he clenched one of the vertical railings surrounding the blue column, and deftly pirouetted to face his wife. The playing had stopped, and his turned was greeted with intense, inquiring gaze. The presentations came so quickly, there was no chance to respond. He smiled, and spoke matter-of-factly: "This is an unusual hour for you to be home." He tried to maintain a blank presentation.

Re'kaba, ever the diplomat, returned Am'riah's evasiveness: "And a strange hour for you as well, husband."

"The current projects have me going day and night. I scarcely know what time it is." Am'riah did his best to present innocence.

"My dear A'mi, all work and no family these days." Re'kaba was also obviously presenting quite deliberately. Her use of the diminutive had an unexpected sting to it. He had not heard it from her lips in so long that its sudden intonation was a bit disorienting. Certain memories tried to arise, but dissolved in obscurity before they could form.

"You did not answer your hail, so I became concerned and checked your vitals. You seemed in distress. Is everything okay?"

"Ah, the hail…I silenced it sometime ago and forgot to reset." He proceeded as nonchalantly as his talents permitted. "In distress? Well, you know how it is. Trying to make advancements when Alhumana keeps us fettered. It makes the simplest task a herculean exercise."

"Funny you should mention the Church. Did you see Ponti Condo's *Locus Omni* today?"

He responded, almost interruptingly: "No!…I was on a secure network, in tough negotiations, and had all notifications canceled." Redshilt feigned interest to deflect his apprehension.

"It said the data was fluctuating abnormally, so that we must be particularly diligent in noting any changes we see that might be contributory." Re'kaba's gaze narrowed infinitesimally, yet it pierced Am'riah's defenses. She noted the twitch at the corner of his right eye, and in sympathy retreated. Releasing her harp ukuleles to float freely, she freed her back-patch and floated toward her husband. She reached out and caressed his face. Instead of relaxing under her touch he tensed; she felt his temperature rise as his face reddened. She withdrew her hand.

"You would share with me your burdens, wouldn't you A'mi?"

Redshilt remained stoic, though this second use of the diminutive had an even greater though different sting. "Yes. Of course. If there were burdens to share. But it is only work, wife. And our work is always a burden that must go unshared." Satisfied with this last reasonable response, he made to shorten the encounter. "I've only come out for little snack, and then I must really get back to work. This time to the office, though." He smiled.

Re'kaba returned his smile, then turned to retrieve her instruments. She had hoped she could crack his shell of remoteness but had not succeeded. Most of all, she had hoped to once again hear her diminutive in his voice: "Reki!"

Avoiding another close encounter with his wife, Redshilt snacked quickly, and without returning to his study, donned a Locator and propelled to the front entrance. The portal opened upon the vast upper spaces of the Quadrant, approaching the curvature of  the Shell as closely as the Forest canopy.  He gave the scene a cursory glance, then propelled to a Ventport just meters below.  Setting his A-nav to the office coordinates and activating the A-cav, he turned his thoughts inwards and away from the day's complications.

CHAPTER 39

Once in his office Redshilt secured all channels, set encryption to the highest levels, muted all notifications, and disabled all telemetry. As a corporate executive he was permitted these divergences from standard operating procedures. Though Excision had weakened the urge to sin, it did not insure honesty, and had done little to quell ambition; and ambitious men, and women, were known to do naughty things! But corporate spying remained an intransigent social bugaboo, so corporate executives were extended these privileges.

At his console, Am'riah Redshilt retrieved the contraband Cap from its hiding place, and logging onto the secret network, began a missive to his co-conspirators. They had adopted a rather archaic term of address, and he used it as he began his missive:

*My Fellow Freedom Fighters...*

Am'riah had composed the missive in route from home to office. More than concerned by the Pontimax's cautions, he felt a greater compulsion to combat this usurper's sway on the minds of free men; to break the strangle-hold his misplaced and outdated morality had on the citizens of the Habitats. Hadn't he, Am'riah Redshilt, done more to add substance and population to the Habitats than this moralizing demagogue? Hadn't he done more to give bounty and reward to the lives of the citizens than the so-called inner peace of Faith? And hadn't his successes, as well as all true human successes, resulted from *doubting* the *status quo*? Alhumana Corporation and its CEO strangled the human spirit, denied the individual free expression, and were more a plague on humanity than its preservation. He would transmit these thoughts to his fellow spirits and was certain its truth would propagate on its own virtue.

On a more practical level Redshilt believed his arguments were defended by pure common sense. Why proscribe activities that have virtually no chance of translating to the real world? The proscription against aggression assumed that someone might actually employ it in a real world circumstance. What was to be gained by it? Every citizen has guaranteed access to every essential of life. And for the more ambitious every opportunity existed to achieve one's heart's desires. Nothing need be taken by force, for all was freely given or easily earned. Certainly perfection demanded effort. But for ordinary men who had no such aspirations, surely life became flat denied these few pleasures; became no more than an unstimulating drudgery.

As a businessman Redshilt chaffed at the chains these proscriptions put upon economic opportunity and development. He knew from what he observed in his own behavior and that of his accomplices that a taste of the forbidden fruit awakened appetites long dormant. And servicing those appetites represented commercial opportunities; new avenues of employment; new products; a whole new industry; all orchestrated and financed by…

He lent no credibility to the argument that mental recreations could and would manifest themselves in social alterations. Or that the actions of a few, permitted a public stage, would have a corrupting influence upon all. There was such a thing as individual responsibility. If one didn't approve of a thing, one would not be forced to partake, could turn away. And the old psychological argument that certain things could harm or misdirect the developing psyche of a child…well, Am'riah was a parent, he knew damn well how and from what to protect his children!

Most importantly, what Am'riah Redshilt was coming to realize was that pent-up desire, pleasure denied, freedom withheld, like the mounting pressure in a boiling sphere, could and would reach explosive proportions. The thought brought that same tingling sensation to his senses that his forbidden mental adventures elicited. He found himself wanting it; hoping for it; working toward it.

CHAPTER 40

Re'kaba Morgana-Redshilt, scion of the Clan Morgan, heiress to the financial house of the same name, product of the legacy of the 12 families, watched her husband depart. She drifted slowly across the open space, impelled by the unseen currents and vortices his hasty exit had created in the room's atmosphere. And though just moments before they had shared this space, already the memory of it seemed stale and tasteless, like old bread on the verge of molding.

It had not always been so. In fact, it had only been in the last few years that any real change in the relationship had obtained, even after six decades together. He had always been an ambitious businessman – banker; financier; entrepreneur – but always those things had been his *work*; she and the children were his *life*. Now that was gone. Though he feigned work the cause, Re'kaba knew from the financial reports that his work now suffered the same neglect as his family. Something had taken hold of his interest and passion and energies. She did not know what it was. She would find out.

After her time in the Corps, Re'kaba's capacity for solving puzzles had recommended her for a career in the forensic sciences. She had a unique capacity for weaving seemingly disparate bits of data into plausible, and more often than not, proper explanations for aberrant occurrences within the Habitats. Such complex and finely structured systems as the Habitats almost daily manifested anomalies that demanded immediate investigation, to determine the impact and possible danger to the systems' balances. She had become pre-eminent in being able to read the subtle clues, the nuanced implications of these anomalies, and to report to the Elders of the Habitat. Before long, the accuracy and acumen achieved in her reports had gained her the notice of the General Council. After an interview and a mere 15 minute deliberation, the Council Elders deemed her abilities sufficiently exceptional to appoint her to the post of Inspector General, whose extant appointee was badly in need of retirement.

It was as the newly appointed IG that Re'kaba had been summoned by the CEO of Alfarms Corporation to examine and report on a series of significantly reduced crop yields for a certain species of *lens culinaris* occurring within several Habitats. Her investigation determined that a genetic hypersensitivity to gamma radiation within certain of the cultivars caused failure of a signal transduction for genes regulating the quantity of ovum production. Reduced ovum resulted in reduced fruit. She alone had noticed a correlation between the crop failures and gamma radiation levels at the time of ovum production, something even the plant geneticists had missed. She presented her report to the Board of Directors of

Alfarms Corporation, whereupon sat the newly promoted CEO of Alfinance Corporation, and dauphin of the Clan Redshilt, Am'riah Redshilt. Though only visible as ocular projections on eyescreens, the young Redshilt was so taken by the young IG, and particularly the intensity of her gaze from the eye screen that immediately after the meeting he had begun to make inquiries.

As members of the 12 families, Redshilt and the young Morgan were exempt from the normal protocols. Redshilt instead employed a *shadchan* to announce his interest to the Don of Clan Morgan. Filled with anticipation, and a little dread, as all young men are when first they test their attractions to the opposite sex, Redshilt anxiously awaited a first report from the matchmaker. What he did not know was that Re'kaba Morgan had been as taken with his intense scrutiny via the eye screen. In the end the services of the *shadchan* proved only ceremonial. The natural attractive forces between Am'riah and Re'kaba alone brought their orbits into alignment.

But now those orbits had gone askew. And as the past years' indifference to their relationship had tempered her conjugal needs, her husband's increasingly aberrant behavior had inflamed her professional curiosities. As a proper IG should, she would investigate the increasingly anomalous activity of Am'riah Redshilt, to determine if it involved consequences for the Habitats.

CHAPTER 41

The Mortuary Worm's presence had not gone unnoticed. As Ho'jin Sada meditated quietly in his cocoon it passed slowly overhead, stopping to sample the air with it distended antennae. These organs were sensitive enough to discriminate to the single part per billion; sensitive enough to detect a single organic molecule exuded in the breath or mechanically discharged from the surface of the skin. It was particularly sensitive to those molecular metabolites that indicated autolytic processes at work.

These processes, by which an organism recycles essential materials, are an ongoing process in all living organisms. They are a part of the continuing repair process. In a young, healthy organism, the processes are minimal. In an older or diseased organism they become more prevalent as greater repair is needed. Eventually, as rejuvenation is outpaced by deterioration, the processes begin to dominate, the resulting metabolites becoming abundant. Any increase in such metabolites always attracts a Mortuary Worm. They can be seen to hover near the windeyes of homes with sick children. They were always in abundance near the assisted care and hospice abodes of the elderly. Ho'jin Sada did not know if his notice of the Worm was the result of his age and the subsequently greater palpability of death, or because ensuing events had made him more attentive to mortal things.

The Abbot was preparing for his next meeting with the Pontimax. As with all encounters between complex human personalities, its outcome was uncertain. Sada's rational mind instructed him to use all of his powers of persuasion to impel the Pontimax's in the directions of prophylaxis, a culling of the damaged fruit. But, ironically, as humanity had struggled toward freeing itself from irrational, instinctive behavior by removing the offending parts from the brain, in spending his life in the service and sustenance of mankind, Sada had gone a long way to repairing and enhancing those structures whose deficiency had spared him Excision. He now actually felt the emotional pangs of compassion and sorrow as those nascent regions secreted their neurochemicals transmitters.

Sada knew from the historical record kept by the Brethren that the procedures dictated by *The Third Testament* had obtained with mixed success in the past. On more than one occasion the sitting Pontimax had not summoned the strength of will to do the necessary, resulting in the massive spread of aberrant behaviors. Only upon passing of the pontifical staff was the remedy found in a new Pontimax possessed of the will to act. But by then, entire Habitats had gone into irreversible decline, and deaths sometimes counted to billions.

In fact, once early in the history of the Habitats, it had even taken the successions of two Alhumana CEOs to find a man willing to act, the result being the loose of two-thirds of the extant Habitats and a threat of total extinction. Afterwards, only herculean effort, unshakeable faith, and incredible sacrifice prevented oblivion.

Ho'jin Sada did not know which course present circumstances would take. Es'paul Condo seemed a sufficiently strong man, but of a compassionate nature perhaps to ready to err in favor of mercy. The Abbot would continue to pound home the facts and hoped that their weight would tip the balance. He had to impress upon the Pontimax that Faith and Prayer were all well and good, but that sometimes salvation could not wait for the eternal, or the intercession of God, but required the action of man on his own behalf.

As Ho'jin Sada continued to meditate, the Mortuary Worm, which had exited the Alcove, yet lingered near its portal, occasionally extending it antennae to sample the air, undulated translucently in pale blue light from the Cylinder Sea to hold its place in the corridor.

CHAPTER 42

Once in his office Am'riah Redshilt opaqued the windeyes and immediately went about the task of disabling all telemetry and encrypting all communication links. He donned the contraband Cap and immediately tuned into the Cause network. Here he kept all the files pertaining to his participation in and support of the Cause's works and objectives, to which he had now become totally dedicated. They so closely paralleled his inclinations that he believed they were the path to realizing his goals – to free humanity's mind from the moral enslavement of the church, thereby opening whole new avenues of experience, and subsequent economic opportunities. Now, with the Pontimax's pronouncements becoming increasingly autocratic, even arrogant, and his recent behavior more erratic and difficult to understand, Redshilt felt more justified than ever to challenge his, and Alhumana's authority.

A good offense always surpassing other tactics, Redshilt decided to continue his pursuit of an Audit of Alhumana Corporation. Retrieving minutes from the last Board Meeting, he again examined Ponti Condo's strange request – a request for a considerable sum to reactive old archeological digs on Earth. Redshilt had already financed extensive mining and archeological expeditions on the surface and deep into the interior of the planet. All reports indicated that everything that might be of economic or historical importance had already been extracted. Particularly the site Condo was wanting to reopen. The historical record had shown for generations that the area had been thoroughly studied and nothing of interest ever found. Every indication was that Amagon had been totally obliterated in the last great, nuclear conflagration. And now, besides his ever more fervent calls for total adherence to the Church's principles, this useless, and possibly expensive obsession with William Proffit, Condo threatened to undo the progressive liberalization that had occurred over past decades, not the least because of his, Am'riah Redshilt's, dedication and effort. Surely the Pontimax's most recent actions warranted a scrutiny of his tenure as CEO of Alhumana Corporation. And all of this without considering his rumored visits to the Core and sojourning with Gleaners! Ponti Condo was obviously a troubled man.

Before he began the work of appealing the Audit in earnest, however, Am'riah Redshilt felt the need for a little rejuvenation, something exciting to stimulate his senses and his creativity. Putting aside the files for the time being, he pulled up the latest Cause offerings. As he perused the growing catalog of "adventures" he carried on a small internal dialog: *What is it they are so afraid of? They think that what goes on in a man's head is automatically neuronal pathways corrupt the entire of a healthy, going to spill out into the world, like some mephitic miasma? How can a little auto-stimulation of normally dormant or barely existent intelligent, productive mind? Sure, some of the stuff was a bit excessive, particularly the erotic stuff. But how could exercising a little aggression, or eroticism, do anything but relieve stress, clear the mind, and rekindle the fire of creativity and ambition? How could a little deviancy among friends threaten the existence of the species? It couldn't of course, and the whole hullabaloo was merely a distraction, to take one's mind away from the truth – that there were those who desired nothing less than to control their fellow men, from how and when they prayed, to whom and where they penetrated. Such hypocritical absurdity!*

As the dialogue played in his mind, a new entry in the playlist caught his attention: "*Assassins: Change the Fate of Mankind – Assassinate the Pontimax!*" Caught by the title, he scanned the Abstract.

*It is the year 10101. Humanity has been reduced to unthinking, procreating automatons. Habitat after Habitat is built, allowing population to increase unbounded. This mindless procreation creates an ever increasing demand for production of Habitats. Human existence for the average man is reduced to a continuous, monotonous labor. Only the Pontimax and his cronies at Alhumana enjoy a life with any diversity. Join the plot to assassinate the Ponti, and set the human race free!*

Redshilt could not restrain the incredulous smile spreading across his face!

## CHAPTER 43

Exceptional empathy had been one of the characteristics that had recommended the young Es'paul Condo to the clergy. As early has his primary schooling it was obvious that he analyzed the interactions with and among his classmates by assuming the perspective of each. He became by nature the class peacemaker, settling disputes between his peers when even the discipline imposed by the teaching mothers failed. That proclivity now reasserted itself as Condo struggled to find some way to assuage the current crisis.

He first considered the problem of acquisition, which persisted in certain individuals beyond Excision. It was a manifestation of the old territorial imperative by which humans as a lesser species had competed, albeit unknowingly, to provide for the survival of their particular genetic code. Adequate resources meant adequate sustenance for offspring; adequate space meant increased opportunity for encounter and breeding. Unfortunately, though, these primitive urges, once supplanted in the cortex, became divorced from their original evolutionary facility and took on a life of their own. No longer serving the external exigencies, they served only the inner life, manifesting themselves as "desires" – meta-phenomena perceived by the ego as separate from the physical world; self-promulgating, self-fulfilling, self-justified: manifested in such arguments *as art for the sake of art,* or *love for the sake of love*. Acquisitiveness could be tolerated when it buttressed superior intellects or talents, so long as it did not result in deprivation to others. In the presence of abundance it was not a problem. And the Habitats *were* abundant. But there was also the problem of eroticism. Like acquisitiveness, remnants of old, hardwired behaviors had impressed certain traces upon the cortex. These old behaviors were purely stimulus/response pairings that had evolved over time resulting in successful procreation. Originally set in motion as the result of pheromones attaching at specific receptor sites and causing a cascade of neurochemical impulses that on the one hand prepared the reproductive organs for function, while on the other hand bathing "pleasure" centers in the brain with neural opiates. But like acquisitiveness it too had become divorced from its original function, and now represented merely a desire to bathe the pleasure centers in opiates. Divorced from the procreative faculty by which it had evolved, it often took on the most bizarre of forms. It too could be tolerated to a degree, so long as it did not excessively or intentionally misdirected the species from its primary function.

Last and most troubling was the problem of aggression. Like acquisitiveness, it was the remnant of the ancient territorial imperative. It had found another purpose as well, however. It also served to preserve the individual organism. In the advent that the intruder upon an organism's territory was not a specific competitor, but instead a predator, acts of aggression often succeeded in driving the danger away. This binate efficacy served to insure its evolutionary success. So important to survival of the species in its infancy, the trait now permeated the cortex, and in ways both large and small influenced every human action, conscious and otherwise. It had been the taming of this megalithic impulse that had inspired Excision. The roots of the great tree were cutaway, in hopes that the limbs would whither. But having become as ethereal as consciousness itself, like an arboreal orchid aggression persisted, even seemed to thrive on nothing more than air.

Every mantra, every prayer, every ritual proffered by the Church was intended to suppress this most tenacious and dangerous of the instincts. But now it seemed that ground was being lost. Though fragile and cut off from its root, the surviving neural pathways were easily fortified, even made to proliferate by their simple use. Stimuli that caused the firing of a particular network resulted in strengthening the network through myelination; the mere act of observing aggression revivified it. The Church's proscription against exposing oneself to expressions of aggression were grounded in scientific fact. Unfortunately, men like Am'riah Redshilt suffered no scientific bent. For them all "laws" were arbitrary, and subject to submission to their talents – even the laws of Nature!

The current crisis obtained from the fact that these vestigial remnants of once essential behaviors were finding common cause and reinforcement. The anti-Excisionists were allying with the virtual experientialists were allying with the eroticist – and the whole coalition gone underground for obviously nefarious reasons. In some instances all three were joined in a single individual. And all were expanding their territories, their space for opportunity, consciously aware of the consequences or not.

Condo's empathic element allowed him to perceive each individuals increasingly elicited desires. The ant-Excisionists wanted to experience an unedited existence; the virtual experientialists wanted to actualize every past, present, and possible combination of sensory inputs for adventure's sake; the eroticists wanted to examine every possible avenue for increasing orgasm's endorphin intensity. He sympathized with individuals whose level of cerebral existence was insufficient, and who resorted to these lesser pursuits to fill otherwise empty moments in their existence. He empathized, he sympathized, but try as he might, he could not understand.

How could the long path of human history, littered with the ruins and tragedies so often repeated become something again neglected. On Earth, man's record had been one of predictable occurrence – a civilization arose by hard work, sacrifice, and a dedication to core principles. But soon the work of the builders became sufficiently distant memories in the minds of their descendants, and the present seemingly forever abundant and secure, so that old proscriptions became unwanted bondage; old rituals the objects of ridicule; old customs replaced by their inverses. And always the result was the same: misery and ruin.

The current danger lay in the fact that as each of these apparently minor human aberrations gradually expanded its territory in the realm of human commerce - spiritual, political, and economical - the greater became the opportunity for further expansion. Give the anti-Excisionists free reign in the market place of ideas, those who had never considered the ideology or even heard of it would now find themselves confronted by it and forced to decide. Give the virtual experientialist's free reign in the market place and their misanthropic gratifications would find new adherents and addicts. Give the eroticist's free reign in the market place and they would have the whole world as fruit for their picking, turning, and exploiting. How could they not see? And yet, obviously they couldn't. It was not a failure of the system to disseminate it needs, but the failure of certain individuals to perceive the needs of the system. It was like a man preaching to the ants that have invaded his domicile. No matter how factually precise his argument; no matter how eloquent his rhetoric; no matter how sincere his implorations – the ant is an ant and continues in its antly ways.

Having been avoided by his predecessor's mysterious and sudden death, and perhaps even more previously, the impact of the problem could now be read in the statistics. Its resolution was becoming imperative. Yet, as Es'paul Condo ever more precisely understood the problem, the more intractable it seemed. He still resisted concluding the obvious solution to which his predecessor had eluded and then evaded, and to which the Abbott Ho'jin Sada, elder of the Brethren of Gleaners, seemed determined to steer him. But the unbearable weight that descended upon his heart at its least consideration drove him to struggle ever more desperately for some alternative. Even the words of *The Third Testament* brought him little comfort: "In time even the sacred Tree of Life is afflicted. It is the loving, the caring gardener that severs the diseased limbs, sacrificing wholeness and symmetry, yet in the certainty that spring will bring new buds and virginal sprigs to flourish in their stead."

CHAPTER 44


Just as Es'paul Condo now spent inordinate amounts of time at his Alhumana offices, Sar'ha Condo was spending more time at the Convent. She had only peripheral knowledge of the circumstances her husband now confronted. However, she knew they were of profound importance by the consummate changes they had engendered in him both physically and psychologically. The man she knew as husband and father to her children was gone. She did not know whether his absence was for a while or forever. She called upon her teachings at Convent to steel herself against the loss. She recalled a passage from *The Third Testament*: "All is transitory in the face of the eternal. Our suffering today fades in light of the joy our children's children's children shall know on our behalf. For through them are our lives eternal."

While at the Convent, Sar'ha assumed the habit of the Sisterhood, following the rites and rituals she had learned as a young girl. She prayed and meditated and took Communion. And she sought counsel with the Mother Superior, who as the feminine counterpart to the Pontimax, was the only one with sufficient resources to inform her current misery.

The present Mother Superiro and Abbess to the Convent had been confirmed for slightly more than a century now. She had been the Mother Superior at the time a young Sar'ha Kier had first been place in the Convent. She had also chaired the committee which had bestowed upon the neophytic Kier the obligation as Executive Breeder. Though a multitude of young women had passed through her tutelage in the interim, Sar'ha had always maintained her interest, not the least because she had become wife to the Pontimax. Now a much matured version of the woman sat across from her, seeking her wisdom and solace.

.

The Mother Superior's Cell was located near the top of one of the Forest's Great Bamboos, where the intermodal diameters just began to decrease, and branches and leaves appeared. Hidden away at the center of the one of the great Forest Quadrants in an area designated a Refuge, where ordinary human traffic was not permitted, a dozen genetically engineered descendants of the earthly *Bambusa oldhamii* rose from the Core Sphagnum to nearly the height of the surrounding trees. Seven of the great culms were mature and constituted the home of the Abbess and Convent. Well-engineered and well-tended, these mature culms had a useful life of nearly 700 years. Five of the culms were half-way to maturity, while as many more shoots were just emerging from the Sphagnum.

The Abbess's Cell had been home to two of her predecessors, and would certainly suffice for the remainder of her tenure. With such a history its interior had become well-appointed with accumulated artifacts. The interior walls and carvings, and in fact every aspect of the domicile, had acquired that deeply lustrous and darkened patina that only cleanings and polishings by the loving hands of generations of acolytes could bestow. The whole was dramatically lit by crisscrossing beams of light entering through the many ornamentally carved windeyes. Seated in a ring as dramatically carved as its adjacent windeye, the Mother Superior and the Sister faced each other and shared presentations deep in meaning and affection. The Abbess spoke quietly, reassuringly: "From the day you entered Convent it was obvious you were intended for important things; destined to be called to serve in ways few ever know. Such callings do not come without a price."

The Sister Sar'ha presented: *I understand.* The Abbess continued: "Though to be the bride of the Pontimax is an honor many a girl may wish, the obligations it entails lie beyond what such juvenile fantasies can imagine. You were taught early that conjugation with the man gave you no special place in his professional priorities. You were also taught that for those chosen, obligation to the Species exceeded all else. Now you must live that reality."

"Yes, Mother." Sister Sar'ha Condo's response was muted. Though Excision successfully mitigated emotional responses arising in the basal ganglion, it did almost nothing to deaden emotional states originating in the cortex. What Sar'ha now felt was not pain of external origin, but impulses descending from cortex to ganglion, resulting in autonomic stimulation of the vagus nerve with its attendant muscle tightening in the chest, known more commonly as "heartache."

Sensing Sar'ha's pain, the Abbess began a narrative whose understanding she hoped would be a balm to this besieged Nun. "It is the Creator's design that women should suffer. For we are the mothers of humanity, and every injury, every disappointment, every loss suffered ultimately becomes ours through our children. It is this suffering that tempers our souls and steels our determination, for not the greatest of suffering can diminish the joy of a single birth – the coming into existence of a new and separate soul, set forth on a journey to discover Creation."

Though told a thousand times over, the Abbess' story remained a catharsis. Its practical aspects brought understanding; its deeper meanings brought solace and hope. The old woman's eyes slowly closed as her mind ventured into the memories that were the storehouse of her wisdom.

"When humanity first ascended, we were creatures with but two useful limbs. The others were mere pegs with which we combatted the acceleration of gravity. In the first Habitats, we continued that struggle, replacing gravity with centrifugal force. The practical aspects of life continued much the same as on Earth.  But the wise among us realized that imitating our earthbound existences only continued our limitations and did not truly set us free to live in the heavens.  Yet, our physical limitations presented problems. Human existence is not free of humorous contradictions," a recollection of which now brought a smile to the Mother Superior's otherwise tranquil countenance. "To live free of gravity, however, presented formidable challenges.  The immune system suffered in its absence; the physiological functions of certain systems required it, the two most prominent being the digestive and the lymph systems.  And there was the decalcification of bone.  Extended exposure to micro-gravidic conditions would render the individual incapable of surviving a return the Earthlike conditions."

The Abbess' smile broadened. "As it turned out, it was the procreative act that presented the greatest challenge.  The inflexibility inherent in a structure evolved to continually combat gravity proved clumsy and inept floating free in space.  The degree to which gravity assisted conjugation was not easily replaced.  In the end, it required the assistance of specially designed devices to provide the needed confinement and impulse to accomplish productive couplings."

The Sister, her eyes also closed, joined the Mother Superior's smile with her own as she recalled the illustrations of these devices in her Convent textbooks.

"And how brave must have been those first women, volunteering to conceive, gestate, and labor in the first weightless Habitats. Though it was known that exposing the developing embryo to weightlessness brought about many early adaptations in the lesser species, what hope and fear, expectation and dread those first mothers must have experienced. Without gravity, the physical act of parturition was encumbered, and required assistance. But as generations born free of gravity accrued adaptations, birthing lost its pain for mother and child alike. We often forget the sacrifices those first Sisters made and from which we so blessedly benefit today." A bit of mischief showed itself at the corner of the old Abbess's eyes. "Why, in this day we can scarcely imagine how unsatisfying it must have been to embrace a lover with only *two* limbs." She shared a wistful smile with her junior colleague, then continued on a more somber note. "Of course, our existence, albeit freed from our own primitive defects, does not come with a guarantee. We only trade the vagaries of earthbound existence for a different set of uncertainties, first and foremost being the cosmic winds. We know not on which day a deadly wind might blow – a hurricane of gamma rays broadcast by a dying star or voracious black hole – an unseen traveler hurling through our midst unannounced but deadly. Already Habitats have been lost to such natural disasters. We prepare as best we can, but in the end a greater power than ours decide our fate."

Mother Superior opened her eyes, which being sensed by the Sister, was reciprocated. The Abbess' tired eyes presented: *I have something I must tell you.* Sar'ha acknowledged.

"Though *freedom* seems forever the preeminent desire of men, it is an illusion. *The Third Testament* tells us: 'No man who must breathe to live is ever *free*.' It is ever so. More importantly in these times, the freedom for all men to know all things brings a greater danger than a little well placed ignorance. Take the Arks, for example. Though rumor and legend abound, their true existence is not acknowledged. They are our safeguard against the cosmic winds, built to shield against intense radiations, save for the improbable nova of our own sun. And here we keep for a year at a time the selected millions who would carry on the Species should catastrophe befall the rest of us. You *may* remember your time there, devoid of true sunlight, sustained by technology alone, and yet possessed with the knowledge and tools of the race."

At the Mother Superior's bidding, a flood of suppressed memories flashed through Sar'ha's consciousness. Yes! She did remember! A small metal Cell, with spartan furnishings, hours spent studying the rebuilding plans, meditating, praying - these memories hidden from her all these years as a bit of well-placed ignorance!

The Abbess read the understanding in the Sister's face, and continued. "Can you imagine the outrage if people knew that only a few were chosen? It is not practical to make each and every Habitat an Ark. Life in such a dungeon would be no life at all!" Sar'ha acknowledged the truth of it with nod.

"Our Species has come far in the millennia since Ascension. Yet we remain as far removed from perfection as ever. And our Excision, as sophisticated and precise as it has become, cannot undue what millions of years of evolution accomplished. Our humanity lies solely in our cortex, but that organ is the child, the offspring, the outgrowth of something as ancient as the Worms."

As a practicing Excisionist, Sar'ha well understood the continuing challenges faced by the researchers and experimenters: how to remove enough without removing too much; how to differentiate residual pathways in the cortex from independently evolved, original pathways. Even with the power of the CQC, exact mapping was impossible because the brain was a self-stimulating organ. Thoughts that arise as meta-phenomena from the mass of external stimuli become a source of internal stimuli, giving rise to new thoughts, all of which become memories. In this ever changing landscape, it was impossible to exactly map the neuronal structure, or to tell exactly where and how far residual pathways rising up from the basal ganglion penetrated the original structures of the cortex. The shadows of instincts had a forest of myriad synapses in which to hide. The best that could be done was to hack away the underbrush in hopes of preventing a conflagrating resurgence.

The Abbess remained silent, observing through the changing presentations in Sar'ha's eyes the growing understanding.  When tranquility had again presented in the younger Sister's gaze, she continued: "Just as we in the Sisterhood fight to protect our genetic diversity while diminishing our earthly passions, so the Pontimax and the Church struggles to keep humankind on the true path, fighting the doubt that forever threatens our true purpose.  And, as our ways are the tender ways of a mother, so must theirs be the sterner ways of the father.  We work to free the mind of the sources of doubt; they in turn must protect us from those minds possessed of doubt."

The Mother Superior watched the darkness of full understanding descend upon the Sister.

CHAPTER 45

Am'riah Redshilt was immediately taken by the extreme realism of this new virtual experience. As convincing as some of the more recent creations had been, always there lingered the realization that the experience was virtual, not real - just as a dreamer at some level is aware of the dream. But this time, just seconds into the simulation he was losing himself entirely. As he inspected his surroundings they so convincingly represented his office in the finest detail, even to the occasional dust bunny clinging electrostatically to the surface of his console, that at first he suspected some malfunction of his Cap. A quick glance at the console indicated it was operating properly, however, and engaged in the intended virtual program. The starkness of the reality was so intense as to be a bit alarming. He made a conscious note to himself to reality check every few minutes. He even set the alarm on his virtual chronometer to remind him. Scarcely had he depressed the set button when an authoritative tap on the shoulder startled him, causing his Locator to spin him to confrontation with its author.

"T'var'sh Redshilt, welcome!"

Redshilt was again startled, this time to hear in human voice the salutation by which members of the Cause had chosen to personally address one another. Though he had by now seen it symbolically represent thousands of times and heard it pronounced by surprisingly imitative voice applications, never had he heard the word spoken so convincingly in a human voice. The figure which had pronounced the word now hovered before him as realistically as any virtual image he had experienced. Dressed in a non-descript Maintenance Corp fatigue, the figured bowed its head slightly in greeting, a flutter of gossamer flings responding to the change in momentums and keeping the figure precisely at eye level with Redshilt.

"I am T'var'sh Krulic...but you may call me Hersh'ma." The figure bowed its head again in deference, stabilized by another flutter of gossamer flings.

The gentle turbulence created by the speaker's Locator wafted ever so gently upon Redshilt's face, again creating a sense of incredible reality. Never before had he experienced such minute detail. He reached out to touch the figure, partly in alarm, partly in disbelief, partly in curiosity, as one reaches out to a phantom in a dream. He first touched the fabric of the fatigue, and then the embossments of its insignia, and finally - irresistibly, suspiciously, disbelievingly – he brought his hand against the soft flesh of the figure's face. As if stung, he withdrew his hand expeditiously. Lifting his head, he focused his gaze on his vexer's eyes. His consternation was not assuaged. The detail was so exquisite that he saw his reflection perfectly portrayed in the dark apples of his interlocutor's eyes. Sensing distress and excess adrenalin, Redshilt's Locator began removing him to a safer distance.

T'var'sh Krulic was sympathetically amused by Redshilt's behavior, the corners of his large, almond eyes curling into a smile.

"Amazing what we are capable of when not fettered by an outdated, over-zealous theocracy, don't you think?" Hersh'ma Krulic cocked his head clownishly, as if to better hear the reply of his anxious onlooker.

"I can hear the Pontimax now quoting the *Third Testament*: 'Do not forsake the God-given reality for the imagined worlds of men!'" Krulic mimicked a pontifical tone.

"A bit of hypocrisy, don't you think? Spending all his days under his Cap, using the technology to impose the world as imagined by one William Proffit on the entire of humanity."

Hersh'ma Krulic crossed his arms and legs and took on the countenance of a tolerant school master waiting for a reluctant student to respond.

Directly the bewilderment and uncertainty in Redshilt's eyes was replaced with an urgent interrogation. "This technology exists, and we are denied it!"

"Not only denied, but forbidden! It is a Class I Sin to be caught in possession of the technology. You don't want to know what the penance is." Krulic tilted his head, cocked an eye, and arched his brows to emphasize this final point.

"Be he, Condo – he and his cult have this technology?" Vestigial pathways long dormant in Redshilt's cranium, innervated. What had previously amounted to little more than a continued agitation gained momentum as impulses lit up synapses and irritation blossomed into true rage.

"They have no right! No right to deny ME what I want – what WE want! I will not be chained to their puny interpretation of existence! We live like insects, mindlessly breeding and building, and to what end? To live a couple a centuries waiting for answers that never come? Surely it cannot be a sin to want more from life! I was thrust into this world without my consent; I will die also, without consent, alone in my vanishing. How can anyone or anything, real or imagined, presume the right to dictate how I shall live the interim?! Damn this hypocrite! Damn them all!"

Redshilt's face crimsoned and the veins in his neck engorged and pulsed. He glared defiantly, not at Hersh'ma, but at the entire of existence.

As if oblivious to Am'riah Redshilt's tirade, Hersh'ma Krulic began calmly and quietly: "I cannot say if the Pontimax possesses this technology, this ability to produce an undetectable alternate reality. But certainly others beside ourselves do. Perhaps they are controlling us with it now. Perhaps they control the Pontimax."

"What are you saying?" Redshilt's present state of agitation reverberated in his remarks. "I am of the 12 families! If the Church doesn't control it, we do! Who are these *others* you allude to?" Redshilt's was not a polite request.

Exempt of affect from Redshilt's rage, Krulic continued in his previous, mild manner: "I only suggest it is possible, T'var'sh. Certainly it is the Pontimax who has the ultimate authority. He is gate keeper, the one who holds the key to this prison that now constrains you - constrains US!"

Redshilt rejoined forcefully: "Yes – the Pontimax! He is the key…" A sudden understanding flared in Am'riah's eyes. "This is no game! This is not about vicariously satisfying an urge for revenge… you mean to assassinate the Pontimax!"

If ever a smile betrayed an unacknowledged truth, the bow of Krulic's lips bounded by the blush on the apples of his cheeks were heralds preceded by a trumpeting host. Again he began quietly: "You are not alone in your rage. Each day the legions of dispossessed grow – tens of millions spread throughout the Habitats, soon becoming hundreds of millions and then billions, as the cause finds new advocates."

"Yes, we must rise up and cast off this cloak of tyranny! Is the plot begun?" Redshilt now spoke feverishly, orgiastically. "We must begin today! The whole of my resources I make available to the cause! We must find this man who hides behind a mask and put an end to him and to any who aspire to his station!" For Redshilt the die was cast.

"T'var'sh Redshilt, the plot is afoot as we speak. The plans are laid. Return to your place and await its execution. Our day of triumph or defeat comes soon." With these final words, Krulic reached around Redshilt and tapped a key on his console. The program terminated, and the fatigue clad emissary of the Cause vanished before Redshilt's eyes. The transition from the virtual world to the real world was otherwise seamless, undetectable. Again he found himself somewhat disconcerted and disoriented by the transition. His fervor remained undaunted.

Still charged with resurrected emotions Redshilt turned to his console, engaged his back patch, and quickly connected to the Cause's secure network. He was anxious, in fact ecstatic, at the prospect of sharing with his disciples these new revelations.

## CHAPTER 46

As Sar'ha Condo exited the ornately carved portal of the Abbess's bamboo Cell she encountered a woman anxiously awaiting the opportunity to enter. By her dress, the make of her Locator, and her ornamentation it was clear the sojourner was Executive class. It was obvious by her demeanor that she was not a Sister of the Order. The impatient glare she visited upon Sar'ha spoke of a woman not practiced in the courtesies of life at the pedestrian level. Beyond these few observations, Sar'ha had little interest in the woman. Matters of vastly greater consequence now populated her thoughts.

Re'kaba Redshilt was unaware of any discourtesies on her part, and in fact had noticed little about the woman exiting the Abbess's abode save for the fact she seemed distracted and therefore did not clear the portal as expeditiously as she might have, which was annoying. In her rush to enter it was necessary for her A-cav to activate to avoid actually coming into physical contact with the exiting woman. Its small jostle further aggravated her already agitated disposition.

Re'kaba was not a Sister, but like many in the Executive class bolstered her sense of self-worth through charitable contributions of time and assets to persons and institutions dedicated to humanitarian pursuits, not so much for the sake of the humanitarian pursuits, of course, but more for the bragging rights. Still, she was not an entirely disingenuous woman. A real concern for her husband and her marriage compelled her, though not out of love or compassion, but instead out of a sense of duty to her class and thereby to herself and her offspring. Am'riah's increasingly aberrant behavior and subsequent diminishing productivity threatened his position and by marital affiliation her own. As she was oblivious to any discourtesy on her part toward the exiting sister, Re'kaba entered the Abbess's abruptly, showing not the slightest deference, oblivious to the old Abbess's well-tempered sufferance, and stated her demand as matter-of-factly as one might address a servant: "I need your help! I must find some way to help my husband. His behavior threatens our position – all that we are entitled to! I cannot pursue ordinary means: no doctors; no behavioral technicians; least of all counsel from Alhumana! Why, any such action would certainly raise suspicion of incompetence! We would surely be decommissioned! Relegated to some lesser ministerial post! We would never recover from such humiliation." Re'kaba's involuntary impulses sent agitated signals to her Locator, so that she darted and bobbed like an agitated humming bird as she spoke.

The Abbess sat quietly as Re'kaba Redshilt disgorged her egotistical lamentation, slowly rolling the beads of a rosarium through her fingers as was the habit of her waking hours. She felt no affront at this woman's lack of social graces or deficiencies in the arts of human intercourse. Instead, she listened intently, extracting from each ocular presentation, from every element of body language, the greater meaning that her words only intimated. She saw on the exterior a woman well practiced in the art of concealment, whose mild exclamations barely interrupted a staid decorum. And yet she sensed beneath the well regulated exterior a soul near panic; a soul that possessed no underlying fundamental beliefs to provide comfort or sustenance in time of trouble. Unlike her previous audience, whose face showed well the anguish and worry for one loved, and yet whose inner strength stood unshakeable in the face of any outcome, the poor wretch now before her was as hollow as a porcelain doll, existing only on the surface, consigned to oblivion if that surface shattered.

Receiving no immediate reply from the Abbess and unable to read beyond the inscrutable countenance, Re'kaba continue her prosecution: "It is well known that the Sisterhood wields considerable if covert influence at all levels, from the executive suites to the guild halls to the theocracy. Surely my generous contributions to your causes earns me some claim to their benefits!"

This last claim was directed at the Abbess with one of those ocular presentations not easily categorized. It fell somewhere between *I have something I must tell you* and *I have something I must ask you;* it contained nothing what-so-ever of *I understand* or *I am at peace*. In fact, it most closely resembled that expression so oft countenanced by the ancient men of Earth, who, before the Ascension new it all too well! They called it *FEAR*!

Re'kaba Redshilt's pleadings engendered a great empathy within the Abbess, calling upon all the vast store of wisdom a century at her post had procured. In sum, she knew that only Truth and Knowledge could provide the balm for this tortured soul. The inscrutable facade she had so meticulously maintained during the plaintiff's appeal now softened, undulating between *I understand*, *I have something I must tell you*, and a reassuring *I am at peace*." She closed her eyes and hummed the gentle mantra of the rosary, as if lulling a baby, and when she detected a calming, a resignation in her audience's respiration, she opened her eyes again, and looked deeply into the now pliant Re'kaba Redshilt's eyes.

She began: "My dear child…It is true that we of the Sisterhood claim some voice in the destiny Man. But it is not as you imagine. We are and ever have been the fertile ground from which the tree springs. But it is the sun and the wind and the rain that determines how it shall grow. And we have no mastery over these things."

The gentle monotone of the Abbess's voice soothed Re'kaba. But the words as yet held no meaning.

Still, the peaceful countenance of the old woman, the mellow light of the Cell's interior, and the gentle scent of incense lulled her. She deactivated her Locator and let herself settle into the Abbess's ornately carved ring.

The Abbess continued: "We of the Sisterhood have come to understand the great order of things. And in this understanding has come a great and blissful freedom from Doubt, and a deep and abiding Faith. For one who accepts the Truth of things lives beyond fear."

The *kalc* of the rosarium at that moment came between the Abbess's fingers, and she raised it to examine it, holding it high and within Re'kaba's sight. Made of gold, the encircled, inverted and broken cross seemed to possess its own light as the beams from the windeyes danced and played upon its surfaces. It had a nearly hypnotic effect on the Abbess's petitioner.

"The *kalc*, symbol of a thousand origins and legends and as many meanings…Yet in this place and at this time it is our symbol. It symbolizes the mother, the birthplace of man; as well, the birthplace of hope, and the future. It is an inner place, requiring sanctuary – protection from the wider world and it vagaries."

Re'kaba had transcended her earlier state of anxiety, and now become a receptive vessel, her peaceful visage flashing *I understand* as each morsel of wisdom from the Abbess was digested.

"Consider this – when in the entire history of the Species have women gathered in the hundreds, the thousands, the tens of thousands, to engage in mutual slaughter to satisfy misplaced instinctive urges?"

The Abbess did not wait for Re'kaba to signal understanding, but proceeded rapidly. "If nothing else, this indicates a difference between the sexes so fundamental as to be irrefutable; so fundamental as to symbolize the underlying framework of this creation – woman must create; man must control!"

Re'kaba presented *I don't understand* and *I have something I must ask you* so rapidly as to be unable to give voice to either condition.

The Abbess continued: "The first ten thousand years of human history record the fact: women gave birth to sons on Earth who then slaughtered each other for control of it!"

The Abbess was so demonstrative in her declaration of fact that its impression upon the now pliable mind of her petitioner was indelible. The doubt signaled by the wavering ocular presentations vanished from Re'kaba's eyes. Now tranquil and untroubled, she presented *I understand*.

"And what record do we have of man's second ten thousand years?" The Abbess paused to let Re'kaba consider the question.

"Woman has surrendered the outer world to men. But in her control of the inner world, the world of true creation, she and she alone decides *which* men shall be born!"

Dendrite expansion and synaptic formation now proceeded at such a rate in Re'kaba's cerebrum that she curled and retreated into Prayer as involuntarily as an infant succumbs to sleep. The Abbess reached out withered yet gentle hands and feet and caressed the now catatonic daughter with all the affections and concerns of a true mother.

CHAPTER 47


E s'paul Condo's sojourns in the Core now became so frequent and prolonged that the Brethren provided him with quarters. As well, upon his arrival at the Core he quickly abandoned his work khakis in favor of the simple, saffron-colored sack worn by the Brethren. He even made attempts to navigate without his Locator, using his feet to grasp at the Sphagnum and propel himself. He was sure he made a comical sight. He also noted the beginnings of the tell-tale staining of his feet.

On this day Condo had awakened early in the woven cocoon that was his bedclave here. Having accomplished his morning ablutions via a Worm, he dressed quickly, and pulled himself effectively albeit clumsily along the Sphagnum shaft in the direction of Elder Sada's apartment. Gaining the portal, he paused momentarily to listen for any stirrings within. Hearing only Sada's slow, unlabored breathing, he crossed the threshold and waited silently, studying the wizened, mahogany countenance of the sleeping Gleaner, noting the pronounced REM.

Directly Ho'jin Sada's eyelids began to flutter over the rapid eye movements as the world of dreams gave way to the dream world of reality. It was if he had sensed Condo's arrival by some unregistered sense so that as he woke he signaled no surprise, but broke straightway into dialogue. "Brother Condo, you arrive early today with your basket full of questions, all wanting precise, little answers." Sada smiled mischievously, always enjoying the small pricks he delivered to Condo's fading certainty; not with malice, but with the knowledge that it is by the small cuts and barbs of life that wisdom obtains.

"I have read the most recent reports." The pronounced sadness in Es'paul Condo's voice permeated every vapor in Sada's chamber. "My mind does not yet want to accept the reality that my senses and my reason reveal. Millions upon millions across the Habitats now in moral and intellectual turmoil as malignant ideas spread their seeds and give growth to long dormant residuals of instinctual behavior. We have come so far! How can it be that our past still haunts us so?"

Ho'jin Sada did not respond immediately. He allowed the vocalization of Condo's laments to echo through his consciousness for a moment, allowing that internal debate to which Condo was the only participant to once again commence.

"Brother, Man did not create Man. He who authored the elements authored Man and He alone is privy to the Grand Design." Sada was quoting from *The Third Testament.* He knew at this point it would give Condo little comfort. But comfort was not the question at hand. What lay at stake was the future of humanity.

"Brother Sada, how can it be that we can conjure limitless energy from the substance of space, design organisms for specific functions, create Habitats in the vacuum of space, and yet we cannot control the wanderings of the human mind?"

Sada did not hesitate to answer: "Because we did not create the human mind! Even the CQC at best mimics us; it can never replace us. For ten thousand years man has dreamed of becoming the "creator" – of an artificial intelligence. And in that quest he has produced some magnificent machines. But in the end they are only that – machines! Devoid of soul; lacking the desire for life that propels mankind onward. For all our attempts, our clever contrivances, science fiction notwithstanding, no machine as yet has ask the most human question of all: 'Why am I here?' We tell ourselves: 'If only the machine becomes complex enough, it will come alive!' The CQC easily matches the complexity of the neuronal structure of a human mind; it can mimic us to such a degree that we can be fooled most of the time. But in the ten thousand years since its inception, it does not of its own volition demonstrate the two most fundamental aspects by which we define our humanity: empathy and altruism. We have programs that duplicate these behaviors in the machine – but we are the authors of those programs!"

Sada closed his eyes and breathed deeply and regularly. Condo could see the bulge of the old monk's corneas as they danced under closed lids, as if Sada were deep in REM. Condo knew his mentor was searching the deepest recesses of his memories, looking for those bits of wisdom, those true life anecdotes that prove a point more efficaciously than the cleverest of constructed arguments. Condo also noticed how much the old figure had shrunken in these past months since their first meeting – excess skin increasingly folded over the continually shrinking frame, the flaming orange hair mere surviving tufts scattered irregularly over the still immense pate, yet all now almost lost among the gathered folds that formed the collar of his saffron garb. Less than a year had passed, but it seemed as though Ho'jin Sada's years had finally caught up to him.

Upon opening his eyes, Sada noted the intense scrutiny of Condo's gaze and immediately understood that during his momentary repose he had been the object of the Pontimax's closer examination. "I see the Gaksei contemplates the mortality of the Sensei." He smiled.

Condo was immediately struck by the absolute truth of it! Yes, he was again Gaksei, and like so many before him, upon realizing time with a beloved Sensei would soon find its end, was filled with a melancholy and tangible apprehension.

As Ho'jin Sada inspected the countenance of his interlocutor, he noted the changing presentations – at once: *I have something I must ask you*; *I have something I must tell you; I don't understand; I understand* – everything but *I am at peace.*

"I see the apprentice already mourns the passing of the master." Ho'jin Sada's remark was without emotion; without ridicule; without sympathy. He looked high over his right shoulder, and with a little jerk of his head indicated that Condo should follow his gaze. Just visible within the confines of a small, dim portal, Condo could make out the translucent, undulating form of a Worm. Its presence could signal only one thing: As telomeres are exhausted, genetic sequences breakdown, resulting in the creation of malformed proteins. These malformed proteins act as prions, spreading deficiency throughout the organism, resulting in aging, and ultimately in death. Mortuary Worms sense the presence of these prions and their metabolites, and when certain thresholds are obtained, become the constant companions of the dying, interceding long before the discomforts and terrors which ancient men so often encountered obtain. *I understand* washed all other presentations from Condo's eyes.

"I am done with telomere augmentations. Done with organ revitalization. Done with gene therapy. I am done with life!" Sada's fervor startled the Pontimax. Ho'jin Sada regained his composure, and continued in quite mundane fashion: "We have behind us tens of thousands of years of human thought and endeavor. No doubt tens of thousands of years of similar pursuits lie in man's future. But I have grown impatient in my old age…" Sada paused for a moment to measure the effect of his words on his hearer. "How long can a man wait for his answer?" The question was rhetorical. The old monk continued immediately: "I must have my answer now! And I am certain beyond doubt that I will not find it here – in this place; in this time; in this life! So I MUST see what comes next...*or doesn't*."

The old monk's eyes closed again, and immediately the darting began, though this time Es'paul Condo believed that Ho'jin Sada had truly retreated to sleep and to dreams – though he could not know if they were dreams of things that *had been*, or dreams of things *yet to come*.

## CHAPTER 48

Sar'ha Condo knew within her heart of hearts that the husband she so loved, admired, and honored existed no longer; that her mate of two broods would not bring forth a third. With the support of her Abbess and Sisters she was coping with this new reality, but she still longed to better understand its purpose – its necessity! She recalled that most ancient of adages: *Women are from Venus; Men are from Mars.* She tried to console herself by recalling the teachings of the Sisterhood:

> *Man is not our equal, but we must submit to him.*
>
> *Our purpose is to wrest the seed from man.*
>
> *We must play upon his passion so that his reason serves our purpose.*
>
> *As man masters the universe without, we must master the universe yet to be born.*
>
> *Our ova are sacred, clay only for the hands of the Creator to mold.*

Sar'ha could go on and on with the lessons so deeply engrained in her psyche. But it brought her little comfort. She turned to the more colloquial questions that defined her circumstance: *What does 'love' mean to man? A man professes to love a woman above all things; marries her; brings forth children; swears his undying devotion... yet, when the first war drum beats, he is off with his fellows to partake of the slaughter.*

Why could men left unrestrained never see the truth of war? In fact, the old, corrupt, and incorrigible among them *invented* the causes for war, sending the best and youngest and brightest among them to die upon the battle field, while their dissolute protégés bed the women and foster the succeeding generations. And most importantly: "Why must some men be called to greater sacrifice than others?

Sar'ha Condo knew there were no absolute or even satisfactory answers to these questions, down the ages to the present. She and her Sisters understood the entire of the social structure of the Habitats depended on Alhumana Corporation's effectiveness in restraining the residual and forever resurfacing instinctual urges. She knew that her Es'paul, as Pontimax, carried upon his shoulders the responsibility not only for his own children, but for the children of all humanity now and to come. And though she and her Sisters were not privy to all, she understood by her own reasoning and the intimations of the Abbess that below the surface of seemingly idyllic life in the Habitats smoldered ancient and as yet unescapable realities. She could only imagine the circumstances that now so burdened her husband; circumstances that would ultimately take him away from her.

CHAPTER 49

Re'kaba Redschilt departed the Abbess's cell forever altered. She had awakened from her Prayer with a new neuronal mapping that fundamentally changed not only her personality but the very processes by which her brain perceived the world. Though deep in REM she had been continually aware of the Abbess's comforting embrace, and through it developed a bond like none she had known before. Upon awakening she had immediately confessed her conversion and prayed for postulancy, which the Abbess granted with a simple kiss to her forehead.

With a lightness of spirit so tangible she forgot to set her Locator, Re'kaba begin a slow, graceful, spiraling down from the height of the Abbess's cell. Each revolution of her descent brought some new visage with color and form so intense she seemed to have entered a new reality. In fact, she had. She would have descended in such a state to the quarantine boundary at the Sphagnum Core had not a Novice arrested her descent and activated her Locator. Upon looking into Re'kaba's eyes the Novice understood immediately that a transformation was in progress, and so as not to interfere, set Re'kaba's Locator homing function. Oblivious to everything but the Novice's smiling eyes, Re'kaba returned the smile as the young

Sister-to-be released her as propelletes extended and thrust her homeward.

Re'kaba was as an infant born – she did not recognize the world she now transited, but had to take in each vision, each touch, all sensation as new data, to be assessed with an all new rubric. Her newly minted algorithm processed that data differently; her rational mind began to fill with new and delightful conclusions. Old and well entrenched ideas occasionally resisted this new phenomena, but once challenged by her new rationality they quickly retreated, leaving only a knowing smile on this restituted soul. Too soon, it seemed, Re'kaba arrived at the portal of her home cubicle. She quickly transited to the interior. She took no time to admire the superficial accoutrements as had previously been her tradition; there was no swell of pride or accomplishment to reinforce the old behavior. She proceeded directly to the quarters of her third brood.

Though Re'kaba was no stranger to worry, she found herself suddenly beset by a new and strange emotion. With recently acquired understanding, she knew it to be *true guilt* – that emotion from which her ancestral traditions and social station had isolated her. The sensation became more intense as she remembered how seldom she had ventured here. It was the domain of nannies and tutors and teachers – not on the regular itinerary of a woman of her position – at least, not until now.

The thing that she noticed most about the place was the smell – it was awash in the scent, the perfume of her children!  As she pulled herself along the handrail, past each bedclave, she knew – *she knew without knowing* – here slept Ha'nah; here slept Job'ka; here slept Ad'ma; here slept Ma'ier!  She rotated slowly to take in the sights of this place where her children slept and studied and grew!  As the full burden of her new understanding descended upon her, her breast quavered, and nearly sobbing, she whispered: "How could I not know?!  How could I not have understood?!"

What few memories she possessed of her first two broods flashed through her mind and the guilt grew ten-fold.  If only she could trade all the spangles of her position and wealth for the time lost with those precious children!

Swallowing hard to assuage the guilt, it going down her throat like a bundle of daggers, Re'kaba gave voice to her new resolve so that it might be forever recorded in the vibrations of the universe: "Men will do what men will do.  But I am a mother, and I shall do as the Creator intended!"

With that simple utterance money, status, Am'riah Redshilt and the worries he had foisted upon her - all were relegated to some inferior and henceforth inconsequential corner of her life.

CHAPTER 50

Ho'jin Sada and Es'paul Condo made their way slowly down the greenly luminescent shaft toward the blue glow of the Cylinder Sea. They were engaged in intense discourse as they "walked" along, the old monk moving smoothly, well practice in the art; the novice missing his grip occasionally and floundering, to be set right again by the firm grip of the master.

"Place an obstacle between a man and what he wants and serotonin levels plummet, inhibitions fade, and aggression rears its ugly head." Sada knew perfectly well that the Pontimax already possessed these physiological facts. He stated them now only out of argumentative tradition. "Further, exposure to aggression lowers serotonin levels in observers or objects of aggression. It is, in fact contagious." As Condo did not offer rebuttal, he continued: "It is this contagion we now consider."

Es'paul Condo now rejoined: "The answers to contagion are: prevention; quarantine; vaccination; elimination." There was the echo of catechism in his tone. He fell silent.

Sada continued his train of thought: "Unchecked contagion leads to epidemic. The epidemic of aggression is war."

Condo picked up the thread, quoting from Sun Tzu: "The supreme art of war is to subdue the enemy without fighting."

Sada turned to the Pontimax, delighted at his remark. "Yes! Exactly! For all our wishful thinking, it is now as it has always been! Aggression can only be met with aggression! The individual may turn the other cheek, but a society, a civilization that turns away from aggression condemns its citizens, its progeny, to misery and untimely death! Therein lies the quandary – the very precepts by which we live as brother and sisters, regulating the behavior between and among us, giving us peace and prosperity within the Habitats – does not apply to the whole of the social animal."

Ho'jin Sada watched closely the countenance of the Pontimax Es'paul Condo as the full burden of his office came to bear. If the masks of agony and ecstasy, drama and comedy, fear and hope, life and death could meld into a single form, it now molded Condo's features. His face truly became the inscrutable Mask of the Pontimax. All the joys in life in this moment dissolved before the flood of reality, of inevitability, of absolute necessity. All that remained were eyes staring into an abyss, with no reflection of what they were seeing. Sada knew the look all too well.

Ho'jin Sada and the distrait Pontimax passed silently through the crystalline portal into the transparent Cell projecting into the Cylinder Sea. Condo let his momentum carry him forward, drifting slowly toward the glass that separated the Cell from the waters of the Sea. He spread his limbs to stop his glide as he encounter the smooth curve of glass, and then ever so gently supported himself against the tender embrace of the water masses gravitational field. It was the strongest gravitational force he had ever experienced in his own flesh, and though minimal, his mind now magnified it to the level of the simulated gravitational fields of the Interfaces. He imagined himself a man on Earth relentlessly struggling against this enslaving force, every waking moment spent combating it chains, fighting to overcome its imposed limitations. Men fought and killed one another for the resources necessary to engineer prosthetics to ease its burden, to simply the labor of gathering the essentials to life from within its grip . For a man without the power to combat gravity depended on the charity of others, or perished.

As had happened on previous occasions a strange, delicate, elaborately articulated organism swam into view. The beauty of its structure, the improbability of its design and function could not be avoided. Es'paul Condo escape his morbid reverie, and a smile came to his face. He pretended a dialogue with the creature: "Well, my little friend, what manner of life are you? Are you plant…or fish…or at last the Creator's ultimate creation – evolved here as you could not have evolved on the unforgiving Earth, which would not suffer such whimsy. Why, you make the most elaborate of star fish, the most audacious of jellies, the most arrogant of fin, fur, or feather seem absolutely mundane!"

This chance encounter provided Condo with the respite he needed. The morose reverie broken, he turned and propelled himself off the glass and across the open space to where Sada waited, a Locator in hand for the erstwhile pedestrian. He slide into the device and fastened its buckle. Its propelletes now under the command of his motor nerves, he turned to face his nemesis.

"Tell me, my dear brother, Ho'jin Sada, Elder of the Brethren, what choices do I have?"

CHAPTER 51

Am'riah Redschildt had spent a fitful night's sleep in his bedclave. His mind had wandered between vengeful imaginings of conquest and the disjointed world of dreams, where success and failure, fear and courage, sanity and madness can blend so smoothly together as to be indistinguishable.

Whether cogitating or dreaming, the tingle of the bedclave's wake-up call brought him to full consciousness. He spent only a few seconds reviewing the night's phantasmagorical exploits when the day's purpose step boldly to the fore. "Today is the day! Today is THE DAY!" his mind's voice shouted. He slithered from the bedclave's embrace, and propelling himself to the nearest handrail, executed a dozen well-formed arguments with himself as he transited the small distance.

*"Indeed, this would be the day of days! Tyranny would end! No longer will 'the self for all' be the moral chains that bind me! From this day forward it will be 'I for myself'. Today men will know freedom again!"*

Exhilarated by the thought, Redschildt realized he had never felt so alive! Today he and his brothers-in-arms would cut the head off the serpent. Today the figurehead of that monstrosity which came between Am'riah Redschildt and the things he desired would be toppled; headless, surely the beast would collapse, die under the force of its own nimiety. And the plan itself was SO exquisite!

Of course, everything would have to proceed with absolute precision. But Am'riah had faith in his cohorts. Particularly T'varish Krulic, who seemed to have the necessary inside connections. Though anonymity was the intent within the Habitats, no complex society can function effectively without some accounting of its members. Such was the case in the Habitats. Every citizen was accounted a number and a place. Am'riah trusted that Hersh'ma had successfully secured that information.

And the method? Well, how superb! The ubiquitous Worm – waste manager; physician; mortician – and now most sublimely – assassin. By a mere management of molecules the Worms transitioned seamlessly from one occupation to another, without so much as a twinge of conscience!

Am'riah Redschildt let these thoughts replay in his mind as he made his way to the bathing chamber. They so pleased his sensibilities that he could not contain a smile, and even chuckled – an almost childish giggle – at the grandness of his design.

If ever a man felt vindicated; felt certain that life had at last played him the winning hand he deserved,

Am'riah was now that man. Privilege, prosperity, even power had not been sufficient, did not measure up to the freedom he was about to acquire - the freedom to pursue his utmost desires, unfettered by arbitrary obligation to his fellow man. So deeply ingrained was this belief that even that primitive element of the vertebrate, the pituitary, could not resist its impulse, and poured endorphins into his blood stream.

Arriving at the bathing chamber in this heightened state, Redschilt quickly shed his sleeping silks, and wanting even more, turned to face the embracing Worm. Every nerve ending already alight, ecstasy paled in comparison to the sensations as the Worm engulfed him.

## CHAPTER 52

Re'kaba Redschildt had moved her bedclave from the conjugal bed chamber to the children's' quarters. Her husband's self-destructive course no longer occupied her thoughts. She now knew that her life did not revolve around his but rather she was the center of orbit for her children. She no longer feared loss of status or wealth. She knew that with her new found purpose, her life and the lives of her children could proceed as well in the meager cells of Hydrofarm workers as from high on the Partitions.

Some small disturbance had awakened her early on this morning, so she slipped quietly from her bedclave, and passing from child to child as they slept, breathed in the sweet, warm vapors of their exhalations. Oh! How she wished that she could have all of her children as such again, to lavish on them the mothering they were denied. But of course, she could not. All the more determined then to dedicate her every waking moment to the nurture, education, and edification of this, her final brood.

As she gazed with adoration at her sleeping angels, sounds issued from the central corridor. She pulled herself to the sleeping chambers portal to listen. What at first seemed incoherent babel she soon realized was her husband, seemingly have a conversation with himself. She could not make out the words, but from the lilt in his voice, punctuated by an occasional, nearly hysterical cackle, she gathered he was quite pleased with something, or more likely with himself. Oddly, after all the past months of torment and worry over his behavior, she felt not the slightest interest in whatever it was that now entertained him. Having shed unkindness along with other previous imperfections, she felt no malice toward him, sincerely hoping that whatever the cause for his behavior, he would find happiness in it. She had found hers.

## CHAPTER 53

Sar'ha Condo was surprised to find her husband home when she and the children arrived. He met them at the blossom end of the Pod, smiling broadly, embracing each in turn, acting as if all the reticence, remoteness, and absences of the past months were suddenly absolved, and life returned once again to normal.

"Let's go swimming!" he offered jocularly, producing the family's set of fins from a closet just inside the entry. The children squealed with delight; Sar'ha rolled her eyes in mock disdain, eliciting an elfish, mischievous grin from her husband. He leaned close to her so the children wouldn't hear. "I'll tend to you later, Madame!" he whispered in a naughty, breathless voice. Sar'ha blushed irrepressibly.

With youthful agility the children were quickly suited up and swimming away in a swirling, twirling knot of limbs and fins. Es'paul helped Sar'ha into her kit and passed her a well-provisioned pack as he fitted himself.

"We might as well make this a picnic too?!" he implored from under raised brows.

On impulse Sar'ha reached across the small space separating them and with finned limbs somewhat clumsily embraced her husband and kissed him rapaciously on his mouth. Then she spun about, and with a childish enthusiasm swam after her brood, leaving the pack floating in front of a bemused but delighted Condo.

They swam; they soared; they frolicked. The boys flushed birds from the foliage and gave chase in a ballet of whirling forms. The girls stopped and sampled the fragrance of every blossom they encountered. In this fashion the family ascended ever higher into the canopy, stopping in the midst of an arboreal orchard to enjoy their meal upon the mat of close grass that carpeted the upper limbs of the trees. Later, continuing their ascent, they burst into the open space between the treetops and the Habitat's shell. All fell idle and silent, basking in the full, filtered light of the setting sun. Instinctively huddling, they watched as the great, reddening orb descended below the horizon of the far partition, the beginning hum and harmony of Ensymphonium beginning to crescendo behind them. Daylight gave way to dusk, and then to night. Above them the shell's plague cleared, opening before them the vastness, the splendor, the infinite mystery of Creation.

## CHAPTER 54

By design Es'paul Condo awakened before his wife and children. He was counting on the sedative effect of tryptophan rich foods on which his children had engorged until late hours, and the passionate and nearly night long intimacy with Sar'ha to keep them all sleeping late into the morning.

Slipping quietly from the conjugal bedclave, Condo grasped a handrail and propelled himself out of the chamber and into the Pod's central corridor towards his study. He would spend a little time putting things in order and reflecting before the new day dawned. Fetching a back patch from a hook at the entrance to his study, he deftly cinched it and proceeded to his desk and seated himself. Sliding his Cap from its drawer and quickly donning it, he began at the controls of his console much as a virtuoso attacks a magnificent arrangement of music. Fingers and toes flew across keys and buttons and switches. Soon his course was plotted, his mind melded with the CQC via the Cap, as Condo began his report to the Brethren concerning the resolution of the matters at hand. With the aid of the Cap he reviewed memories in contracted time, so that a day's worth of thought compressed to mere seconds. He let the recent days play out one by one before his mind's eye...

*He was in Ho'jin Sada's chamber deep within the Core Sphagnum. In his always avuncular tone, the Elder of the Brethren proceeded: "Expirations and extinction have not always resulted from disease or calamity, as you must now suspect. In fact, the majority have occurred, and I suspect will always occur, in response to infectious "isms". He smiled at his own use of this colloquial reference for 'ideology'.*

*"We have been assailed by every ism imaginable! And not just those of an intellectual nature! Aside from the current hedonism, there have been infections of animalism, masochism, sadism – even cannibalism! One particularly dangerous outbreak of fatalism came so close to success that its practitioners were actually able to smuggle sterilizing compounds into a majority of the Habitats! They were so certain that life, that human existence itself, was so demonstrably useless that human extinction was the only appropriate course. Had their compounds been successfully disseminated within the Habitats...well, we would not be here having this discussion."*

*The Elder continued: "We know what the result of inaction will bring. History makes that absolutely clear! Each delay brings only greater misery, greater destruction, and greater loss of life. We hesitate to address the infection when it counts hundreds, and then we must answer it when it counts thousands; we hesitate at thousands of infections and then we must deal with millions.*

*Unfortunately, as the populations of the Habitats now constitute trillions of souls, infections hardly become noticeable until they affect millions. Such is the present case. If we delay, we shall be facing BILLIONS of infections!"*

The argument was not lost on Condo. He fast-forwarded to a succeeding day.

*He, Sada, and Hersh'ma Krulic were contemplating the Cylinder Sea from within the crystal control room. Hersh'ma spoke first: "Of course, for the solution to work as intended, the cultists must maintain an absolute belief in their cause and the possibility of its ultimate success – until the very end."*

*"My younger Brother is correct," Ho'jin Sada interjected. "If we are to be merciful, compassionate – then we cannot show our hand. If they suspect they have been detected, a panic will ensue. Panic engenders fear. The ultimate fear for the unprepared is the fear of death. We must spare them this suffering!"*

*Hersh'ma continued: "You know, Brother Condo, that a plot for your assassination is afoot. In fact, it quickly comes to fruition. I know, because I have been a party to it. It is not wise to let infections fester and spread. Better to apply some poultice to draw the infection out. I have provided that poultice by supplying the cultists with your citizenship number and your place."*

Strangely, Condo felt no betrayal at this revelation. He had long since surrendered to the reality that he was but a pawn in a game much older and more significant than himself. Again he fast-forwarded to the point where Sada had described the mechanism by which the solution would be accomplished.

*"It is a simple task, the rearrangement of a few molecules, accomplished remotely, easily, using a Device. Each Worm will be encoded with a triggering molecule that once detected will place it in assassin mode. Those triggering molecules will be segments of DNA belonging to all the known cultists. Of course, the method devised for your assassination is the same, courtesy of our brother Hersh'ma. But you will be safe here. The Worms become unresponsive once they enter the Core Sphagnum. All of their energies turn to digestion, and occasionally reproduction."* Ho'jin Sada enumerated the process as nonchalantly as one might describe the tending of a garden.

Finally, Es'paul Condo, Pontimax and CEO of Alhumana Corporation, Church to the Habitats, reviewed Elder Sada's apologia for the coming act:

*"The Third Testament tells us a man can have no better life than to die peacefully."* Ho'jin Sada *paused momentarily, his presentation indicating a moment of internal reflection, perhaps as he compared this writ to his own mortal circumstance. As quickly, his focus returned and he continued:* "What better moment for a man to

*perish as in that instant when he reaches out for the thing desired, with all the joy and anticipation and certainty of obtaining it? This is the gift we bequeath to those who would trespass against us. Death will come quickly, painlessly, ecstatically in the maw of the Worm, which is the Creator's arbiter of all things!"*

Satisfied that he had considered all things, Condo finished what would be his last official act as Pontimax and CEO of Alhumana Corporation, and as per agreement with the Brethren, placed the data chip in a medallion which now hung around his neck. It would be gleaned from his personal effects.

Condo slipped quietly from his chair, and gliding along the handrails made a final pass by the chambers where his wife and children now slept peacefully in their bedclaves. The love he felt for them magnified the ache growing in his heart – the ache he new was soon to be mirrored in their hearts. But his Faith was strong. He new that these small aches would pass, and paled in comparison to joy his actions guaranteed to countless generations as yet unborn.

## CHAPTER 55

As if by a Divine plan, at the very moment the spiritual leader to the Habitats Es'paul Condo entered the bathing chamber of his home Pod, the old and withered Gleaner Ho'jin Sada emerged from his woven cocoon. As if connected by some ethereal orchestration the men slipped from their coverings in unison: Condo out of his sleeping silks; Sada from his saffron sack. With a single breath they addressed the infinite: "May God forgive us!" As one they turned to face the Worm.

Life in the Habitats goes on. May it ever be so!

## THE END

www.ingramcontent.com/pod-product-compliance
Lightning Source LLC
Chambersburg PA
CBHW032203190626
46810CB00017B/14